THE HALFADAY CREEK SERIES BY
JAMES B. HENDRYX

Skullduggery on Halfaday Creek
The Saga of Halfaday Creek
Adventures on Halfaday Creek

Visit www.jamesbhendryx.com for more information on
forthcoming installments in the Halfaday Creek
uniform matching series.

SKULLDUGGERY ON HALFADAY CREEK

James B Hendryx

SKULLDUGGERY ON HALFADAY CREEK

JAMES B. HENDRYX

ILLUSTRATIONS BY
PETE KUHLHOFF

INTRODUCTION BY
PATRICK NEWCOMB

ALTUS PRESS • 2013

© 2013 Altus Press • First Edition—2013

EDITED AND DESIGNED BY
Matthew Moring

SERIES EXECUTIVE CONSULTANT
Richard Hall

PUBLISHING HISTORY
"To a Life of Adventure" by Patrick Newcomb, originally published in *Traverse, Northern Michigan's Magazine*. Copyright © 1987 by Prism Publications, Inc. Reprinted by arrangement with Prism Publications, Inc.
"Black John Goes Outside" originally appeared in the October 10, 1944 issue of *Short Stories* magazine (vol. 189, no. 1). Reprinted by arrangement with the Estate of James B. Hendryx.
"Cush's Third Wife" originally appeared in the December 25, 1944 issue of *Short Stories* magazine (vol. 189, no. 6). Reprinted by arrangement with the Estate of James B. Hendryx.
"One Good Turn Deserves Another" originally appeared in the August 10, 1939 issue of *Short Stories* magazine (vol. 168, no. 3). Reprinted by arrangement with the Estate of James B. Hendryx.
"Evil Companions" originally appeared in the September 25, 1939 issue of *Short Stories* magazine (vol. 168, no. 6). Reprinted by arrangement with the Estate of James B. Hendryx.
"Murder on Halfaday" originally appeared in the November 10, 1939 issue of *Short Stories* magazine (vol. 169, no. 3). Reprinted by arrangement with the Estate of James B. Hendryx.
"Hanged by a Thread" originally appeared in the April 25, 1943 issue of *Short Stories* magazine (vol. 183, no. 2). Reprinted by arrangement with the Estate of James B. Hendryx.
"All in the Day's Work" originally appeared in the January 10, 1936 issue of *Short Stories* magazine (vol. 154, no. 1). Reprinted by arrangement with the Estate of James B. Hendryx.
"Reward–$1,000" originally appeared in the August 25, 1940 issue of *Short Stories* magazine (vol. 172, no. 4). Reprinted by arrangement with the Estate of James B. Hendryx.
"Ten Thousand New Lakes" originally appeared in May 1955 issue of *Field & Stream* magazine (vol. LX, no. 1). Reprinted by arrangement with the YGS Group and the Estate of James B. Hendryx.

THANKS TO
Theresa Burau Baehr, Deborah Fellows, Robert Loomis, Richard Moore, Patrick Newcomb, Rick Ollerman, Julie Rhodes, Jeff Smith, Cynthia Whyte, & the Leelanau Historical Society

TABLE OF CONTENTS

TO A LIFE OF ADVENTURE

PATRICK NEWCOMB

IN 1921, JAMES B. HENDRYX arrived in Suttons Bay much the way the famous character of his novels, Black John Smith, arrived in Halfaday Creek—with a dubious, unconventional and colorful past.

Before Black John fled to Halfaday Creek, he had held up the United States Army in Alaska and ran off with a battleship, at least so said Old Bettles, a Dawson sourdough, and like Black John, an invention of Hendryx.

"It was only part of the army, a major and three common soldiers, to be exact; and the loot was about forty thousand, lacking a few dollars, and not a battleship," says Black John in the novel *Grubstake Gold*. "The incident was more in the nature of a sportin' event than a theft."

Likewise, Hendryx had committed his particular peccadillo (as Black John would put it) in the spirit of fun and good sport. As a reporter for the *Cincinnati Enquirer*, Hendryx was sent to Joliet, Illinois, to cover the execution of a man named Jenkins. After he witnessed the hanging and wrote the story, he inserted a colorful headline which, either through a copy editor's carelessness or Hendryx's own craftiness, slipped into the morning edition of the newspaper. The good citizens of Cincinnati awoke to the news of the day: "JENKINS JERKED TO JESUS AT JOLIET."

The uproar that ensued chased Hendryx from his job as a reporter to an outlaw life of fiction writing—a profession, loosely speaking, more suited to his outlandish wit and raw, rogue talent. In 1915, he published his first novel, *The Promise*, a story about lumberjacks in the Northwoods. By 1921, the money from sales of his adventure novels and stories was coming in steadily enough for Hendryx to purchase a house and 360 acres of forested land on Lee Point, south of Suttons Bay.

After plumbing was installed, Hendryx moved his wife, Hermione, and family into the rambling three-story house, which had been built in the 1890s by Judge Burch from Boston as the centerpiece of what was to have been—but never became—a lakeshore resort. Harold Titus, a fellow writer and companion on fishing trips to Northern Michigan, had alerted Hendryx to the near-wilderness piece of property. It was here, on the shore of Grand Traverse Bay, where Hendryx settled down to a somewhat civilized life of hunting, fishing and writing.

Like Black John, who tricked out a slick profit on all of his enterprises on Halfaday Creek, Hendryx prospered at the abandoned resort on Lee Point. While raising a family of two girls and a boy—Hermione, Betty and James Jr.—he wrote 57 novels and countless short stories, most of them set in the Wild West and the Yukon gold rush days. The adventures of Black John Smith, Corporal Downey of the Mounties and Connie Morgan intrigued generations of readers in the '20s, '30s and '40s. Black John, with a quick-draw wit and a double-barreled sense of justice, outsmarted interloping outsiders and kept the miners and reformed outlaws of Halfaday Creek (in his own words) as "moral as hell." Corporal Downey, meanwhile, using more conventional law enforcement techniques, tracked down and brought to justice men who dared to break the law in the rugged Yukon Territory of gold rush days. In Alaska, the boy adventurer Connie Morgan hit the trail and lived out the wilderness fantasies of every reader of *The American Boy*, a popular magazine that serialized many of Hendryx's novels.

Born in 1880, Hendryx was 40 years old when he moved to Lee Point. He brought to his novels and stories the richness of his own experiences punching cattle in Montana and prospecting for gold in Alaska. Hendryx's father owned and edited the *Sauk Centre Herald*, in Sauk Centre, Minnesota, and his great-great-grandfather was William Henry Harrison, ninth president of the United States. Still, Hendryx largely ignored his illustrious political and literary heritage while growing up. He preferred hunting and fishing and the lessons of the woods and lakes to any learning to be had in the classroom. By his own account, young Hendryx was expelled 24 times by the superintendent, mainly because he thought it was more important to run his trap line than to sit in class.

As a teenager, Hendryx explored the woods and streams of Sauk Centre with Claude Lewis, the older brother of Sinclair Lewis, the Nobel Prize-winning author. "Sinclair was three years younger and he was a pest when we were kids," said Hendryx in an autobiographical sketch published by *Ford Times Magazine* in February 1951. "He was always wanting to drag along with us when we went anywhere. You couldn't get rid of him."

Hendryx studied law at the University of Minnesota, but left after two years with the notion that he had learned enough law to keep him out of trouble. His good sense and his knowledge of the law kept him out of trouble a few years later when he was a ranch hand in Montana. Out on the range, he had become acquainted with Kid Curry and his brother, Lonnie, two members of the notorious Wild Bunch, which was led by Butch Cassidy and the Sundance Kid. Asked to join a posse that was forming to bring in the Curry brothers, Hendryx had the local harness maker tear up his saddle. "There was an unwritten law that you couldn't be forced into a posse without your own saddle," Hendryx said. "The Currys were neighbors and I didn't want any trouble with them."

From Montana, Hendryx and a friend headed to the gold fields of Alaska, a trip they financed with $1,400 won in a poker game. They were at the tail end of the gold rush, however, and except for the plots and characters mined for use in later novels, Hendryx spent much of the 14-month stay in Alaska chopping cordwood.

Simply stated, his credo was, "Never let your work interfere with your fishing." Nevertheless, many a fish swam free in Grand Traverse Bay while Hendryx, a prolific author, worked on the two or three novels he published every year. He spent the mornings writing in a small log cabin hidden in the woods near the big house, typing the stories hunt-and-peck style with his index fingers. Both the cabin and his bedroom inside the house were stocked with maps that he could pull out to check the geographical accuracy of the travels of his characters in Alaska and the Yukon.

"He almost never took a vacation," says Robert Loomis, Hendryx's son-in-law, remarking that even on his long trips to Canada, Hendryx took along his typewriter and worked on his stories. "But then again," Loomis adds, "his whole life was a vacation."

While Hendryx spent the mornings enlivening the drama on Halfaday Creek, he sometimes devised plots to liven things up on Lee Point. One morning in the cabin, he took a razor and shaved a number of gaps in his big handlebar mustache. His daughter, Betty Loomis, remembers how as a girl, she met him coming back from the cabin in the afternoon. "Daddy," she said, "what happened to your mustache?" Acting puzzled, he ran his fingers over the gaps in his mustache. "Oh

THE FIFTH MAN
by Manning Coles

A CRIME CLUB SELECTION

MANNING COLES and Tommy Hambledon, his chief character, are fast building a reputation for themselves that has few equals in the field of mystery and adventure fiction. Tommy, with a very special brand of humor and an amazing amount of common sense, has a way of getting in and out of almost incredible difficulties, for Manning Coles, without seeming to do so, creates an atmosphere where anything can happen and everything does.

His latest adventure is concerned with the mysterious comings and goings of a man with many aliases. Tommy first comes to know this man as the fifth of a party of British prisoners to be landed on the south coast of England from a German submarine. He looked pretty much like a German fox, and no one was more surprised than Tommy when he turned into a first-rate British hound.

Readers familiar with *Green Hazard*, *Without Lawful Authority*, and other Manning Coles books need not be reminded of the hairbreadth escapes and magnificent bluffs which his characters execute. THE FIFTH MAN is in the same tradition as these earlier volumes and promises as exciting a tale as any of its predecessors.

This novel has not been serialized in any form prior to book publication.

DOUB
W

WEST OF THE M lies a land of u colorful and exc Old West as i romance. A lan where great he and tumblewee violent and ra You'll be famous West Bliss Lomax, reading the Western is c Always look

my!" he said. "I fell asleep in the cabin and the squirrels musta sneaked inside and nibbled away at my mustache."

In later years, he worked in a room upstairs in the main house. The family remembers how he used to laugh out loud while writing his stories. "You'd hear the clicking of the typewriter and then the sound of him laughing," Betty Loomis says. "Then more clicking and more laughter."

A tall, lean, rugged man with sparkling blue eyes, Hendryx invariably wore wool pants and a flannel shirt, sporting always his handlebar mustache and ten-gallon hat. "Even in the middle of summer, it seems he was always dressed for winter," says his daughter, Mittie (Hermione) Swartz. "The kids in high school called him Trapper Dan." The showman in Hendryx relished the role of cowboy and backwoodsman and he often rode his horse in full western attire in the parades held in Suttons Bay and Traverse City.

In Wild West tradition, the Hendryx place on Lee Point resembled a

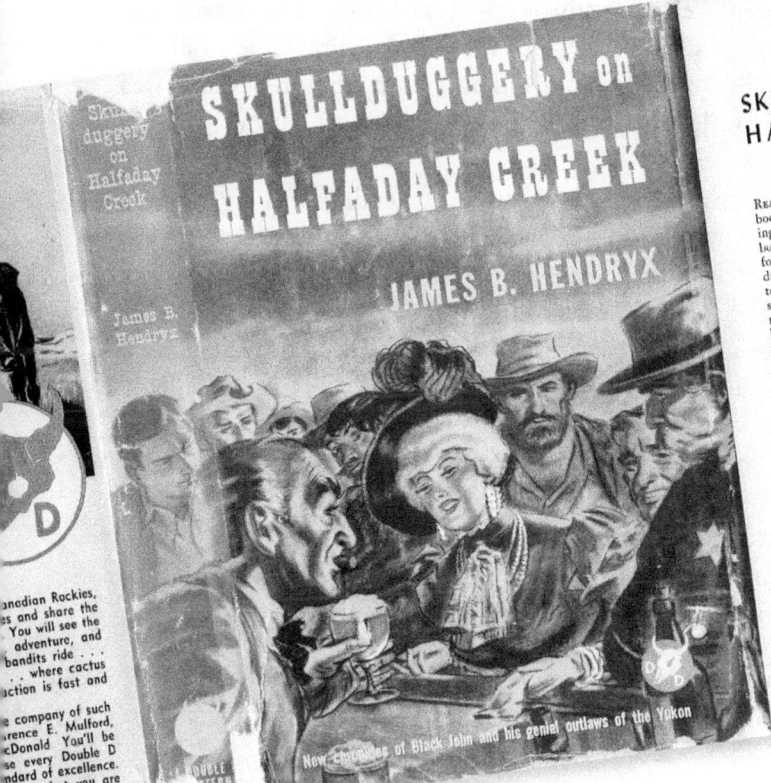

S.O.J.L.C.
Price, $2.00

SKULLDUGGERY on HALFADAY CREEK

JAMES B. HENDRYX

James B. Hendryx

New Chronicles of Black John and his genial outlaws of the Yukon

DOUBLE ETERN

SKULLDUGGERY ON
HALFADAY CREEK

JAMES B. HENDRYX

READERS of James B. Hendryx's previous books will have no difficulty in remembering Halfaday Creek on the Alaskan-Canadian border, or Black John, the one-man police force who metes out justice to a variety of dubious characters. For those who are new to these tales of the Northwest, we need only say that Halfaday Creek is the home of a number of outlaws who find it convenient to have a border to step across when the law appears, and that Black John spends most of his time keeping the "crick" clear of swindlers, gold thieves, unwanted wives, and cardsharps.

In this story Black John evens up the score with a number of old enemies. On a trip "outside" to his boyhood home, he perpetrates a clever swindle on a too-zealous banker who once had caused trouble over his father's mortgage; encounters his friend Cush's third wife on the way to the "crick" to make trouble for her husband, and engineers the hanging of some high-grade ore thieves.

This is accomplished with Black John's usual imperturbability and good humor and the fact that he comes out a few thousand dollars ahead on each of the deals no way lessens his moral stature.

Black John's many fans will find him resourceful and unpredictable as ever there is no slackening in the pace of life on Halfaday Creek.

anadian Rockies,
es and share the
You will see the
adventure, and
bandits ride . . .
. . where cactus
action is fast and

e company of such
arence E. Mulford,
cDonald. You'll be
se every Double D
ndard of excellence.
re of what you are

large spread in the hills of Montana. He built a corral where he broke wild horses himself until his wife convinced him to hire a cowboy from Montana to do the hazardous work.

Over the years, the house was the site of an endless number of all-night poker games. The players included James Milliken—father of former Governor William Milliken—Harold Titus and Carl Detzer, both fellow writers, and sometimes a priest from Leland who had to leave early on Saturday nights in order to be able to say Mass on Sunday mornings. "One of the enduring memories from childhood is the sound of poker chips clinking downstairs as I went to sleep in my room," says Mittie. Hendryx also spent many Saturdays at Jud Cameron's barber shop and pool hall, playing cribbage and poker with the gang.

When more people settled in Northern Michigan, Hendryx sought a wilder country and bought a cabin on Basswood Lake, north of Thessalon, Ontario, where he took the family on summer vacations. Up in the Canadian wilderness, Hendryx would put a pack on his back and a canoe above his head and take off alone on weeklong trips in the backcountry. His instructions to this wife concerning his return were simple: he would be gone for a week, but if he did not return in seven days, she was to allow him three more days before she sent anyone in search of him.

Though an excellent horseman, Hendryx was regarded by those who rode in a car with him as a terrible and terrifying driver. He valued a car with big tires and plenty of ground clearance so that he could fly over rugged logging trails to his favorite hunting and fishing spots. One day, while washing a blue station wagon that he had owned for years, he suddenly dropped what he was doing, ran inside the house and dragged his wife outside to look at the car. Blue wheel covers were visible where the water had washed away the layers of mud. "Look!" he said. "The wheels match the car!"

Sometimes when snow closed the roads on Lee Point, Hendryx would ask the hired man to clear a path to the shore, and the spirited writer would motor over the ice to Traverse City. One time, after a day of poker playing and grocery shopping in town, the car broke through the ice on the return trip. Hendryx salvaged some of the groceries before the car sank. A farmer happened along and yelled, "What in the world are you doing, Jim?"

Hendryx yelled back, "I'm starting a grocery store, you darn fool. What did you think I was doing?"

Hendryx appeared as the featured guest on the television show, *This Is Your Life,* in May 1956. When asked by host Ralph Edward if he would do anything differently if he had the chance to live his life over, Hendryx replied, "I'd do twice as much of it."

Hendryx died of lung cancer in 1963. He had always smoked, but he laid off the bottle later in life after "doing a pretty good job of drinking" when he was young.

"He was a nonconformist in the best sense of the word," says Betty Loomis. "He might have broken some rules, but he never did so to hurt anybody."

"He didn't live by the book," agrees Hendryx's son-in-law Fred Swartz. "He wrote the book."

BLACK JOHN
GOES OUTSIDE

BLACK JOHN SMITH elevated a foot to the brass rail before the bar, as Old Cush, proprietor of Cush's Fort, the combined trading post and saloon that served the little community of outlawed men that had sprung up on Halfaday Creek, close against the Yukon-Alaska border, set out bottle and glasses, and shoved the leather dice box toward his customer.

"Beat them three treys in one," announced the big man, as the little cubes came to rest on the bar. "I feel lucky this mornin'."

Cush returned the dice to the box and rolled them out. "Mebbe you don't feel so damn lucky lookin' at them five aces," he taunted. "That's a horse on you."

"I feel luckier'n ever," Black John grinned, as he gathered the dice and rattled them noisily with his hand over the mouth of the box. "In the first place you strained yer wrist by shakin' five aces agin three treys, when three fours would have answered the purpose. An' not only that, by shakin' the best hand possible in one shake, you've practically precluded the possibility of shakin' even a mediocre hand in the next few attempts. You see, Cush, success or failure in dice shakin' rests squarely upon the law of averages."

Cush scowled and eyed the hand that waved the dice box back and forth. "If it rested on big words that don't mean nothin' when you git 'em said, you'd be the best dice shaker in the world. But before you roll out them dice take yer hand off'n the top of the box—jest in case a couple of aces er sixes, would git stuck between yer knuckles an' sort of help out yer law of averages."

"What! You don't mean to imply that I'd cheat, do you?"

Cush replied, his gaze fixed on the box that continued to move back and forth in the other's hand. "Any honest man, any pore man, or any friend of yourn could trust you with the last damn ounce of dust, er the last roll of bills he had in the world, an' he'd never lose a nickel. But when it comes to shakin' dice fer the drinks, there ain't no ornery, low-down trick you wouldn't pull off, if you was let to. Roll out them dice now—an' see that you roll 'em free."

The big man's grin broadened as he cast the dice. "Four fives. Let's see you try to beat 'em."

Cush cast the dice and scowled at the pair of deuces that rewarded the effort, gathered them and cast again. He left a pair of sixes, shook the remaining three dice twice more without getting another six. And returning the box to the back bar with a grunt of disgust shoved the bottle toward the other.

"The drinks is on me," he admitted. "Anyone could beat two sixes in three shakes."

"All of which goes to prove what I was tellin' you."

"Shakin' dice don't prove nothin', except sometimes a man gits a free drink: an' sometimes he pays double. What the hell you got on yer other shirt fer?"

"The feel of spring has got into my blood. I'm obsessed by nostalgia."

"My second wife used to have it. Sort of draw'd down one side of her face. She claimed it hurt like hell. She used to tie a baked onion on it, an' after while it would let up."

"You'd recommend that treatment, eh?" grinned the big man.

"Why shore. It done her good. I never had it, myself."

"Okay. I'll take your advice."

"But cripes, John. Where the hell you goin' to git an onion? I'll bet that right now there ain't an onion this side of Vancouver!"

"All right. To Vancouver I'll go, then."

"What!"

"Yup. I'm goin' outside."

"Huh. Outside that drink yer standin' in front of."

"No. I meant it, Cush. If there's no onions in the Yukon, I'll go where onions are. I'm takin' yer second wife's word for it—if onions cured her, they'll ondoubtless cure me."

"You mean you'd go clean down to Vancouver on her say-so? You never lived with her. You don't know what a damn liar she was—the way she carried on with that C.&O. conductor whilst I was tendin' bar back in Cincinnati."

"Hold on, Cush!" grinned the big man. "Yer gettin' kind of mixed up, ain't you. Here, it wasn't only three, four weeks ago, you claimed that was yer third wife—an' it was a *B.&O.* conductor!"

Cush mopped somberly at the bar with his rag. "I ain't mixed," he replied somberly. "Both them roads runs into Cincinnati—an' they both got conductors."

"An' while I'm outside, I might's well take a trip back home an' see how pa's gettin' along. It's be'n quite a while sence I come away, an' he's gettin' along in years. I'd kind of like to know about my brother, Willie, too. Last I heard he was doin' time in Atlanta fer some mail robbery he was mixed up in. Trouble with Willie, he never learnt that honesty is the best policy. An' it ain't that he didn't have the chanct to—what with Pa bein' a preacher."

"Mebbe he's got pardoned," suggested Cush.

"Not if the Government knows its stuff, he ain't."

"Er he might of got turned loose fer good behavior, er some-thin'."

"Not Willie."

"But if he was turned loose, would you be fetchin' him back with you?"

"No. We don't want Willie on Halfaday. He couldn't be depended on to stay moral. We might have to hang him."

"Course yer only kiddin'—about goin' outside?"

"No. I'm goin'. My heart yearns fer the scenes of my child-hood. The green hills, an' the open fields, an' the babblin' brooks. The little church at the crossroads where Pa used to preach. The one-room school house with the happy voices of children playin' in the yard. The lowin' of kine in the meadows—"

"What the hell's a kine? An' how could it low?"

"The mooin' of cows, to you. I spoke poetically."

"Yer always speakin' some way that no one kin figger what you mean. Where's this here place at, where you was raised?"

"Far, far back amongst the mountains, of Rhode Island's vast hinterland."

"So you come from some island, eh?"

"Well, it's not an island—"

"No—an' you never come from there, neither! An' what's

more, there's plenty of green hills right here in the Yukon to look at, an' likewise, open country, an' cricks. An' I wouldn't go from here to the door yonder to hear no cow moo, nor to see no church, nor no schoolhouse, nor yet to hear no kids yellin' in the yard of one!"

"You're an iconoclast, Cush—a scoffer at sacred things—a shatterer of ideals."

"I wouldn't take that off'n no one but you—an' as fer scuffin' around an' scatterin' ideas, you've got me beat a mile! Take this here idee about goin' outside to git you an onion! Of all the damn fool things you've ever done, that's the damndest."

"My mind's made up," Black John said. "The homin' instinct is clutchin' at my heartstrings. There's old Grandma Smith—I wonder if she's still alive?"

"She's prob'ly jest as alive as she ever was. You never had no more Grandma Smith than I did. But honest, John—layin' all kiddin' aside—you wouldn't leave Halfaday? Cripes—what would we do if you wasn't here? There ain't no word but you kin handle the damn cusses that comes driftin' in on us. We'd be in a hell of a fix!"

"My absence will only be temporary— not much longer'n a prospectin' trip—say two, three months, at the longest. I really mean it, Cush. I'd like to see Pa agin—kind of see how he's gittin' along—mebbe slip him a little change, er somethin'. He might be havin' a tough time, sort of old, an' alone, like. Willie shore ain't be'n no comfort to him."

Cush shrugged. "All I got to say is— hurry back, John. I won't say no word to hinder you from goin'. Yer old pa shore needs all the comfort he kin git—what with two boys like you an' this here Willie saddled onto him!" He turned to the safe. "How much money you takin' along?"

"Oh, about ten thousan' in bills, an' say fifty pound of dust."

"Fifty pound of dust! What the hell would you do with dust down in the States? Cripes, that comes to damn near thirteen thousan' dollars!"

"That's right. How the hell do I know what I'll do with it? I never seen the time a little dust wouldn't come in handy. Weigh it out, Cush, an' I'll be pullin' out."

II

BELL RINGING, AND brake-shoes grinding, the train slowed to a stop before the little wooden station. Half a dozen passengers alighted, as many more got aboard, the conductor waved his arm, and with a puffing of black smoke and hissing of steam the train gathered momentum and passed on down the valley. On the platform Black John's eyes swept the little town whose main street straggled parallel with the creek, flanked by frame dwelling houses banked in irregular rows along the steep hillside. A low rumbling and splashing of water reached his ears and his glance settled on the slowly turning wheel of the old wooden grist mill beside the pond. Fat bodied flies buzzed noisily as they swarmed about a trickle of sticky liquid that oozed from a cask near the freight room door.

The big man removed his broad-brimmed black hat, mopped at his brow with a blue cotton handkerchief, and became aware that the platform was deserted save for himself and a stoop-shouldered man who noisily pushed an iron-wheeled truck bearing an assortment of boxes and parcels over the uneven planking. Reaching down he picked up the heavy leather valise from the platform and nodded to the man with the truck.

"Hot," he ventured.

"'Taint bad," replied the man, and disappeared with his truck through the gaping door of the freight room.

Crossing the track Black John walked down the street past the stores with their wooden false fronts, past the post office where the little group of stragglers waiting for the mail to be distributed eyed him with half-hearted interest, past the only new building in town—the neat one-storied brick structure with the words MERCHANTS STATE BANK stencilled in gold across its plate-glass window.

But there was nothing half-hearted in the glance accorded him by the shrewd gray eyes of Judson Grimm, the banker, who stood in the open doorway of the new brick building. Those eyes took in every detail from the high-laced pacs, the checked flannel shirt, open at the throat, the black hat, and the heavy black beard of the passing stranger. Speculative wrinkles creased the banker's forehead, as his gaze centered on the broad back now almost out of sight in the distance. He was aroused by the voice of Clem Whipple, one of the bank's directors, and the town's leading merchant, who with a black book in hand from between the leaves of which the ends of bills and checks protruded ostentatiously had stepped across the street to make his daily deposit.

"'S'matter, Jud? Figger he's a hold-up man?" he grinned.

Grimm shook his head. "No, I don't reckon we've got to worry any more about hold-ups, what with the new vault, an' time lock an' burglar alarm. I was just a-wonderin'."

"Musta come in on the down train," Whipple said. "Prob'ly some fella some coal company sent in on to sort of look the country over. Or he might be goin' to prospect for oil."

"Oil!"

"Yep. Oil. Time's comin', Jud, when there's going to be more money in oil than what there is in coal."

A GRIN of condescension twisted the thin lips of the banker. "You must have been readin' about these new fangled gasoline buggies, or automobyles they're makin'."

"That's right. An' I'm tellin' you the time's comin' when they're goin' to be quite a thing."

"Quite a thing maybe for race tracks, or maybe to run on city streets where there's stones or brick pavin'. But just let 'em try to run 'em on the country road! Gosh—when the sand won't stop 'em the mud will."

"When enough folks buys 'em they'll begin hollerin' fer better roads—an' when enough folks holler loud enough they most gen'ly always get what they're hollerin' for."

"But enough folks won't never buy 'em. They cost anywheres from two thousan' dollars up. How many folks can afford to pay that much just for somethin' to ride around in?"

"They'll make 'em cheaper. I'm tellin' you, Jud, time's comin' when I'll be sellin' more automobiles right here in town than I sell buggies now."

"You!"

"Yes. Me. When the time comes I'm go-in' up to the city an' get holt of the agency for these parts. An' I'd be willin' to bet I'll be makin' more money off'n em than I'm makin' out of my store an' implement business put together."

"An' when you get up there them city slickers'll try to sell you stock in their factory, or stock in some oil wells, an' they'll clean you out slicker'n a whistle."

"A man might do worse than buy stock in a good automobile fact'ry."

The banker shrugged. "It's your money, Clem. Fool it away if you want to. But when they clean you out, an' you come to the bank for the money to start over again, don't forget that I warned you."

The other grinned. "I rec'lect the time when you was runnin' the feed store an' you loant old Nate Bascome a hundred dollars fer to work that there gold mine he claimed he found in some cave back in the hills."

The banker frowned. "Gold's different," he retorted. "Gold's somethin' you can turn into good hard cash any time you want to. It ain't a machine that'll break down or get mired down in mud an' sand. The Government'll take all the gold a man's got an' pay spot cash for it. Just you try to sell the Government one of these automobiles, an' see what luck you'd have!"

Whipple grinned. "I never see you sellin' the Government no hell of a lot of gold. Out in the hills they're still laughin' about how old Nate put one over on you."

Judson Grimm's face flushed angrily, and his scowl deepened. "They are, eh? Well let me tell you, Clem Whipple, that if you an' all them laughin' hyenas out in the hills know'd what I know, you'd be laughin' out of the other side of your mouth. I'm tellin' you now—old Nate found that gold!"

"What!"

"Yes, sir, he found it. I'm no damn fool. I'm a business man. I can buy an' sell any three of them laughin' jackasses out in the hills. I'm makin' this bank pay, ain't I? You'd ort to know. You're a stockholder, an' a director, to boot. I'm makin' money for the bank, an' makin' money for myself, too."

The other nodded. "You're makin' the bank pay, Jud. No one could say you ain't. But there's plenty of folks that think you're too hard—foreclosin' on folks that could of paid out if they was given more time to, buyin' up paper an' clampin' down on folks, an' the like of that."

"Notes an' mortgages are contracts. If a man makes a contract he's got to live up to it er suffer the consequences. That's the law. I ain't never gone contrary to the law."

"I ain't sayin' you ain't got the law on your side, Jud. But if old Nate found gold, where is it? I never heard about any gold mine bein' worked in the hills."

"He found the gold, all right. I never loaned him that hundred dollars till I'd sent the samples he fetched in to the city an' got an assay on 'em. Them samples was rich, all right—'high grade ore,' they called it in the report. I let him have the money then, an' he was goin' out an' fetch in a couple of ton of the ore. He claimed his mine was in a kind of a cave—but he never let on where. But the damn revenooers shot him before he ever got the ore out. Trouble with Nate—he had too many irons in the fire."

"Then you still believe there is a mine somewheres back in the hills?"

"I know damn well there is. I seen the samples, an' had 'em assayed. Fer a couple of years I spent my spare time pokin' around in the hills huntin' that cave—but there's hundreds of little caves, an' I never located the right one. But some day someone's goin' to find it. An' when they do, believe me, I'm goin' to get in on it!"

Whipple shrugged. "Mebbe you're right, Jud. Well—good luck to you. I've got to make this deposit an' get back to the store. The mail's all sorted. I see folks comin' away from the post office."

III

BLACK JOHN TRUDGED along the dusty road that followed the course of a creekbed deeper and deeper into the hills. Now and then he would swing the heavy valise from his shoulder, wipe the sweat from his forehead, lie down on his belly and drink deeply from a roadside spring. He passed numerous cabins perched in their irregular clearings that scarred the hillsides. Now and then the lips behind the heavy black beard smiled as some native dilapidated buggy, or a pedestrian passed staring in frank curiosity.

The shadows were deepening the narrowing valley as he finally left the road and followed a little-used lane to a clearing half a mile up a draw.

He paused, set the valise on the ground, and stood for a long time leaning on the rail fence staring at the cabin from the stone chimney of which smoke curled lazily. It was a familiar scene—the log cabin with the whitewashed porch in front, the ramshackle stable in the rear, and the privy at the end of the well worn path. Nothing was changed. The bucket still hung at the end of its pole above the stone curbed well, and martins twittered about the bird house canted crazily on top of the wind-broken tree stub—a picture out of the past.

The door opened and a man stepped out onto the porch,

seated himself in the splint rocker, and proceeded to fill a pipe. A hound dog emerged from beneath the porch, yawned, stretched, and ascending the steps curled up at the man's feet.

For several moments Black John gazed at the big-framed, gaunt man, whose snow-white beard cascaded over his shirtfront. "Goin' on seventy, an' nary stoop to his shoulders," he muttered, picking up the valise. "Looks like pictures of Abraham. Wonder if he'll know me?"

Stepping through the turnstile, he made his way up the path. The oldster took the pipe from between his lips and eyed the approaching man. The hound at his feet, cocked an ear and gazed with sad brown eyes, slowly thumping the floor boards with his tail.

"Come up, stranger, an' set," the old man invited, indicating an empty chair without rising. When the other had seated himself he asked abruptly, "You et?"

The black-bearded one nodded and smiled. "Yeah, I fetched a snack along an' et beside a spring. Ma inside?"

The oldster leaned forward regarding the other with piercing gray eyes. He removed the pipe from between his lips. "You— son! Well, now, I'm powerful glad to see you. Ma's gone. Passed away three year now, come New Year's. A misery ketched her. It was the Lord's will. You be'n away a long time."

"Yeah, it's quite a while. But things ain't changed none."

The other shook his head slowly. "No. There's been bornin's, an' marryin's, an' dyin's. But the hills don't change."

"You still preachin'?"

"Yes. Still carryin' on the work of the Lord. One Sunday in the Sharon church, an' the next at Mt. Sinai."

"Pretty good pay?"

"I can't complain. Mt. Sinai pays me a hundred dollars a year, an' Sharon eighty. They don't never quite make the full amount, but they do all they can. I get a lot of meals, what with preachin', an' callin' on sick folks. Then there's the farm, an' the marryin's.

I get two dollars, or a couple of hens, an' now an then a shoat—accordin' to what they can afford. It all helps out. Sim Beckle give me ten dollars the time I married his Sally off to Tom Mason."

Black John grinned. "Sally Beckle—she was Sim's oldest gal, wasn't she? The squint-eyed one? Sim must of thought it was worth that to get shet of her."

"She wa'n't pretty, nor yet young. But she was a good worker."

Black John's eyes swept the weed-choked clearing, and came to rest on the three or four acres of plowed land. "You mentioned the farm," he said. "Looks like yer sort of behind with yer plowin'."

"No. My corn's all in. What with preachin', an' visitin' sick folks here an' there amongst the hills, I ain't got time fer a great deal of farmin'. Besides that, the land's runnin' lean. Fact is, son, there ain't manure enough in one mule to keep a forty-acre farm goin'."

"Have you tried gettin' more mules?"

"No. It wouldn't pay. They'd eat their heads off."

"Looks like yer sort of stalemated," Black John grinned. "It don't look like you could make a livin' fer you an' a mule off'n that little patch of corn."

"No. But I don't have to worry about it no more. This is the last crop I'll be takin' off the place."

"Figgerin' on movin'?"

"Got to. Judson Grimm's done foreclosed on me."

"You mean Jud Grimm that runs the feed store in town?"

"He used to run the feed store. He's a banker now. Makin' a lot of money, they say. Dresses up in store clothes every day. Didn't you see the new brick bank in town?"

"Yeah, I noticed it. Seen a man standin' on the steps when I come by. Didn't recognize him as Jud Grimm—but sense you mention it, that's who it was, all right. He give me a kind of hard-eyed stare when I went by—like he was sort of appraisin' me."

"Judson Grimm is hard-eyed, an' hard-hearted," the old man replied. He coaxes folks into borrowin' more money than they can afford to borrow from the bank to buy things they don't need, an' then when the time comes an' they can't pay it back he forecloses on 'em. There's Zeke Hardy, over on Sand Crick, an' Joe Massy, an' Sam'l Patten—Jud's took all their land away from 'em. There's plenty more I could name, too. An' there's the widder Semple—he tuk her cow, an' her mule, an' her hens, an' her two geese, an' her plow, an' wagon—he tuk even her bed an' her cook stove when he foreclosed agin her on a chattel mortgage he got her to sign fer the hundred dollars he loant her to visit her sister in Atlanty."

"More vitriol in his soul than milk of human kindness, eh?"

"I've went to him more'n onct—not fer myself, but fer others, to see if I couldn't git him to ease up on 'em—to give 'em a chanct to save their land—but it wa'n't no use. Might's well talk to a stone. Judson Grimm never done a kind act in his life. Fer's anyone knows, he never had a kind thought in his head. He's all fer makin' money, Judson is. He does it all legal, too. He's a good business man. There can't no one git the best of him."

"H-u-u-m-m," Black John mused, "an' interestin' case, to be shore. An' one that, in all equity should be dealt with. You know, Pa, there's some folks claims I'm a pretty good business man, myself. I might do a stroke of business with Jud Grimm that might net some slight profit, an' teach Jud a lesson besides."

The old man's brow drew into a frown, and he peered intently into the other's eyes. "There can't no one git the best of Judson Grimm, an' do it honest," he stated with conviction. "An' remember, son—the Lord laid a heavy hand on Willie fer departin' from the straight an' narrow path. Don't you go tryin' to git the best of Jud by no questionable method—like holdin' up the bank, er nothin' like that. They've got a new burglar alarm on it—an' besides it wouldn't be right. Look at what happened to Willie."

"Good gosh, Pa! I hope you don't include me in the same

category with Willie! Why robbery is as crude as it is immoral! By the way, I assume that Willie is still down in Atlanta thinkin' it over."

"Yes. He got twenty years. The Govmint's hard on a man that robs a mall train. Not that I'm sayin' Willie didn't have it comin'. He hadn't ort to done it. But Willie was a good boy, in the main. Fact is, son, I allus figgered he was the best of the two of you. You was inclined to be wild. That's why I sent you to the theological seminary when you got through school. I figgered you was smarter'n Willie, an' would learn to be a preacher. Then, couple years later I got a letter sayin' they'd throw you out fer some prank you done. Me an' ma figgered you'd come home. But you never come."

Black John grinned. "No, I jest sort of kep' on agoin'. You see, Pa, there's a lot of young hickory growin' right handy—an' I had a lot of respect fer yer good right arm. Big as I'd got to be, I know'd you was bigger. An' besides, I didn't care much fer farmin', nohow. An' there was too many abstruse p'ints in theoretical theology fer my limited intelligence to master—so I decided to forego the ministry, too."

"Them p'ints you speak of kin be forgot. I never went to no seminary. I jest preach the Word like it stands in the Bible, in a way folks kin understand, an' leave all them p'ints fer the city preachers to wrangle over."

"It's jest as well," approved Black John. "But gettin' back to Jud Grimm. You claim there ain't no one ever got the best of him in a business venture, eh?"

"That's right. That is, no one but old Nate Bascome. An' that was before Judson was a banker—whilst he was still runnin' the feed store. Nate he took Judson in on a gold mine deal."

Black John's eyes lighted. "A gold mine? Was Jud interested in gold?"

"He was—an' he is yet, from what I hear. Everyone here in the hills knows about it. They still laugh about the time old Nate took Judson fer that hundred dollars."

"A hundred dollars, eh? Gosh, it must of be'n quite a deal!"

"It couldn't of hurt Judson no more if it had be'n a hundred thousan'. He's allus braggin' about what a good business man he is. He'd holler till you could hear him a mile if he lost a dime."

"How was this here Gargantuan swindle worked?"

"Well, old Nate, he run a couple of stills back in the hills in a couple of caves. Then one time the revenooers found his stills an' smashed 'em up, an' confisticated all his licker. So Nate was broke. Well, he wanted to git a fresh start, so he begun pokin' around the hills an' hintin' here an' there, about a gold mine he'd found. Judson Grimm heard about it, an' he got Nate in the feed store one day an' ax him about this gold mine. Nate told him he'd located a vein of gold in a cave, back in the hills, but he couldn't git only a little of the ore out, on account it was stuck in the rocks. He 'lowed if he had a hundred dollars he could buy him a drill, an' a pick, an some powder, an' caps, an' fuse, an' begin minin' his gold.

"Judson tried to git him to tell where this here cave was at—but old Nate wouldn't. But he showed him some samples of rock, an' Judson sent 'em off somewheres to be assayed, an' pretty quick he got a report that they was high-grade ore. So Judson gits Nate to sign a paper givin' him a half interest in this here mine, an' he gives Nate a hundred dollars fer to buy the stuff he needed. Nate he goes to the city an' blows in the hundred fer copper tubin', an' new mash ba'r'ls an' a lot of stuff, an' hunts up a new cave, an' starts his new still. But the revenooers was onto him—an' they surrounded him an' when Nate shot it out with 'em they killed him. Nate's boy, Sam, was in on the fight, an' he shot one of the revenooers an' skipped out, an' ain't never b'en heered from sence. Judson hollered his head off, an' tried to git his hundred back on Nate's widder—but her lawyer told her Jud couldn't do nothin' about it. That paper Nate signed wa'n't no good, on account of it didn't have no property description onto it. Well, Judson hunted around in the hills, off an' on, fer years—but he never found Nate's mine."

Black John's brow drew into a puzzled frown. "But them samples Nate showed Jud? This here's a limestone an' granite country. There's no quartz in the hills, nor any other gold-bearin' rock. Where'd he git them samples?"

The old man smiled. "Well, son, I reckon I'm the onliest one in the hills that knows about them samples—an' I never told nary soul. When Nate got shot, he lived half the night through, an' I went there to offer him what comfortin' words I could from the Book. He repented fer everythin' he'd done incloodin' cheatin' Judson Grimm. He told me that them samples was fetched from Californy by his grandpa years ago, an' had be'n layin' around on the fireplace shelf ever sence. Nate he rec'lected 'em, an' it give him the idee. I'd of told it around fer a good joke on Judson, except that I know'd he was goin' to a lot of work, an' a lot of trouble, an' wastin' a lot of time huntin' that mine—an' I figgered it wouldn't hurt him none to keep on huntin'. Judson was mean an' graspin' even before he started the bank."

Black John nodded thoughtfully. "You done right, Pa," he approved. "An' if I was you, I'd never breathe a word of this to any livin' soul as long as you live. A man as hard an' as graspin' as Jud Grimm is, had ort to be punished fer the things he's done to folks—an' fer a man of his ilk, there ain't no worse punishment than livin' right here in the hills, knowin' there's a fortune layin' buried in some cave—an' he can't do nothin' about it."

"That's right, son. It's the Lord's way of punishin' him. I shore won't do nothin' to interfere with the workin' of His will."

"Okay. Now—take the farm here, Pa—I s'pose you'll sort of hate to part with it, eh?"

For a long time the old man's glance shifted here and there about the clearing. Finally he removed the pipe from between his lips.

"No, son I don't reckon I'll care much. Ma's gone. An' you boys is gone. An' like I said, the land's gittin' leaner every year. I'm gittin' older, too—seems like it's harder an' harder to git the work done."

"Where do you figger on goin'?"

"I ain't give it no thought. I'll go somewheres. I'll make out. I'll have my preachin' money, an' I'll find somewheres to live."

"The old place ain't changed none," Black John said. "Everything jest the same as I remembered it. I s'pose that old cave is still jest like it was when me an' Willie used to play robber, an' hole up there."

"Yes. Way over in the back corner. That part of the field's all grow'd up to bresh. So long sence I've be'n over there I'd most fergot about the cave."

"How'd you like to go to town tomorrow an' pay off the mortgage on the farm?"

"Why—son, I can't. It's three hundred dollars, besides the interest. I ain't got the money."

"I'll let you have the money."

"You got that much?"

"Oh shore. I told you I was counted a good business man."

"Before I'll touch a penny of it I'd have to know it was come by honest. Remember Willie."

"The facts speaks fer themselves—Willie's in, an' I'm out."

"Even if I got the farm back, what'll I do with it? The land's gittin' porer every year—an' I'm gittin' older. I'd jest have to mortgage it agin. That is, unless you'd stay an' help me work it, son! The two of us could work along together. We could git another mule, an' mebbe a couple of cow an' some sheep, an' bring the land back. Then Sundays we could divide up on the preachin'. You could have Mr. Sinai, an' I'd keep Bethel. That way we could make a go of it."

BLACK JOHN gravely shook his head. "No, Pa, I don't hardly think it would work out. You see, I've got a little rusty on my farmin' an' my theology has kind of suffered a relapse, too. I figgered if you was to pay off the mortgage you'd sell the farm to me."

"But if you don't aim to farm why would you want to buy it? Mebbe," the father added, "it's on account of old mem'ries you've got of the place you was born an' raised?"

Black John grinned. "No, I wouldn't care to lay out much cash on them old mem'ries. Fact is, Pa, you tried to whale the word of the Lord into me an' Willie through the wrong end. This here purchase would be in the nature of an investment."

The old man eyed him shrewdly. "Son," he asked abruptly, "what kind of a business you be'n follerin', that folks would say you was a smart business man?"

"W-e-l-l, I've dabbled in whit you might call speculation, now an' then. My reg'lar vocation is prospectin' fer gold."

"Gold. You be'n way out West?"

"Yeah, quite a piece."

"You better stick to your prospectin', son. Land here in the hills is goin' down—not up. This hull forty ain't worth much more'n what the mortgage an' interest calls fer."

"That's ondoubtless true, Pa. But I've got a kind of extry special reason fer wantin' to buy this partic'lar piece of property. It's on account of the cave."

"The cave!"

"Yeah. As I rec'lect it me an' Willie used to crawl through a kind of passage in under some tilted limestone slabs for twenty, thirty feet an' then the cave widened out into a considerable room. Me an' Willie kep' a couple of old blankets in there, an' wood an' matches, an' when we know'd you'd be layin' fer us fer some bit of hell-raisin' we'd got into, we'd knock off a couple of hens, an' drag 'em in there an' lay low fer a couple of days till you got cooled off. What with the seepage water, we got along okay. I rec'lect we rigged one of them slabs so when it was braced from the inside you couldn't git past it."

The old man nodded. "Yes, I used to git powerful angry with you boys—the way you carried on. But mebbe I was too hard on you. I figgered it was fer your own good. But—the way Willie turned out, mebbe I was wrong."

"Don't look at it that way, Pa. We never got a lick amiss. Trouble with Willie, his moral fibre prob'ly wasn't as tough as mine."

"But what would you want with the cave now?" the old man persisted, a twinkle in his shrewd gray eyes. "I'll promise not to whale you—even if you was to fill up on corn licker."

"The fact is, Pa, I come back here to the hills where I can be absolutely ondisturbed while I'm puttin' the finishin' touches on an invention I'm workin' on."

"What kind of invention?"

"Well, it's a—a universal solvent."

"A what?"

"A universal solvent. A chemical compound that'll dissolve anything. It's like this—water will dissolve sugar an' salt, an' sech like things. Acids of different kinds will dissolve different metals. An' strong alkalies will dissolve other things. What I'm strivin' fer is a chemical that'll dissolve anything—no matter what it is."

"You mean wood, er glass, er metal, er rubber—er anything you could git holt of?"

"That's right."

The old man was silent for several minutes. Finally he spoke. "When you git it—what you goin' to keep it in?" he asked.

Black John gulped, choked slightly in his beard, and regarded the other with twinkling eyes. "That, Pa," he replied impressively, "is the finishin' touch I was referrin' to. I've got the solvent, all right. That part was fairly easy. It's the container that's botherin' me."

"You mean you done invented somethin' that will dissolve anythin'—an' now you got to go to work an' invent somethin' it won't dissolve?"

"That's right."

"Seems like, son, yer kinda workin' in circles, ain't you? What good is it goin' to be when you git it?"

"What good is it! Cripes, the Government'll take all I can make of it at a mighty good price. Jest think what it would mean in road buildin', fer instance—no more hills, no more big rocks to move er build around—jest pour on some solvent—an' presto, the hill er the rock is gone, an' they can go ahead an' lay a level road. An' in war—jest think what it would mean in war—load a cannon with solvent an' shoot it at a fort er a ship—an' when the shells explode an' blow the solvent around, there ain't no more fort, ship, guns, er soldiers—they're all dissolved an' run off down the crick."

"Hum—looks like you got somethin' there, son—if it works."

"Oh, it works, all right. But it's got to be kep' mighty secret till I perfect the container—that's why I thought of the cave. Don't tell a soul what I'm doin' in there—don't even tell anyone who I am. An' jest to keep folks from pesterin' you about what's goin' on here, it might be a good idea fer you to move to town."

"Move to town!"

"Shore. We'll slip into town tomorrow. You go to the bank an' pay Jud Grimm what's owin' him, an' get the mortgage. Then you deed the farm over to me. I'll give you a good bargain. Money ain't no object to me."

"But—son, when I deed the farm over to you, folks'll know who you be—it'll be right there in the deed."

"You deed it to John Smith. That's all they need to know about me—"

THE OLDSTER frowned. "But, son—it don't seem right, somehow. It's like lyin'. You ain't John Smith, an'—"

"To all intents an' purposes I am. Listen, Pa—it's like this. You know how authors uses pen names, nom de plumes, some call it—like Mark Twain, an' Artemus Ward, an' a lot of others. Them ain't their real names. They're names they took to keep folks from pesterin' 'em fer their autograph, an' invitin' 'em to dinners, an' makin' nuisances of themselves generally. It ain't considered lyin'. Why there's good authority for it in the Good Book—St. Paul's real name was Saul—an' what I claim, what's good enough fer St. Paul, is good enough fer me. Takin' our cue from the Good Book, an' these here various authors, us inventors has adopted the same system to keep from bein' pestered. I've used the nom de plume of John Smith with gratifyin' success. It's shielded me from much onwanted notoriety, here an' there— sort of let me go about my business onmolested by certain parties who might seek to curtail my various activities."

The old man nodded. "I reckon you're right, son. I guess, seein' how St. Paul done changed his name there can't be no harm in it. An' it's mighty comfortin' to me to know that you rely on the Book fer guidance. Well, I reckon it's time to turn in, if we're goin' to town tomorrow. I'll sleep better knowin' that Judson Grimm ain't goin' to beat me out of the farm."

IV

DESPITE HIS YEARS the old man set a pace the following morning that aroused Black John's admiration. "You shore ain't feeble on yer legs," he said, as they came to the outskirts of the town. "We've covered that six miles in jest a little over an hour."

"I kin make it quickern' the mule kin—that's why I don't bother to hitch him up. Sundays I walk clost to twenty mile an' preach twict to boot."

"Let's stop in here," Black John said, pausing before the livery stable.

A man in shirt sleeves got up from a chair. "Want a rig?" he asked. "Where to?"

"Got a horse that's sound an' gentle? One that can do twenty mile an' come in with his head up?"

"Yup."

The big man's eyes swept the array of vehicles that lined one side of the shed. "That there rubber-tired buggy—the one with the red wheels—how much?"

"That's accordin' to where yer goin'."

"I'm buyin'—not hirin'. How about that black mare there in the second stall—she all right?"

"Best horse I got in the barn, sound as a dollar, an' a woman can drive her."

"Okay—how much fer her an' the red-wheeled buggy?"

"Well—I—I didn't aim to let her go. I—"

"How much?"

"Well—I'd ort to git a hundred an' fifty fer her. An' that there buggy—I'd ort to git a hundred fer it. It's good as new."

Black John pulled a roll from his pocket and peeled off some bills. "Here's yer money. Hook her up."

Ten minutes later he tied the horse to the hitchrail in front of the bank and followed the oldster inside. Stepping to the wicket window the old man faced the banker. "How much is owin' on my mortgage, Judson?" he asked.

Grimm scowled. "Now listen, Parson, there ain't no mortal use in tryin' to borrow another cent on that farm. I've loaned you more already on it than I'd ort to. The land's petered out, an' you know it." He consulted a record. "The mortgage comes due on the first of August, an' I can't extend the time another day. I've extended it too many times already."

The old gray eyes met the other's gaze squarely. "I didn't ask to borrow any more on the farm, nor yet fer no extension. I asks how much is owin'—up to now."

Again the man consulted his record, figured a moment, and passed a slip of paper under the wicket. "There you are—three hundred an' eighty-one dollars an' sixty-two cents, to date."

Reaching into his pocket the old man drew out a roll, counted out three hundred and eighty-two dollars, which he shoved toward the other. "There you be," he said. "I've got thirty-eight cents comin'. Give me them notes, an' the mortgage."

Grimm's eyes widened at sight of the roll. The scowl faded from his face, and the thin lips smiled. "Well now, Parson, I don't like to be hard on no one—'specially a preacher. If it ain't right handy for you to pay off the mortgage, s'pose you just pay the interest. That way, I'll extend it fer another year—might even let you have another fifty on the place."

"Give me the notes an' the mortgage. I done sold the farm."

"Sold it! Who to?"

"To John Smith."

"John Smith! Where's John Smith goin' to get the money to pay fer it? He can't get it here! He's no good—"

"It ain't the John Smith you mean. It's this man, here."

"Oh!" The gimlet eyes of the man behind the wicket shifted to the big man who stood with an elbow on the wall desk that held an inkwell, a couple of pens, and a pad of deposit slips. "Say, ain't you the man that come in on the train yesterday?"

"Yup."

"You don't look like a farmer."

"Nope."

"If you're lookin' for a farm, I can show you some good ones. This farm of the parson's ain't nothin' but a side-hill forty that's all run down, an' never was no good in the first place."

"That's jest the kind of a place I'm lookin' fer."

"You a coal man?"

"Nope."

"Prospectin' fer oil, maybe?"

"Nope." Black John turned to the older man. "Come on, Parson—get yet papers an we'll be gettin' along."

The banker thrust the mortgage and the canceled notes beneath the wicket, and the two left the bank. Black John grinned to himself as he caught the expression of consuming curiosity with which the banker watched their departure.

As he untied the horse Black John motioned the old man to the driver's seat. "You handle the reins," he said, "an' we'll sort of drive around an' see if we can find a house fer sale."

"A house? Clem Whipple's old house is fer sale er rent—all furnished ready fer someone to move in," the oldster said. "Clem he build him a big house further up the street, an' they jest moved in last month. Clem's woman she has a baby about every year, an' she fin'ly pestered Clem into buildin' a bigger house. Clem he runs the big store yonder where them binders an' mowin' machines is alongside of."

In the store Black John came directly to the point. "You got a house fer sale?" he asked.

"Yes—it's the one right next to the store, here."

"Furnished?"

"Sure. Figgered it might rent better that way. I built me a new one an' bought all new stuff. But I'd ruther sell than rent."

"How much?"

"Well—it's in good shape—no busted winders, good tight ruff. Runnin' water an' 'lectric lights. Good privy an' a one-stall barn out back. I'd ort to git twelve hundred fer it, jest as it stands. How do you want to pay?"

"Cash."

"You mean—cash money—right on the spot?"

"Yup. Make out the deed to the parson, here. Show a clear title, an' it's a deal."

THE THREE proceeded to the court house, and a couple of hours later, as the two were driving back into the hills, the oldster spoke. "You must have a sight of money, son—the way you throw it around. I'll bet you could of made Jim Baxter throw off twenty-five dollars on this here rig, if you'd of dickered a little—an' that house, I'm shore goin' to take a sight of comfort in it. I'll be mighty proud to live in town. It's a fine house. But if you'd belittled it an' found fault with it, Clem would prob'ly of throw'd off a hundred dollars fer a cash money sale. You claim folks figgers you're a good business man, but dog me if I kin see why they would—payin' the first askin' price fer stuff that-a-way."

"I don't never stop to shoot skunks when I'm on a moose hunt."

"What?"

"Oh, jest a way of speakin'," the big man grinned. "Now you remember, Pa—don't never let on that I'm your son, to no one, at no time."

"I've give my word. It'll be a little further to walk out to Mt. Sinai on Sundays, but I won't mind. It's worth it—livin' right in town."

"Walk! You ain't got to do no walkin' from now on, Pa. That's what I bought this rig fer."

"You mean this here rig—it's fer me!"

"Shore it is."

The old man was silent for a long time. "A good drivin' hoss, an' a red wheel buggy—an' rubber tires. Son, I never expected to see the day when I'd own a rig like this."

"It'll beat walkin'," the big man grinned, "an before I forgit it, here's five hundred dollars you better shove in yer pocket fer to kind of keep you goin'. Costs money to live in town—what with horse, feed, an' all."

"You're a good son—it makes me feel kinda bad—the way I used to whale you when you was young. I done it fer your own good, but—it makes me feel kinda bad. Anyways, you've turned out a fine man."

"Don't you feel bad about it, Pa. It was ondoubtless them whalin's that forged me into the sterlin' character that I am. Without 'em, I might of gone to the dogs."

"Out in the hills the folks is sure goin' to wonder how come I got a rig like this."

"Jest tell 'em you traded the farm to John Smith fer the rig, an' the house in town."

The old man smiled. "It's a good thing you earnt the reputation fer bein' a good business man somewheres else. 'Cause folks around here sure ain't a-goin' to think so. They'll figger I skun the eyeteeth out of you."

"They might change their minds later," Black John replied, dryly. "The reputation of bein' a fool never hurt no one—if he ain't one."

V

TOWARD THE MIDDLE of the afternoon, two days later, Jud Grimm followed Clem Whipple to the door of the bank after Whipple had made his daily deposit. Whipple paused on the step and pointed down the street. "There comes that feller now—the one that come in on the train t'other day. He sure seems to have plenty of money. He never says, 'I, yes, er, no' when I told him what I helt my house at. Jest forked over the cash like it was small change."

Grimm frowned. "That's the same way he bought that rig off'n Jim Baxter. Just asks how much—an' pulled a roll that would choke a horse, an' peeled off the money."

"I was askin' the parson about him, last evenin' when he come in the store. But he don't know nothin' except the fella come to his place the other evenin'. Claimed his name is John Smith, from out West somewheres.

"Claimed he wanted to buy the parson's farm, an' the parson traded it to him fer that rig, an' my house. Looks like the feller ain't got good sense. Cripes, the house alone's worth two farms like that there side-hill forty!"

"Besides that, he gave the parson the money to pay off the mortgage the bank held on it."

"Yeah—an' he must of give the parson quite a chunk of money on top of that, 'cause he had quite a roll on him when he bought some stuff in the store."

"I offered to show him some good farms, but he claimed the parson's farm was jest what he was lookin' for."

"He don't look like a farmer."

"I'd say he's a damn fool."

"Well, you can't always tell. He might be up to somethin'—like prospectin' for oil, or coal."

"I ask him that right here in the bank, an' he says he ain't."

"Well—whoever he is, I got to get back to the store. There comes Joe Bracken drivin' up fer that mower I sold him yesterday."

A FEW moments later Black John paused before the door of the bank and nodded to the man who stood in the doorway. "Howdy," he said. "I'd like to make a little deposit."

Grimm's gimlet eyes lighted. "Step right in, Mr. Smith. Fine day!" He passed through a swinging gate and stepped behind his wicket. "Jest make out a deposit slip at the desk, Mr. Smith. Always glad to make new friends. That's what we're here for—to accommodate our customers."

The big man smiled and advanced to the window. "This here ain't exactly the kind of a deposit you're used to handlin, I reckon. It's gold."

"Gold!"

"Yeah. I ain't had much time to work on my vein yet. Jest took out a little to see how she's comin'. Didn't get started to work till damn near eight o'clock this mornin'. Knocked off at noon. Here it is—must be three, four ounces." As he spoke, he shoved an envelope toward the other, who picked it up, his face showing surprise at the weight, as he balanced it in his hand. Opening the flap, he peered inside.

"How do I know this is gold?" he asked sharply, a gleam of suspicion in his eyes.

Black John grinned. "Wouldn't nothin' but gold be that color, except it was brass—an' I never heard tell of minin' no brass. Besides, brass wouldn't be nowheres near as heavy as what that is."

"Jake Simms, he's a jeweler. He'd ort to know gold when he sees it. Time to lock up, anyhow. His shop's only a couple of doors down the street. We'll show it to him."

"Okay. I'm shore he'll tell you it's gold—once he gets a look at it, an' hefts it."

The jeweler emptied the grains into a small scale. "Three and a half ounces," he said. "That's gold, all right. Nothin' else that heavy, an' that color. I can put the blowpipe on it, if you want."

"Go ahead," Grimm said. "Might's well make sure."

The jeweler stepped to his work bench at the rear of the shop, and a few minutes later he returned. "It's gold, all right," he reiterated. "Pure gold. Not no alloy in it, nor nothin'."

"What's it worth?" Grimm asked.

"Twenty sixty-seven, is what the Government pays for it," the jeweler said. He turned to Black John. "I'll buy it off'n you, if you like."

The big man shook his head. "No. I reckon I'll keep it. Well, I must be gettin' along."

Grimm followed him out of the store. "Come on over to the bank," he said, "an' make your deposit."

Black John shook his head. "I don't like to put you to the bother of onlockin' the bank agin, jest fer a piddlin' three an' a half ounces of gold," he said. "I'll be depositin' plenty of it, onct I get a-goin'. Prob'ly fetch in a batch couple of times a week. I wouldn't like to keep no heft of it on hand. Someone might steal it. An' bein' as yer goin' to handle a lot of it from now on, I'd feel better about it if you'd ship this here little batch in to the Government, er some assayer, an' get a report on it. You could send it in by registered mail."

"That might be a good idee," Grimm agreed, and drew a notebook from his pocket. "Here, I'll give you a receipt for them three an' a half ounces."

Black John waved the receipt aside, with a grin. "Never mind the receipt. If I figured I couldn't trust you with three an' a half ounces, I wouldn't be figurin' on depositin' prob'ly hundreds of pounds of it with you, would I?"

"Hundreds of pounds of it!"

"Oh, shore. When I get a-goin' I figure I'd ort to be gittin' out anyways a pound er so a day."

"Gettin' it out of where?" The big man noted that the gimlet eyes were fairly gleaming with avaricious excitement.

"Why—out of my mine, of course."

"You mean—you found a gold mine on that forty you bought off'n the parson."

"Well—I don't know's you could say, I *found* the mine. You see, I know'd it was there before I bought the farm."

"But—how could you know that? You ain't been around here only a couple of days."

Black John grinned. "That's right. But I know'd it, jest the same. It's a kind of a long story—but it b'iles down to me runnin' onto a feller out in Nevada last month that was in bad shape. I was workin' a proposition that wasn't doin' none too good, back in the mountains—an' this feller was workin' another one about six mile from me—an' he was goin' good. Yeah, he had a mighty good thing there—takin' out plenty of high-grade ore.

"I was hittin' fer town that day, an' I stopped in to see if there was anythin' he needed that I could fetch out to him. An' by cripes, I found him pinned down to the floor of his tunnel by a big rock that had dropped down from the top. I seen he was in a bad way—all smashed up. This here rock must of weighed tons, I couldn't do nothin' but fetch him some water, an' give him a swig of licker out of my flask.

"He kind of revived when the licker took holt, an' he told me he know'd he didn't have long to live, an' how he hated to die there alone. I told him I'd go to town fer help—but he know'd, an' I know'd it wasn't no use, bein' as town was twenty miles away, an' I was afoot. So he says if I'd stay there with him to the end, he'd put me onto the best damn proposition I ever heard tell of.

"Well, I didn't take much stock in it, but I hated to go off an' leave a man to die alone in misery, so I stayed with him, an' then he tells me about this here farm of the parson's, here in the hills, an' how years ago his pa had found a gold mine in a cave on the back end of this here forty. He claimed the person didn't know nothin' about it, an' his dad was goin' to wait till he'd took out some more gold, an' then buy the farm off'n the parson. But in the meanwhile, the old man got shot by the revenue men. He claimed he was in on the fight, an' that he shot one of the officers, an' had to skip out. That's why he never dared to come back an' work this mine.

"Still, I didn't take much stock in it, an' Sam seen I didn't. 'John,' he says, 'you got to believe me. You ain't doin' none too-good where yer at. I know it, an' you know it. I'm dyin'. I'm done. That there mine back East ain't never goin' to do me no good—even if I dasted to go back an' work it. Yer doin' me a mighty good turn, by settin' here with me till the end, an' I aim to show you I appreciate it. Go back an' work that mine, an' you'll get rich—an' it won't take long, neither. I'm a dyin' man, John,' he says, 'an' I swear I'm tellin' the truth—an' to back it up, I'm givin' you what cash I've got on hand—ten thousan' dollars—it's in under the loose board in my floor back of the stove. You might's well have it. It won't never do me no good, where I'm goin'.'"

"Well, I set there with him till he died a couple hours later, an' then I went in his shack, an' shore enough there was the ten thousan' in bills, right where he claimed it was. So I took the money an' come here. I figured that even if he was lyin', I'd come out ahead—even if there wasn't no parson where he said there was, an' no cave, an' no gold. With that ten thousan' I'd get a chanct to see the Eastern country, an' if the mine didn't pan out, I could go back to my own claim, there in Nevada.

"But he was right. The parson was here, an' the cave's right where he claimed it was—an' best of all, the gold's there. It's even better than he claimed it was."

"What was this man's name—the one that told you about the cave?" Grimm's voice trembled slightly from suppressed excitement.

"Him? His name was Sam Bascome. Er at least that's what he claimed it was. Well, so long, banker. I got to git over to the store. I want to git a pick, an' some powder an' caps an' fuse. See you in a few days."

A MONTH passed, during which Black John made bi-weekly deposits of gold, each a little larger than the last, until his fifty pounds of dust was credited to his account. It was near closing time the day he made the last deposit. "You better figure her up, banker," he said. "I reckon I'll draw out the amount of them deposits in cash—ort to run a little better'n sixteen thousan', at the Government price."

Grimm eyed him shrewdly between the bars of the little wicket. "You mean you're drawin' it all—closin' out your account?"

"Hell, no! Not closin' out my account! Jest drawin' down what money is comin' to me. You see, banker, I found out my vein is widenin' out as she goes down. It's gettin' so's it's more'n I can handle, alone. Then, workin' in a cave, that way, it ain't so good, neither. It's so dark in there I've got to keep four, five lanterns goin' all the time, an' it's damp an' onhealthy. I feel the rheumatiz beginnin' to ache in my bones a-ready. I didn't want to make no move till I found out what the vein was goin' to do—but now I know it's widenin', instead of pinchin' out, I figure it's time to sort of expand."

"How do you mean—expand?"

"Well—first off, I want to take the roof offn that cave—cut into the hill till it's all open above the vein. I couldn't ask no crew of men to work in there, the way it is."

"Crew of men! I thought you was workin' alone!"

"I have b'en up to now. But not no more. Like I said, the job's gettin' too big fer one man to handle. Cripes—by puttin' on a crew of men I could be takin' out ten, fifteen times as much as what I am now. So I'm goin' to start a company."

"You mean, incorporate a company—sell stock—an' all that?"

"Yeah—I guess that's the way they'll do it. I don't know

nothin' about sech doins'. That'll be up to them. I don't care how they work it—jest so I git my share of the gold."

"Up to who? Who do you mean by 'them'?"

"Why, them New York fellas—the ones I'm goin' to see—the ones that's got to organize the company, an' put up the money. That's why I'm drawin out my cash—so I can show it to 'em, an' tell 'em how long it took me to get out that much gold—an' they'll know I ain't tryin' to put nothin' over on 'em."

"But—why are you goin' to New York? Why not—?"

"That's where the money is—yes, sir— right there on Wall Street. That's right where all them big companies git's started."

Grimm glanced at the clock on the wall. "Closin' up time," he said. "Wait till I lock the doors. Then come on inside here, an' let's talk this thing over."

"I don't want to miss the train to New York. I done bought my ticket when I come past the depot."

"The train don't leave fer two hours. In the meantime, you an' I can talk business." He locked the doors, and led the way inside the railing. "Set there," he said, indicating a chair near his desk. "Don't you know," he began, "that if you was to go to New York with this proposition, them big money men will clean you out slicker'n a whistle?"

Black John shook his head. "It's my mine. How could they?"

"They'll do it, all right. You wouldn't have a show. They'd organize a company of some kind, an' ball the papers all up with 'whereases' and 'be it knows' an' all such nonsense, till you won't know where you're at—but they will. You won't be no-wheres—an' they'll have the mine. An' they'll have it legal. There won't be a damn thing you can do about it. Even if they did give you some stock—it would only be a small amount. Cripes, they'd issue thousan's of shares, an' sell 'em, an' wouldn't give you only enough to keep you from squawkin'.

"What you want is a partnership—not a corporation. Yes, sir—just you an' one partner. Then you know that whatever the mine makes, you get the half of it. An' that partner ort to be a local man."

"Yeah—but there ain't no local man got enough money fer to buy a half interest in my mine."

"How much do you figger it's worth?"

BLACK JOHN pondered. "Well, a proposition that kin make better'n sixteen thousan' clear profit in a month, had ort to be worth quite a bit. That's damn near two hundred thousan' a year. Not only that—but the vein's widenin', like I said. No tellin' what she'll pay when I get a crew in there."

"But the vein might narrow down agin—or it might run out altogether."

"That's right. A man's got to take a chanct on that. But I've done consid'rable minin'—an' I know it ain't apt to. I'll bet you a thousand to one, that the vein'll keep on widenin'."

"You ain't named your figure fer a half interest in the mine."

"You mean—*you* want to buy a half interest, go into pardnership with me on it?"

"Well—I might. If the price is right."

"How much you got?"

"How much do you want?"

"I wouldn't take a damn cent less'n two hundred thousan'. That's only one year's profit—with only one man workin' the mine. But it's got to be all cash money."

Grimm considered. "That's more cash than I could lay my hands on, jest at the moment."

Black John nodded. "That's what I told you—no local man would have enough cash. That's why I'm goin' to New York. I'll bet they can raise that much."

"I could dig up a hundred thousand—an' give you my note for the balance."

"Nope—two hundred thousan', cash money. That's my price. I won't come down none."

"By God, I ain't going to let this chance slip!" Grimm exclaimed. "I believe I can arrange to get the money in the city."

"In New York?"

"No, no! We won't have to go as far as that."

"I got to have every damn cent in cash money—no notes, no checks, no bank drafts nor no other kind of paper. Good U.S. bills is the only kind of paper that talks with me."

"Okay. We'll go up on the train. But what do you want with that much cash?"

"I'll tell you, banker. I'm goin' to deposit it in the city bank. You know, this here's only a small bank, as banks go—an' if anything was to go wrong—well, I'd ruther my money was in some big bank. It ain't that I don't trust you. Hell, our monthly deposits here will be more, from now on, than you've ever took in before. I jest want to kind of spread my money around—jest in case."

"Okay. I think I can turn over the cash as soon as the bank opens in the mornin' up in the city. I'll let the girl open the bank here in the mornin', an' I'll catch the noon train back."

"I'll have to get my ticket changed then," Black John said, "an' here's another thing—I see you've got signs up here that you sell life insurance."

"That's right. Want to take out a policy?"

"No. But you know, banker, I feel sort of mean like—buyin' that farm off'n the old parson, for practically nothin', you might say."

"You bought it fair an' square. He ain't got no kick comin'. A bargain's a bargain. He prob'ly figgered he got the best of you. So did we all. When I git the best of someone, you bet I don't lose no sleep over it. I figger if they got the worst of it, that's their hard luck. It ain't nothin' to me. If a man gets took in on a hard deal—that's his fault. I've had 'em come whinin' to me about their hard luck when I've foreclosed on mortgages on 'em. But it don't do 'em no good. If a man ain't got sense enough to hang onto what he's got, he'd ort to lose it."

Black John nodded. "I guess that's a good way to feel, all right. But, somehow, I don't like to take advantage of no one. This here insurance company—they put out annuities, don't they?"

"Sure."

"Okay. The old parson, he told me he's seventy. How much would an annuity cost that would give him, say a hundred dollars a month fer the rest of his life?"

Grimm picked a small book from his desk and thumbed the pages. "Here it is—age seventy—let's see—hundred a month. It'll cost eleven thousan' dollars."

"You mean if I pay in eleven thousan', he'll get a hundred a month long as he lives?"

"That's right."

Black John drew the money the banker had paid him, from his pocket and counted off eleven thousand. "Here you are," he said. "What do I get to show I paid it?"

Grimm smiled. "We'll go right to the main office just as soon as we get through at the bank tomorrow mornin'. They'll fix you up—pay me my commission, too. Come on—we better be getting down to the depot."

LEAVING THE metropolitan bank the following morning, the two stepped across to the office of the insurance company, where the annuity was arranged. "You've jest about got time to go back to the bank an' deposit that cash before train time," Grimm said, as they left the building.

"That's right," the big man agreed. "I'll drop over there right now. You go on down to the depot. Be'n a long time sence I've be'n to a city. I might stop over tonight an' see a show."

Grimm frowned. "Them shows is a waste of money. They soak you two dollars fer a ticket—besides yer meals an lodgin' at the hotel. It's a waste of money."

Black John grinned. "You know, I kinda wish we'd fetched that old parson along. Chances is he never seen a show."

"Looks to me like you'd blow'd in enough on that old fool already," Grimm retorted.

"Oh, I kinda hate to consider he might be thinkin' hard of me—about that farm deal."

"He won't think hard of you when he cashes that hundred dollar check the first of every month," Grimm replied.

"That's right," Black John said. "An' I'll bet *you'll* be thinkin' of me when he cashes them checks, too. Here comes a cab. You better grab it—if you want to ketch that train!"

CUSH'S THIRD WIFE

THE WOMAN WAS tall, blonde, and ample of frame—a frame made up of tightly controlled curves. Her eyes were baby blue, but deep behind their disarming softness lurked a hard, cynical glint—a look of wisdom of a sort. Black John Smith, returning to the Yukon from a not unprofitable trip "outside," judged her to be thirty-five, as she faced him across the table at dinner the first evening out of Seattle.

It was July and the ship's passenger list was made up for the most part of excursionists. The incessant babble of voices rose above the rattle of dishes as Black John's glance swept the room. A few sourdoughs, silently and purposefully shoveling food into their mouths, a professional gambler or two, numerous couples—business men, college professors and their wives obviously bent on broadening themselves by travel, and obviously striving to seem perfectly at home, darted furtive glances about them and exchanged a word or two now and then.

A bevy of vacationing school teachers at one table bantered laughingly with a group of vacationing clergymen at the next. At the end of the room three or four tables had been shoved together beneath a painted banner which proclaimed THE B.P.O.E. LODGE OF SAUK CENTRE, MINNESOTA. Certain of the Elks were enjoying themselves so boisterously that Black John grinned as he caught the stony-eyed glares that several of the lady Elks bestowed on their bibulous mates.

The lady across the table seemed to be unaccompanied. Black

John noted that her eyes, too, had been busy, and by their expression he sensed that she knew what it was all about. Once their glances met and she seemed about to speak, but the moment passed, and her glance dropped to her plate.

Later, toward the end of the long twilight, he came upon her standing alone at the rail, her eyes on the high-flung timbered slopes of the rugged coastline. Their eyes met. He paused and raised his hat. "Good evenin', Ma'am. Fine sight, ain't it?"

The red lips smiled as the blue eyes met his own. "Yeah, if there's a lot of mountains I suppose anyone might as well look at 'em. Gee, think of all them trees! What do they do with 'em all?"

Black John grinned. "They ain't done nothin' with 'em yet. Time'll come, I s'pose, when they'll make 'em all into lumber. Too bad, too. Them big spruces has be'n growin' for a hundred years—mebbe a thousan' for all I know. It's a shame to cut 'em down."

"But they ain't doing no one any good up there on a mountain. Someone might better be getting a profit out of 'em. If

folks are going to keep on building houses they've got to have lumber. I'd say cut 'em down. What's the use letting 'em stand there doing nothing?"

"Just a difference in viewp'int, I guess. I'd rather see a tree than a house, any time."

"You might try living in a tree sometime," she smiled.

"Well, lookin' at it from that angle, I s'pose houses are a necessary evil. You off on a vacation?"

"No. There's enough vacationers on this ship, without me. They'll get 'em an eyeful of this kind of stuff, and then talk about it for the next twenty years. You don't look like you're on no vacation, neither."

"No, I'm goin' back home. Be'n outside for a spell."

"You mean you live up here somewheres?"

"Yeah, in the Yukon."

"Yukon Territory? That's where Dawson is, ain't it? You from Dawson?"

"Occasionally. I'm in an' out of there."

"What business do you follow?"

"Prospectin'."

"Prospecting? You mean you're one of these here miners you read about that dig around in the dirt for gold up there in the Klondike?"

"Yes, that seems to size up the situation, in a general way."

"ACCORDING TO what the papers claim, this here Dawson's a wide open town. They say everyone's a millionaire, an' they throw gold around like it was small change. I read how, taken in the summer time like this, it stays daylight all around the clock, and the saloons run three shifts of barkeeps, and never close their doors, and how the gambling joints and dance halls runs wide open all the time."

"Well, barrin' mebbe a pardonable amount of exaggeration an' distortion, the description seems to fill the bill."

"That's what I like—a wide open town where one can have some fun."

"Are you, perchanct, headin' for Dawson for the purpose of participatin' in these here frivolities?"

"Looks like you know a lot of big words for a miner. You make anyone feel like they was talking to some damn lawyer."

"God forbid!" grinned the big man. "The more I see of lawyers, the less I like 'em."

"You and me both. I ain't exactly heading for Dawson, but you bet, I'm going to stop off there and sort of look around. If it's like the papers claim it had ought to be good. Little Annie knows her way around—don't you worry!"

"Yer plight ain't caused me no gray hairs, so far," Black John chuckled.

The woman winked and nodded toward a couple who approached slowly along the deck. "That good looking school ma'm has copped herself a young preacher and by the way he's eyeing her, if his foot don't slip before the boat hits Skagway, it won't be his fault—nor hers either, by the looks of things."

"Yeah, preachers an' school ma'ms is ondoubtless human like the rest of us. Well, so long. I'll be movin' on. There's a game ribbin' up in the smokin' room, an' I'd kinda like to set in on it."

"What kind of a game?"

"Oh, poker er stud, whichever strikes their fancy. Either one of 'em's recommended to while away a monotonous evenin'.'"

A five-handed game was in progress, and Black John drew up a chair, as the kibitzers, including several of the clergy, moved aside to give him room, and bought a stack of chips.

The players consisted of two professional gamblers, a Yukon sourdough, an Elk, and a business man from Chicago. The game was fairly stiff, and at the end of an hour the Elk shoved in his last chip and lost the pot to the sourdough who showed a flush against the Elk's three kings. He pushed back from the table. "That's all for me, gents. You're a little too rich for my blood. I'm quitting while I've still got my shirt."

"Do you mind if a lady sits in?" Black John glanced up at the words to see the blonde standing beside the vacated chair smiling down at the players. One of the gamblers cleared his throat:

"No, Ma'm. It's an open game. But—er, sometimes the bettin's kinda lively. We wouldn't like to see anyone lose maybe more'n they could afford to—'specially a lady."

"Don't worry about me. I know about how the game's running. I've been looking on for ten, fifteen minutes. Little Annie can look out for herself." She seated herself, reached beneath the table, and following the audible snapping of elastic, produced a sizeable roll, peeled off some bills, and returned the roll to its place.

WHEN THE game broke up, sometime after midnight, "Little Annie," as she called herself, was some six hundred dollars to the good.

The next night she sat in the game again, and Black John

noted the glance she cast at the huge roll of bills he drew from his pocket as he paid for his chips. The game started out with seven players, but by midnight three had dropped out. Black John yawned, and shoved his chips toward the banker. "I'm cashin' in", he said. "Never did take no interest in a four-hand-ed game—ain't enough action."

Fifteen minutes later, as he sat in a deck chair smoking his pipe, his eyes on the vast panorama of mountain shapes slipping astern in the moonlight, the blonde dropped into the chair beside him.

"Gosh, big boy, don't you never get tired gawpin' at all them mountains and trees?"

"It's an inspirin' sight. Makes a man feel sort of insignificant an' futile, in comparison with the vastness of nature—like layin' on yer back an' lookin' up at the stars on a clear night, an' won-derin' what it's all about."

"Yeah," the woman agreed, rather vaguely. "Looking at it that way I suppose it is. Just think—if all them trees was sawed into boards what a lot of houses they'd build. You know, I could fall for this country in a big way. I like a big country, and I like a big man. A girl could do a lot worse for herself than marry some prospector an' live up here from now on. I don't mean none of them damn lushers like you read about that throws their money around there in Dawson. I mean some good all around man that maybe likes to set in a game, now and then, or takes a few drinks when he wants 'em, and goes ahead and 'tends to his business. A girl could be happy like that, and the man would be happy too—just them two living together way off up some crick, if the girl was a good cook like me. Ain't that so?"

"W-e-e-l-l, there's other things to look at than just the cookin'." She laughed—and he hastened on. "I mean like if the girl wasn't used to roughin' it. It's mighty lonesome up some of them cricks. An' then there's bears, an' wolves, an' black flies, an' mosquitoes. An' in winter it gets so cold that if you pull a prospect shaft out of the ground an' lean it agin a tree it'll freeze stiff in a minute an' stand right there till spring. An' then, there's the work. Winter minin' takes a sight of wood to thaw out the gravel, an' more wood for cookin' an' heatin' the shack. The man's got to put in all his time diggin' out the gold, so the woman's got to cut the wood an' haul it in to camp. It's a consid'rable chore, fer anyone that ain't used to it."

"It wouldn't be lonesome if they loved each other, and they could shoot the bears and wolves, and nail screens on the windows to keep out the bugs, and if it got cold you could keep putting on more clothes, and I don't mind hard work. I'll bet I could chop wood if I had to." She paused for a few moments, her eyes on the high-flung skyline. "You married?" she asked abruptly.

"Who—me? Oh, shore. Yeah, I'm married, all right."

"Your wife ain't along with you, is she?"

"No. No, she ain't along. You see, we ain't livin' together no more. She up an' quit me."

"What did she quit for?"

"Early this spring, it was. After she'd got the winter's wood chopped an' hauled in I sent her up the crick about seventy mile to knock over a couple of moose an' pack the meat down. That was along about the last of January, an' it was March before she got the meat all packed down an' cut up an' smoked, an' when she got through she claimed the work was gettin' too hard, so she walked out on me."

The woman laughed. "You've got to think up a better one than that, big boy," she said. "You're too kind hearted to treat a woman like that."

"Who—me? I'm counted the hard heartedest man in the Yukon—bar none."

"You can tell that one to the Marines, too. If you're so damn hard hearted why did you lay down the winning hand tonight when that young lad shoved his last hundred dollars in the pot—and then tell him he'd better get out of the game while the getting was good?"

"How do you know what I laid down? I shoved my hand in the discards."

"Be yourself, big boy. I was dealing, wasn't I?"

"Oh!"

"Yeah—I told you Little Annie can take care of herself. You know I've got a hunch that if you and me was to hook up, we could do mighty well—what with the cards, and all."

"How do you mean—hook up?"

"Why, get married, of course. Take it with the gold digging, and what we could do with the cards, we ought to be able to clean up big. I've had a lot of experience with the cards. I could show you a lot of tricks."

"Yeah? An' I've had some experience with gold diggers, too. An' learnt a few tricks from them. But about this here gettin' married—much as we'd like to, I'm afraid we'll have to forget it. 'Course, I was kiddin' you about the reason my wife walked out on me—it wasn't on account of no work I piled up on her—we just couldn't seem to hit it out, so she quit an' went back to the States. That was a year ago. You see, it wouldn't be doin' right by you if we was to get married—an' me not bein' divorced."

"Don't let that worry you any. I've been married twice, and never got no divorce either time."

"Well, of course, that would sort of even things up. But the fact is, Annie, there's a lot more to it than that. I might's well come right out an' tell you—the reason my wife quit me, she couldn't stand the worry an' the strain of never knowin' when some policeman was goin' to step up an' lay a hand on my shoulder. She never found out about my past till after we was married. Fact is, I'm wanted in six or seven states for various jobs rangin' from train stick-ups to bank robberies. You see, I couldn't ask no good woman to share the fate of a criminal."

THE WOMAN laughed, hunched her chair closer, and laid a hand on his arm. "Listen, big boy—you ain't done nothing! There's a ten thousand dollar reward out for me, right now—and has been for years. My first husband's brother posted it when I faded out of the picture right after my husband died, and they dug him up and found out he'd been poisoned and found out I'd bought a lot of fly-paper, and then found the sheets of paper where I'd throw'd 'em after the poison was soaked off. I played it kind of dumb there—I'd ought to of burned them sheets. But I blew before they done all that. It don't make no difference how much evidence they've got if they don't catch up with me. It's been a long time ago—and they ain't got me yet, so I guess they never will. He had it coming to him—the dirty dog! I found out where he'd been two-timing me right along, so I fed him the fly-paper stuff. And as soon as I got holt of the twenty-five grand the insurance company paid over, I beat it. It takes a damn sight smarter man than Joe Berger to put anything over on Little Annie—you can bet your last blue one on that. I claim he got just what he had coming."

Black John nodded. "Yeah, under the circumstances yer act seems reasonable—mebbe not right down benevolent—but reasonable enough fer practical purposes."

"Sure it was. But the damn cops called it murder—and murder don't outlaw. In a few years them bank and train jobs of yours will be outlawed and they can't do nothing about 'em. And just to show you that you ain't the only repeater on the job, I'd have got my second husband the same way if the rat hadn't skipped out on me just when he did."

"Was he two-timin' you, too?"

"He prob'ly was. I heard afterwards how he two-timed his second—I was his third—by keepin' a woman over in Covington. But I don't know's you could blame him much for that—she was playing around with a B.&O. conductor all the time, according to the talk. Anyhow, she skipped out with him. And a year later Lyme married me."

BLACK JOHN'S lips clamped tightly about his pipe stem, as something clicked in his brain. "B.&O. conductor, eh?" he said.

"Yeah—in Cincinnati, it was. Lyme was tending bar on Freeman Avenue, and when I got acquainted with him I seen where if I married him it would be a dandy hideout till the stink about Joe blow'd over. Neither of us said nothing about being married before. And I didn't give my right name. Lyme was drawing down good enough wages so we lived comfortable enough in an upstairs flat. He was quite a bit older'n me, but I didn't figure on sticking around very long, anyhow. I never told him nothing about the twenty-five grand I had salted away, figuring it wasn't none of his business.

"We'd been married a couple of years, and I was looking around for a chance to pull out on him, when one evening he come home and showed me a roll of eleven hundred and sixty-five dollars he won on a three-horse parlay at Latonia that afternoon. Well, it looked like my chance to get out with more than my shirt, so I slipped down to the store and got me a batch of fly-paper and set it soaking way back in under the bed where I figured Lyme wouldn't never see it.

"The next day I went out to see my sister in Cummingsville, and when I got back I found that Lyme had pulled out on me. Yes, sir—can you 'lieve that? Pulling out on a girl like that— taking his eleven sixty-five and his week's wages with him, and leaving me penniless, for all he knew?"

"Sesh perfidy is almost beyond conception."

"That's ten years ago, an' that's the last I ever heard of Lyme Cushing till last month in Frisco."

"Did you run acrost him there?"

"No—but I run across a man that knew him. Listen—you live somewheres up in this Klondike country—did you ever hear of a place called Halfaday Crick?"

"H-u-u-u-m—Halfaday Crick. Yeah, seems like I've heard the name mentioned. Let's see—Halfaday Crick—seems like the talk is that a bunch of outlaws hangs out there, er somethin'."

"That's the place! That's just what this fellow told me down in Frisco. Whiskey Bill Jones, his name is."

"Whiskey Bill, eh?"

"Yes. Do you know him?"

"Well, I couldn't say as I do, or don't. A lot of fellows shows up around Dawson, off an' on. Seems like I've heard the name spoke."

"Well, one night me and some friends was having us a little drinking party in a café, and this Whiskey Bill come over to our table and got mixed up in it someway, and somehow I happened to mention Lyme Cushing's name, and he claimed how there was a man by that name running a trading post and saloon on this Halfaday Crick, up in the Yukon Territory right close to Alaska. I asked about him and according to the way this Whiskey Bill described, him he's the same Lyme Cushing to which I was married that time in Cincinnati. What's more, Whiskey Bill says how Lyme's making big money, what with his trading post and saloon, and being in with some big outlaw name of Black John. So, not having much more than five grand to my name, I decided to hit right out for this Halfaday Crick and get in on some of Lyme's dough—or know the reason why. You bet Little Annie knows her way around. He'll either come across handsome—or else! Running out on a girl like he done! Then—what I figured, me and you could get hitched, and with what you've got, and what I'll have, we'd be damn well heeled."

"H-u-m. The plan has its merits. But it's got its drawbacks, too. In the first place, Annie, I hate to think of you goin' up there amongst all them outlaws alone, that way. Cripes—anything might happen!"

"Don't you worry about me, big boy! Little Annie can take care of herself—outlaws, or no outlaws. Look—there's that drunken U.S. marshal staggering along the deck—the one that was shooting off his mouth there in the smoking room about what he was going to do, and flashing all them blank warrants he was going to get filled out in Skagway. It'll be a damn wonder if he don't fall off the boat."

"Guess that's right," Black John admitted. "He might do just that—might try to climb the rail, or somethin'. Guess I'd better help him to his room an' put him to bed." He rose. "See you tomorrow, an' we can sort of go into this here thing deeper. It might be we can figure things out."

Ten minutes later, with the marshal tucked into bed with his boots off and his clothes on, Black John retired to his own stateroom, and grinned broadly, as he fingered a blank warrant duly signed by the proper authorities.

"I've got a hunch," he muttered, "that Cush is about to play one of the leadin' roles in a drayma."

II

THE TRIP OVER the pass and down through the lakes was uneventful. Those bound for the journey down the Yukon boarded the *Sarah*, and as the boat approached the mouth of the Pelly Black John turned to the blonde, who stood close beside him at the rail. "So yer plumb set on goin' on up to Halfaday alone, Annie?" he asked. "I still don't feel right about not goin' along. What if somethin' should happen to you up there amongst all them outlaws—after you'd got our future all planned out?"

"Don't you worry about me, big boy. It's like I told you, if you was to go along it might spoil everything. According to what Whiskey Bill said, they're a tough bunch up there—and this Black John is the toughest of 'em all. But no matter how tough they are, they won't harm a lone woman—'specially a girl that's only lookin' for her rights. If you was to go along it might look like a skin game of some kind—like the two of us had it all ribbed up to hook Lyme for a bunch of dough. You wouldn't last ten minutes if Lyme was to turn them outlaws loose on you. But chances is, when they hear me tell how Lyme run out on me there in Cincinnati, an' left me alone an' broke in the big city, they'll up an' make Lyme do the right thing by me."

Black John heaved a deep sigh. "Yeah—I s'pose yer right, Annie. But I was talkin' to the captain an' he says this Halfaday Crick is way up the White River somewheres, an' the White runs into the Yukon about eighty miles above Dawson. What you better do is to go on down to Dawson an' hire a guide to take you to Halfaday. If you won't let me go along I insist on payin' the expenses of the trip." He pulled out a huge roll and stripped off two one hundred dollar bills. "That ort to take care of it all right. I'll be waitin' for you in Dawson when you get back. I'm gettin' off here at Selkirk. Want to see a fella about a proposition he wants to sell a half interest in somewheres up the Macmillan."

The woman's eyes were on the roll he crammed back into his pocket. She drew the two bills slowly back and forth between her fingers. "Now listen, big boy," she said. "From now on we're playing this game double, see? Don't you go putting out no cash till I get back. We'll have plenty then. If we're throwing in together, I've got a right to be in on these deals, too."

"Oh, shore, Annie! If we're throwin' in together, it ain't no more'n right you should. The most I'll do till I see you agin would be to lay out mebbe a hundred dollars fer an option—jest enough to hold the deal till you can look it over." The boat gave a long whistle blast, and Black John hastened away and came back a few moments later with his valise. When the gangplank was lowered, he went ashore. "So long, Annie!" he shouted to the blonde who stood at the rail waving her handkerchief. "See you in Dawson!"

WHEN THE boat passed out of sight around a bend, Black John bought a canoe, loaded supplies and a camp outfit into her, and paddled downriver in the wake of the steamboat.

A week later he stepped through the door of Cushing's Fort, the combined trading post and saloon that served the little community of outlawed men that had sprung up on Halfaday

Creek, close against the Yukon-Alaska border. As he crossed to the bar the somber-faced proprietor reached for dice box, bottle and glasses.

"So you got back, eh? It's about time. Beat them three fives in one."

Black John picked up the box and shook three sixes. "Horse on you," he announced, gathering the dice into the box and rolling them out again. "An' how does them five fours suit you?"

Cush shook four deuces and shoved the bottle across the bar. "Huh," he grunted, "you prob'ly picked up some new kind of a trick whilst you was gone. By God, you stayed away long enough to."

"I ain't shook a game of dice since I left here. How's things be'n goin'?"

"'Bout like always. Every guy that don't hast to be no wheres else comes driftin' in on us."

"Oh, shore. Halfaday always did get more'n its share of the sinful. Any specific, or overt malefactions to report? Or are you merely suspectin' some contemplated infringement of rectitude?"

"You shore as hell ain't fergot no big words wherever you was at, an' you prob'ly invented some new ones. If them was s'posed to be questions you was askin'," he added, filling his glass, "would you mind repeatin' 'em in English."

Black John tossed off his drink. "I was merely inquirin' whether or not any crime had be'n committed on the crick durin' my absence, or do you just figure someone aims to commit one?"

"Well—we had one murder, an' one hangin'. An' there's a couple more fellas moved into Whiskey Bill's old shack that said a damn good hangin' wouldn't hurt none."

"A murder an' a hangin', eh? I'd like to hear the particulars."

"There wasn't none to speak of. Couple of fellas moved into Olson's old shack. One of 'em got murdered, an' we hung the other one."

"I trust that the hangin' was authorized by a duly called miner's meetin'."

"Yeah, we called a meetin' an' voted, an' then went ahead an' done it."

"I assume that the evidence was duly weighed."

"Oh shore. It weighed ninety-seven ounces. That's what the one we hung had on him, an' we figgered he must of stole it off'n the one he murdered, which he was broke."

"Was the defendant given a chanct to testify in his own behalf?"

"Yeah, he was like all the rest—claimed he never done it. But hell, anyone knows anyone would lie like hell to keep from gittin' hung—they'd be a damn fool not to."

"But the evidence—" persisted Black John. "Are you shore you hung the right party?"

"Well, they wouldn't of be'n no p'int in hangin' the other one! He was dead a'ready!"

"What I'm gettin' at is—did you deem the man guilty beyond the peradventure of a doubt?"

"I don't know how to deem—an' you know it. But look at it reasonable—here's two fellas. One of 'em gits murdered. An' if the other one didn't murder him, who the hell did?"

BLACK JOHN grinned. "Sounds simple an' logical enough. An' with sech an overwhelmin' preponderance of evidence agin him, you boys ondoubtless arrived at a just solution. That is, providin' yer shore the victim was murdered."

"Cripes—I'm the coroner, ain't I? I know when a man's dead, don't I? If you don't believe he is, you kin go out there in the graveyard an' dig him up an' see fer yerself! He's the second one of them two new graves. The first one's the fella we hung."

"The case is closed," agreed the big man. "My interest in the matter was merely casual, an' don't involve no sech expenditure of labor."

"What I claim," complained Cush, "you'd ort to stick around instead of kihootin' all over hell. Then you'd know what's goin' on. Here you be'n gone better'n two months. An' when you went away you claimed you wouldn't stay no longer'n what a common prospectin' trip would amount to."

"Well, a lot of prospectin' trips lasts two months. Hell, some fellas go on one an' never do come back!"

"Yeah—an' that's the kind I figgered you'd went on when you didn't show up every day."

"The statement seems a trifle ambiguous—but we'll let that pass."

"Where the hell you be'n at all this time?"

"Oh—here, there, an' yonder."

"Did you see yer folks like you claimed you was goin' to?"

"Yeah—all that's left of 'em. I seen Pa an' Willie."

"I thought you claimed this here Willie was in some jail."

"That's right—Atlanta. His was a Federal job. Him an' a couple of other nitwits robbed a mail train—er tried to. The venture proved onsuccessful, an' Willie draw'd twenty years. So before I hit back, I dropped down to Atlanta to see him. Nice place they've got down there—if a man cares for prisons."

"I bet he was glad to see somebody from the world outside."

"No. Nothin' I could say seemed to please him. I started out by callin' his attention to the fact that honesty is the best policy, an' he begun cussin' me out somethin' awful. An' when I reminded him that he wasn't brought up to talk like that, an' how, if Pa could hear him he'd shore be mortified, he cussed all the harder. He called me a damn preacher. You see, he know'd I was headed that way—"

"Huh," Cush interrupted, "you shore as hell never got very fur along with it, I'd say!"

"The matter was taken entirely out of my hands. My theological education terminated abruptly, owin' to certain tendencies I'd developed that seemed somehow incompatible with the curriculum, out of harmony with the divine, an' at variance with the environment of the seminary."

"Godamity! You shore as hell sucked all the big words out of them kricklums er 'vironments, er whatever you call 'em, before you was kicked out! But go ahead—you'd got to where Willie was doin' all that cussin'."

"Well, I seen I wasn't gettin' nowhere tryin' to inject a moral atmosphere into Willie's cosmos, so I changed the subject an' tried to cheer him up a bit by p'intin' out the obvious advantages he had over other folks. I called his attention to the fact that he seemed to be placed amid pleasant surroundin's, an' how he didn't have no cares nor worries—like not knowin' where his next meal was comin' from, an' not havin' to lay awake nights worryin' about someone breakin' in an stealin' him blind—but that didn't make no hit with him, either. He only redoubled his cussin', threatenin' that when he got out he'd hunt me up an' knock hell out of me if it was the last thing he ever done. So I come away from there thoroughly convinced that Willie is ondoubtless steeped in original sin, an' won't never amount to nothin' ontil he changes his viewp'int."

"You claim you seen Willie jest before you hit out fer here. What was you doin' up to then?"

"Oh, a bit of this, an' a bit of that. You see, Cush, I bought me a farm."

"A farm! By God, John! Did you say a farm?"

"That's right."

"You mean yer goin' to quit here an' settle down to farmin' back in the States? Of all the damn fool things you ever done—that's the damndest! You ain't no farmer, John—an' you won't never make one! How long you goin' to be satisfied scatterin' manure around on the ground an' then plowin' it under? Where's the fun in that? An' where's the fun in tossin' corn to a bunch of damn chickens? An' feedin' swill to a lot of pigs? An' milkin' some cows? An' hitchin' up a team of horses an' then whackin' 'em on the hind end all day to make 'em go? What kind of work is that fer a man to be doin'?"

The big man grinned. "I'll admit that the picture you paint ain't allurin'."

"An' you ain't no farmer, neither! How big is this here farm you bought?"

"Well, it's bigger'n some, an' not so big as others. It's what you might call a one-mule farm. I'm inclined to agree with you that my talents run along other lines. I purchased this estate more for its esthetic value than for an agricultural enterprise. Why, just think Cush—from my front porch back there on the farm I can set of an evenin' an' look out acrost the little valley up which the white road winds, an' watch the sun set behind the distant hills. In the foreground I can see the old rail fence an' the wooden privy, twisted slightly askew by the winds of many years, but still—"

"Huh," grunted Cush disdainfully, "I wouldn't take no comfort settin' on no porch gawpin' at no road, an' no fence, an' no wind-racked privy. If it was me I'd move it around back where it belongs."

"Ah, no, my, friend. That onpretentious buildin', viewed against the mighty background—against the vast rollin' sweep of the hills, leads one to meditate an' to contemplate on the utter futility of the puny works of man in comparison with the illimitable grandeur of nature."

"Huh. I still claim I'd rather do my contemplatin' an' meditatin' out back."

"And," Black John continued, "besides this farm I purchased a residence in town, an' a black drivin' mare, an' a red-wheeled, rubber-tired buggy."

Cush peered intently into the speaker's face across the bar. "So—some woman's got you hooked, at last, eh?"

"Not yet, she ain't."

"I mistrusted there was somethin' back of this here farm buyin', horse buyin' trip! An' this here house you bought in town—what do you aim to contemplate from it? Er mebbe it's got a backhouse out in front, too!"

Black John laughed. "Fact is, Cush, I bought the town house

for Pa—an' the horse an' rig, too. An' I bought the farm off'n him. He's right around seventy, an' the farm was sort of gettin' the best of him, what with his preachin', an' all. He was up agin a problem in agronomy that had him stopped—he couldn't get his mule to eat enough to produce manure enough to raise corn enough for the mule to eat."

"Why don't he feed the damn mule twise as much an' give him a dolt of castor ile, then?"

"The plan would seem to have its merits, but would ondoubt-less furnish only temporary relief—sort of burnin' the candle at both ends. I wanted to do somethin' that would sort of put Pa on easy street fer the rest of his life. Here he was walkin' twenty miles every Sunday to preach in a couple of churches which both together paid him less than two hundred dollars a year—an' the farm wasn't even payin' its way. Pa had mortgaged it to the local banker—a hard, graspin' man, who was about to foreclose on him an' not leave a roof over his head. So I paid off the mortgage, bought the farm, an' give pa the house in town, an' the horse an' buggy so he can drive instead of walk to these here churches. An' on top of that I bought an annuity that'll pay him a hundred dollars a month as long as he lives."

CUSH HEAVED a sigh of vast relief. "Then you ain't fixin' to quit Halfaday?"

"Hell, no! I feel, Cush, that my life work is right here."

"Yer damn right it is, John! I'm glad you got yer pa fixed up. That was a fine thing to do. But, about this here farm? What with the old man livin' in town—what you goin' to do with it? Looks like it would be'n cheaper to let that banker foreclose his mortgage an' take the damn farm."

"Not under the circumstances. In fact, Mr. Grimm, the banker, is goin' to do quite a bit of worryin' about that farm."

"You mean you sold it to him—to the same banker that helt the mortgage on it?"

"The very same. Only I didn't sell him the farm—merely a

half interest in a gold mine he believes to exist in a cave situated on the premises. You remember when I left here I took along fifty pounds of dust, an' you wanted to know what the hell I wanted to do with dust down in the States? An' I told you a man never could tell when dust might come in handy. Well that dust did."

"I hope you stuck this here banker good, John. Damn these here bankers that skins pore folks like preachers an' sechlike out of all they've got! I shore hope you stuck him good!"

"Well," the big man admitted, tossing several packets of bills onto the bar, "I made some slight profit on the transaction. You rec'lect I took along ten thousan' in cash besides that dust, which by the way, figgers twenty dollars to the ounce, instead of sixteen like here. That's twenty-six thousan' dollars. I think you'll find in the neighborhood of two hundred an' eleven thousan' four hundred an' fifty in them packages. My incidental expenses run right around a thousan'. I paid two-fifty fer the rig, about four hundred fer the mortgage, twelve hundred fer the town house, give Pa five hundred fer the farm, an' paid eleven thousan' fer his annuity. Added to this was a special two hundred dollar expense I incurred on the river boat comin' in. Altogether I consider the trip well worth while. It was a great comfort to Pa to know that one of his sons turned out good."

III

THE NEXT MORNING, as Black John stepped into the saloon, Cush set out bottles and glasses, and grinned at him across the bar. "I be'n kinda studyin' over all them things you told me about yer trip, an' I come to that there two hundred dollars that you called a special expense you was put to comin' in on the boat. Did one of them river boat gamblers take you fer that two hundred?"

Black John solemnly filled his glass. "No, Cush, it was a woman."

"A woman, eh? I'd shore be interested in hearin' about her."

"Yeah," answered the big man dryly, "I sort of figured you would."

"Was she good lookin'?"

"Yeah—in a mature sort of a way. Big blonde, I'd say risin' of thirty-five."

"Must of be'n pretty slick to take you fer two hundred."

"Well—she knows her way around."

Cush downed his drink at a swallow, and wiped his mustache on the back of his hand. "My third wife was a big blonde. She'd be somewheres around thirty-five by now," he said reminiscently. "Her name was Annie."

"Yeah—that's what she claimed."

"What!" The word exploded from between Cush's lips, as his eyes widened to twice their natural size.

"I run acrost her on the boat. She seemed sort of alone like, an' we got acquainted the first evenin' out. She plays a damn good game of poker, in a crooked sort of way. Seems like a kind of a lovin', trustin' soul, though, at that."

"Lovin', trustin' soul! She's the damndest—"

"Now, listen, Cush," the big man interrupted. "You might be prejudiced."

"Prejudiced—hell! But hold on, John! They must be a lot of big blondes. An' some of 'em would be bound to be around thirty-five. An' a lot of 'em could be named Annie. You shore she's the same one?"

"All I've got's her word for it. That, an' the fact that her story sort of checked with things you've let drop, now an' then—like you bein' a bartender on Freeman Avenue in Cincinnati—an' you makin' that eleven-sixty-five killin' on a three-horse parlay at Latonia. Besides that, she claimed the man she married there was named Lyme Cushing, an' the strikin' similarity in names leads me to believe you're the party she referred to. Besides that she claimed that you was now runnin' a saloon an' tradin' post on Halfaday Crick."

Cush made a queer gurgling sound in his throat, and downed two drinks in rapid succession. "How in hell could she know that?" he asked.

"A friend of yours told her—Whiskey Bill. She run onto him one night on a party in Frisco."

"Friend of mine! By God if he ever shows up here again I'll learn him to go shootin' off his mouth! I'll wham him so hard with a bung-starter they could hear his head pop clean down to Dawson! You mean—she's comin' inside? You mean she's headin' into the Yukon?"

"Not headin'. She's here."

"Where?"

"Well, prob'ly somewhere on the White River, by now. When I left the boat at Selkirk, she aimed to go on down to Dawson, hire a guide, an' come up here."

"Why the hell didn't you head her off? Why didn't you lie to her—er throw her in the river, er somethin'?"

"Who am I to come between man an' wife? There might of be'n times, Cush, when I've committed some act that in its last analysis might be open to question—but comin' between a man an' his wife ain't one of 'em. What I figure, if you two was to get together agin, you might do right well. She seems able, in a financial way."

"But she tried to pizen me! If I hadn't found that fly-paper soakin' in under the bed, I'd be dead!"

"Oh, shore. But what I claim, married folks has got to overlook one another's little shortcomin's if they expect to git along."

"Shortcomin's! By God, pizenin' a man ain't no shortcomin'!"

"Well—mebbe not. But it ain't exactly commendable, neither. But far's I can see, you ain't got no kick comin'. Did she ever mention her first husband?"

"Her first husband! Cripes, had she be'n married before? No, she never told me about no first husband!"

"It was prob'ly an oversight. After all, a woman can't be expected to remember everything. Anyway, she couldn't get hold of no flypaper up here. Of course she might fetch some along, but you could ondoubtless locate it in time to prevent a tragedy. An'—that's an idea. A tragedy—or mebbe only a comedy! Look at the Thespian possibilities of the situation. Cush, we're confronted wtih all the ingredients of a great drayma!"

"You an' yer damn draymas! I won't have nothin' to do with no more draymas—not now, nor no other time! How does it come that every time you think up some drayma, I'm allus in the middle? There ain't be'n a damn time in any of these here draymas of yourn when if anything went wrong, I wouldn't of be'n either married, er robbed, er killed—er some damn thing would happened to me! An' how does it come that it's allus me it would happen to?"

"That," opined Black John, "is merely a coincidence. Hell, Cush—nothin' ever did happen. That's owin' as much to your oncommon ability as an actor, as to my outstandin' acumen as a director. You've played up nobly in every part I've ever cast you in. For instance, if the part called for you to look scairt, you've always given a superb performance."

"Yeah—an' by God, there ain't never be'n no time in none of these here draymas of yourn that I wasn't so damn scairt right up to the end, that it didn't take no actin' to look that way!"

"Exactly! An' thus you inject an air of realism into your role that no amount of practice could hope to attain. That's why I've always cast you for the leadin' role."

"Why the hell don't you take one of these here leadin' rolls yerself sometimes?"

"A good director chooses his cast solely by their fitness for the part. Fer instance, in this present presentation, I deem it inadvisable for me to appear onstage ontil the very end of the play."

"Yeah, an' that's the way you've allus done!"

Ignoring the interruption, Black John continued: "Durin' the entire performance I'll be there in the storeroom with my eye glued to the peek-slot. In the final scene, I'll enter, back stage— through the storeroom door, there, just in time to—"

"Yeah—jest in time to pick me up off'n the floor an' help pack me out to the graveyard, 'cause by that time I'll prob'ly be pizened, er shot, er somethin'! No, sir! I won't have nothin' to do with yer damn drayma. Not where Annie's mixed up in it, I won't. She damn near got me onct—an' by God, I ain't goin' to give her another crack at me! Cripes, I don't never see a sheet of flypaper but what the hair on the back of my neck kinda prickles, an' I git a funny feelin' in the pit of my stummick."

"Listen, Cush—it might be that instead of a tragedy, this here drayma might turn out to be a beautiful romance with a lovin' reconciliation scene at the end, an' a chant to live happy ever after. *Reunited After Many Years*, we could call it, er mebbe *Hearts Aflame*."

"Not with Annie in it, you couldn't call it none of them names. It would be *She Got Her Man*, er *The End of Lyme Cushing*, an' the last act would be where you an' the rest of the boys was cuttin' my name on a new slab. No, sir—if Annie shows up here there ain't goin' to be no recontalliation, er whatever you call it, an' not no livin' happy never after. The minute she sticks her face in the door I'll ask her how much she wants to git to hell outa the Yukon, an' stay out! Cripes, I'll give ten thousan'— twenty-five thousan' to git shet of her!"

Black John reached for the bottle and refilled his glass. "Do you mean, Cush, that if I could figure out some way to get Annie out of the Yukon fer good, you'd pay me twenty-five thousan' dollars?"

"Yeah—you, er her, er anyone else. But it's got to be so she won't never come back!"

"H-u-m, the amount is worth contemplatin'."

"It's worth payin', too—if it'll git shet of her fer good an' all. 'Long as Annie's in the Yukon, I'll be tastin' fly-paper every time I eat. I've be'n afraid all along that one of them damn wimmin would show up—either my first, er second, er third wife—an' of course, it would have to be the worst damn one of the lot! That's jest my luck! If you can't work it, I'll buy her off—but by God, I'll have a bung-starter in my other hand when I do it!"

IV

AFTER GIVING ONE Armed John certain instructions, Black John returned to his cabin, produced pen and ink, and got to work on the blank warrant he had purloined from the drunken U.S. marshal on the boat. When he had finished the warrant was no longer blank. It called for the arrest of one Annie Berger, alias Annie Cushing, alias Little Annie for the murder of one Joe Berger, her husband. Folding the warrant, he slipped it into his pocket. Also he pocketed the U.S. marshal's badge and the handcuffs he had acquired on another occasion, and proceeded to Pot Gutted John's cabin. He was greeted effusively by that worthy who was eating his midday meal. "Well, by God, John, I'm shore glad to see you back! When time kep' a-goin' on an' on an' you never showed up, we'd begun to figger somethin' musta happened to you—like some woman got hold of you, er somethin'."

Black John laughed. "Women's the least of my troubles."

"Yeah? Well, all I got to say—yer lucky. By Cripes, I'll bet wimmin's at the bottom of half the men of Halfaday—er we wouldn't be here! Cush claimed you'd be back in a month. What kep' you so long?"

"Oh, this an' that."

"You missed a damn good hangin'. He spun around like a top—first one way, then the other—jest kep' on a-spinnin' till he run down."

"I trust you didn't make no mistake."

"Hell, no! Anyone could tell he needed hangin', jest by lookin' at him. Ornery lookin' cuss—but he couldn't lie worth a damn. What's on yer mind, John?"

"Me an' Cush is goin' to stage a drayma, an' we want you to take a part."

"What kind of a part?" the other asked a bit dubiously. "An' besides, I thought Cush claimed he wasn't goin' to have nothin' to do with no more draymers."

"He's goin' to have somethin' to do with this one, an' so are you. You're to play the part of a U.S. marshal, an' serve this warrant on the lady in question."

"Lady! Hell, there ain't no lady on Halfaday!"

"There will be. Listen, Pot Gut, your part is a minor one, but it's important. This here Annie Berger, or Annie Cushing, or Little Annie, as she calls herself, is Cush's third wife, an' she's headin' up here to horn a big chunk of money out of Cush, claimin' he deserted her. An' its up to us to save Cush that needless expense."

"I told you damn near every misery a man gits into is on account of some woman!"

"That's right. An' we've got to keep her from gettin' holt of this money. What we've got to do is to help Cush get shet of her fer good an' all."

"You mean, I'll arrest her, an' then we'll go ahead an' hang her. Hell, John—ornery as wimmin is, I couldn't take no joy in hangin' one. It don't seem right, somehow."

"Well, the ethics involved in the indiscriminate hangin' of women might be open to question. But we don't need to go into that, here, because we don't aim to resort to a hangin'. All we want to do is to chase her plumb out of the country. This here Annie is due to show up any minute. I sent One Arm down the crick with orders to hit hell bent back to Cush's the minute he spots her. He'll stop here an' you two come on up to the fort as quick as you can get there. Then you an' me'll slip into the storeroom, an' watch through the peek-hole. It ort to be amusin' as hell when them two gets together. Cush is scairt to death of her on account of her tryin' to pizen him one time, an' he'll offer her big money to get to hell out of the country. Then, jest before he turns this cash over to her, you slip out the back way an' go around an' come in the front door, an' serve this warrant on her."

"But hell, John—after I've got it served, that don't git shet of her! We've still got her on our hands, ain't we? What are we goin' to do with her?"

"That," explained Black John, "is where I come in. I'll make a play of feelin' sorry fer her, an' offer you money to turn her loose. You accept the money—an' it won't be no stage money, neither. You can keep it. That'll be your pay fer playin' yer part. She'll be so damn scairt, she'll hit out of here an' won't stop goin' till she hits the States."

"But Cripes, John—what's she goin' to be scairt of. This here warrant's a fake. You filled it out yerself. I know yer writin'."

"The warrant's a fake—but the murder wasn't. This Joe Berger mentioned in the warrant was her first husband. She pizened him fer his insurance. You might mention that Berger's brother posted a ten thousan' dollar reward for an arrest. That ort to sort of clinch things."

"Why—the damn skirt! Mebbe we'd ort to go ahead an' hang her—lady er no lady."

"No—I'm like you—kinda sentimental when it comes to hangin' women. Besides the crime was committed outside our jurisdiction. You got everything straight, now?"

"Yeah. But about that there dough. If I'm goin' to keep it, don't make it too little. You gotta remember, John, no U.S. marshal would turn a murderer loose fer no chicken feed. It wouldn't look right."

Black John grinned. "Don't worry. The amount will be adequate. You'll be well paid for your time. Stick that warrant in your pocket. Here's the handcuffs—an' be sure to pin that badge on yer shirt. This arrest has got to look official. I'll be gettin' back to Cush's. I figure she'll be showin' up sometime today or tomorrow. She won't spend much time in Dawson. She'll want to clean up on Cush as soon as she can so's to get to work on another roll she's got her eye on."

V

IT WAS MID-FORENOON of the following day as Black John returned his glass to the bar after the third drink and glanced across at the somber-faced proprietor. "I shore wish you'd string along with me in makin' a drayma out of this here comin' meetin' between you an' yer long lost love. We could—"

"I've told you onct an' for all—an' by God, that's jest what I mean—I ain't goin' to have nothin' to do with no more of yer damn draymas—not now nor no other time. When Annie shows up, I'm goin' to dicker with her, an' pay her off an' git shet of her the quickest way I know how! If we was to go foolin' around makin' some kind of a drayma out of it, somethin' might go wrong. Then where the hell would I be?"

The big man was about to reply when One Armed John burst into the room with Pot Gutted John puffing along behind him. "She's a-comin'! She's a-comin', John! She an' a Siwash guide! In a canoe. They'll be here pretty quick. I ketched sight of 'em jest below Pot Gut's shack."

"Okay. You better run along about yer business, now. Cush wants to have a private talk with the lady. Me an' Pot Gut'll slip out into the storeroom." He turned to the man behind the bar: "Be nice to her, Cush," he grinned, "an' maybe she'll take you back. I've often thought that all this place lacks is a woman's touch—an' I've got a hunch, this one's goin' to make a touch all right."

Cush scowled. "Sometimes, John," he growled, "I feel like bustin' you one right between the eyes with a bung-starter!"

In the storeroom Pot Gutted John seated himself on a barrel while Black John took his position at the peek hole, a slit invisible from the barroom side, but which gave the watcher behind the partition command of the entire saloon. Behind the bar Cush fortified himself with a rag. A few moments later he glanced up to see the woman framed in the doorway.

"Hello, Lyme," she greeted. "Just to think—I've found my dear husband at last!" She crossed the room and faced him, leaning her elbows on the bar.

Cush nodded somberly. "Hello, Annie. Yeah—I'm him."

"You don't seem very glad to see me."

"I ain't."

"Well, you might at least set 'em up. I ain't had a drink in God knows when."

"What you goin' to have? I got whiskey."

"Whiskey'll do me," she smiled, and poured a liberal portion into the glass he set before her. When he had filled his own glass she raised hers. "Well—here's to old times—eh, Lyme?"

They downed their drinks in silence, and the woman glanced about the room. "Nice place you've got here, Lyme," she said. "I think I would like to live here."

"It does."

"They say you're makin' a lot of money, up here."

"Who says?"

"Why, Whiskey Bill Jones told me about it. He says he lived here on Halfaday Crick for quite a while."

"Yeah, he lived here, all right. But he's the damnedest liar ever lived, too."

"He says that big iron safe there is just bulging with gold and bills."

"That stuff in the safe ain't mine. The boys all banks their dust here."

"Anyway, there ought to be a nice livin' in it, for just the two of us. You know, Lyme, I believe I'm going to like it here."

"Huh?"

"Sure. Ain't it wonderful, Lyme—me and you spending your old age together, after all these years?"

"Not by a damn sight! If you was to stick around here, I wouldn't have no old age—an' you know it!"

"Why, Lyme—how you talk! Don't you love me any more?"

"No!"

"But after all, you're my husband. You can't get out of that. I've got my rights. A man can't marry a girl and then just walk out on her, like you did."

"He can't, eh? How about that there fly-paper I found soakin' in under the bed?"

The woman threw back her head and laughed. "For Pete's sake, Lyme! Is that why you run out on me?"

"Who the hell wouldn't?"

"Don't you know what I was doing with that fly-paper?"

"Yer damn right I do! You was meltin' the pizen off'n it so's you could feed it to me an' git away with that there eleven sixty-five I won at Latonia!"

"You're crazy! I was soakin' the stuff off that paper to pour around in cracks to get rid of the roaches."

"Yeah? Well, here's one roach you didn't get rid of, anyway. Listen, Annie—there ain' no p'int of us standin' around augerin'. Let's git down to cases. You wouldn't live with me no more'n what I'd live with you. You come up here to stick me fer what you kin git. What's yer figger?"

"How much you got?"

"I might be able to dig up five thousan'."

"Be yourself, Lyme. I wasn't made in a minute."

"I was wantin' to play fair with you, Annie—go fifty-fifty. That's about the half of what I've got."

"Don't make me laugh."

"Oh, well—if you want to play the hog—take the hull ten thousan'! I kin start all over agin. But that's the last damn cent you'll ever git out of me."

"Listen, Lyme—like you said a while ago—let's get down to cases. Whiskey Bill told me you'd made plenty up here. And when he said 'plenty,' he didn't mean no lousy ten thousand. He told me that besides your saloon and trading post here, you're in with some outlaw by the name of Black John. He didn't tell me his last name—but that don't make no difference, one way or another. He told me they're all outlaws, here on the crick, but that they're a damn good bunch of fellows. Now, I want to be reasonable, Lyme. I don't want to gouge you for more'n than you can afford. I'm going to name a figure—and if you don't come across with it, you'll wish you had. Little Annie knows her way around. I'll stick around here and put on a poor deserted wife act that'll make every damn man on the crick despise you, and—"

"What's yer figger?" Cush interrupted.

"Twenty-five thousand—cash money—right on the line."

"Okay. You win."

THE WOMAN smiled. "I thought you'd look at it reasonable, Lyme. You're right about me not wanting to live here in this damn dump. And I don't care no more about you than you do about me. I found a man I can really love. Him and I are going to get married just as quick as I get back to Dawson. He's a great big fine-looking man. I met him on the boat."

"Huh—how much has he got?"

"He's got plenty. I seen his roll. And he must be making good money besides. He's a prospector."

"Did you fetch along some fly-paper?" Cush asked. "There might not be none in Dawson."

"Don't be silly, Lyme. I'm really in love, this time."

"Yeah—that's what you told me, too. What's this here prospector's name?"

"His name is Smith—John Smith. He's a swell looking guy—big, broad-shouldered, and about the handsomest black beard I ever seen."

The lips beneath the yellow mustache smiled, a bit grimly, and as Cush turned toward the back bar to reach for the bottle, his eyes flashed toward the peek hole. A moment later he again faced the woman across the bar. "Have another drink, Annie," he said, shoving the bottle toward her. "So yer goin' to marry John Smith, eh?"

"Yes. Do you know him?"

"Know him! Who the hell don't know him! Why—there ain't a woman north of Vancouver that wouldn't give her right leg to marry him! He's got one of the best propositions in the hull Klondike! You an' him ort to be happy as a couple of rattlesnakes. By Cripes, Annie—it's jest like a drayma, ain't it? Here's you an' me got together agin after all these years—only to part agin—an' you marry a rich man. An' I got to struggle along through life all alone. It's kinda sad, like—ain't it, Annie? What with our great love all mildewed, an' sort of bogged down in its own ashes."

The woman peered instantly at him across the bar. "What the hell you handing me? This last drink must have gone to your head!"

"No, sir—I never was so sober in my life. It's a drayma, I'm tellin' you—jest like you see in a show. Only this time things has shifted, an' I'm doin' the directin' an' someone else is playing the leadin' role—an', believe me, if I was him I'd look scairt—an' I'd be scairt, too! I'm jest a-wonderin' how it feels when a director finds out the shoe's on the other foot?"

"You must be nuts! I don't know what the hell you're talking about. Come on—come across with that twenty-five grand, and let me get to hell out of this bughouse!"

Cush turned to the safe, produced several packets of bills, counted out twenty-five thousand dollars and laid it on the bar before the woman.

As she was about to reach for it, Pot Gutted John stamped into the room, a United States marshal's badge displayed conspicuously on his shirt front. Stepping to the woman's side, he laid a hand on her arm. "Annie Berger, alias Annie Cushing, alias Little Annie I arrest you fer the murder of Joe Berger!"

The woman whirled to face him, a look of terror in her eyes. "It's a lie! It's a damn lie! It's a frame-up!"

"Here's the warrant. You kin tell that to the jedge an' the jury at the trial, mam. Mebbe they might believe you."

"Who's this Joe Berger they claim I murdered?"

"He's a corpse now. He used to be yer husband till you pizened him with fly-paper fer to git his insurance. His brother posted a ten thousan' dollar reward fer yer arrest, dead er alive."

THE WOMAN'S face had gone dead white at the words, her eyes took on a dull, set look.

It was at this moment that Black John strode into the room. At sight of him, a ray of hope lighted the dull eyes. "John!" she cried. "Oh, John!"

The big man stepped to her side. "Yeah, Annie—it's me. I got kinda of worried, waitin' around fer you to come back, so I come on up here to see if anything had happened to you—what with all the outlaws they claim hang out here on the crick. On the way I overtook the marshal, here—and he told me all about it. It's shore too bad, Annie—jest when you'd got our future all doped out."

"How does it come a U.S. marshal can serve a warrant here? According to Whiskey Bill this place is on the Yukon side of the line—and the Yukon's Canada!"

Black John nodded. "He must have lived here before the re-survey, then. Didn't you see that stone monument about three miles down the crick? That's the new boundary established last year."

"But—can't you do something? Don't let this man take me away! My God, John—if he takes me back it means—the hot seat!"

"That's so. But I'm afraid there ain't nothin' I can do. That is"—he paused, and his eyes rested on the huge figure of Pot Gutted John who stood with an elbow on the bar. "That is," he repeated, slowly, "onless I can appeal to this man's better nature.

How about it, officer?"

"Who, me?" Pot Gutted John's eyes assumed a puzzled expression.

Black John spoke slowly. "You look like a kind-hearted man—like a family man—possibly with a wife and little children waiting for you at home. Just think, officer—just stop and think what your act in arresting this woman will mean—to her. It will mean that she will be taken back and dragged before a court of law—and made to suffer all the torture and humiliation of a trial—and then be taken to the state penitentiary and locked behind iron bars until such time as the law sees fit to drag her to the execution chamber, and attach the electrodes to her body, and then turn on the current of electricity that will cause that beautiful body to writhe and twitch. There will be the sickening stench of burning flesh—and then the poor crumpled thing that is left will be taken out and thrown into a rude coffin and buried in a potter's field with no one to mourn her loss. Think of it—can you ever go back and face your wife and little children, knowing that you had brought all this upon a pore defenseless woman? Could you ever expect to enjoy an untroubled night's sleep again—knowing you had wrought this onspeakable horror? No—I say a thousand times no! Am I right—or am I wrong?"

"Yer right, John—I didn't want nothin' to do with it in the first place."

"Jest so! A man of your calibre wouldn't. But it was your duty, as you say it—so you went ahead. That is commendable. But on the other hand, there's your future peace of mind—and your family to consider."

"But I ain't got no—"

"Silence!" Black John thundered. "I realize you have no other course as an officer. But I'm appealin' to you as a man. I know a man when I see one—an' I realize it would be futile for me to offer you a bribe to let this woman go. You can report that you could not find her—an' no one will ever be the wiser. Turn her over to her guide and tell him to slip her out of the country over the Dalton Trail. She has the money to pay him. You will do this—because I can see that you are a man of sech sterling worth that you would not have the blood of this woman on your soul. Here—take this money—a thousand dollars—that should repay you for any expense you have incurred."

He picked up the twenty-five thousand that lay before the woman on the bar and turned to Cush. "I am borrowing this change, my good man," he said. "You ondoubtless know who I am—John Smith—I have one of the best propositions in the whole Klondike."

Cush gulped as Black John counted out a thousand, and handed it to Pot Gutted John. "My advice to you, officer, would be to turn over that warrant to Mr. Cushing, here, so that, if at any future time, this woman should attempt to return hither, he can hand it to the nearest marshal and have it served." Pot Gutted John handed Cush the warrant, and Black John continued. "Go now, and take her back to the guide and order him to take her out of the country." He turned to the woman. "That's all I can do for you, Annie. My advice to you is to pick 'em up an' lay 'em down as fast as God will let you. When you get to the States, you better never show up where anyone that ever knew you will see you. Remember, the arm of the law is long— an' a murder never outlaws."

When they were alone in the room, Cush eyed Black John. "There ain't no stone monument three miles down the crick," he said.

"Yeah? That's ondoubtless why Annie didn't see it. But revertin' to financial matters—I guess I earnt this here twenty-five thousan', all right. However, seein' how you finally fell in with my idea of makin' a drayma out of it—an' even went so far as to some of the directin', I'm willin' to go fifty-fifty." He counted off twelve thousand dollars and shoved the money across the bar. "There's your half—after deductin' the thousan' we paid Pot Gut. It's a good drayma, Cush, that turns out well fer all parties concerned."

ONE GOOD TURN
DESERVES ANOTHER

A BURST OF laughter from a stud table across the room attracted the attention of the little group of sourdoughs who
stood at the Tivoli bar, in Dawson. Deck in hand, the dealer
had halted the distribution of the cards with three up and a pot
in the center of the table to relate a doubtful story to which the
half-dozen chechakos who were playing listened in rapt attention. At its conclusion all roared with laughter, and the deal
proceeded.

"Huh," grunted Swiftwater Bill, "ain't that jest like a bunch
of damn chechakos! Lookin' at 'em a man would think a stud
game was a social event instead of a business enterprise."

Moosehide Charlie grinned. "That's Tom Stiles—him that's
dealin'. He's a chechako, all right, an' he seems to stand ace-high
with all the other chechakos. But they tell me he takes 'em
reg'lar at stud an' draw poker. They say he'd ruther play than
eat. Seems to have plenty of dust, too."

"Yeah," agreed Camillo Bill, "but how'd he git it?"

"He ain't so damn pop'lar down on the Porcupine," supplemented Old Bettles, dean of the sourdoughs. "Me an' Camillo
was talkin' to Dan Cadzow, the trader at Rampart House, not
long ago down to Forty Mile, an' he kind of spilt us an earful."

Burr MacShane nodded. "I heard, up to Circle City, that he'd
doublecrossed Cadzow on a grubstake deal, an' likewise that
he'd beat Old Pop Rooney out of his claim."

"Yeah," agreed Camillo Bill, "an' accordin' to Cadzow, that

ain't the half of it. There was an old-timer named Paddy Dorgan located up the Porcupine jest above where the Crow runs in, that had done pretty good fer himself snipin' the bars an' scoopin' out shallow shafts fer years. Cadzow figgers he must of had somewheres around thirty er forty thousan' in dust cached somewheres. This spring Dorgan disappeared, an' not long after he was missed this here Tom Stiles an' his pardner, a Dutchman name of Dietz, busted up an' Stiles pulled out of the Porcupine country. An' he's be'n spendin' plenty of dust ever sence."

"It might be the dust he got out of the claims he beat Cadzow an' Rooney out of," reminded MacShane.

"No, they never worked the one Cadzow claims they beat him out of," replied Camillo. "An' Dietz is still on Pop Rooney's claim. They didn't have time to take no hell of a lot of dust out of it before Stiles come away."

"Accordin' to Cadzow," Bettles said, "everyone on the Porcupine figgers Stiles an' Dietz knocked Dorgan off an' robbed his cache. Cadzow stopped in at the Forty Mile detachment an' told the inspector about it, an' he sent a constable back with him to look around up there."

"H-u-u-m, thirty er forty thousan', eh?" said Black John Smith, who was in Dawson on one of his periodic trips to exchange gold dust from Halfaday Creek for bills. "The amount is worth contemplatin'. It would be a damn shame if a venture like that was got away with. It savors strongly of underhandedness. Does Stiles know the police is investigatin' the incident?"

"YEAH, HE knows it," replied Camillo Bill. "It was three, four weeks ago Cadzow an' the constable hit back fer the Porcupine country, an' a couple of days later I was standin' here at the bar, an' Stiles an' some other chechako was here, too, an' Jake Simms come in an' told me he jest come upriver from Eagle an' he met Cadzow an' the constable goin' down river to check up on a fella named Dutch Dietz who was suspected of knowin' somethin' about a murder up there. I seen that Stiles was listenin' an' watched him out of the tail of my eye. He went kind of white, at first, an' then throw'd three, four drinks into him without lettin' on he'd heard anything. He's still here, so I guess he figgers Dietz won't squawk, an' the constable won't be able to locate Dorgan's corpse. Anyhow, he don't seem to be worried none," he added as, following a fresh burst of laughter from the stud players, Stiles rapped on the table and loudly ordered a round of drinks.

"He shore makes a good fella of himself amongst them damn chechakos, even if he does rake their chips acrost the table," opined Moosehide.

"Wonder what kind of a fella this Dietz is?" speculated Black John.

"Jest another damn chechako," Bettles replied. "Accordin' to Cadzow he ain't got neither the brains nor the guts that Stiles has. He can't even write writin'. Draws his letters with a lead pencil, like kids does. An' Cadzow says damn near every word is spelt wrong. He knows, 'cause sometimes Dietz fetches a list of supplies to the tradin' post. He figgers if Dorgan was knocked off it would be Stiles done it—with Dietz jest trailin' along."

"The hell of it is it ain't only the damn chechakos he's makin' a good fella of himself with," observed Burr MacShane. "He shore is playin' up to Old Bill Rodney's gal."

"Yeah—she's a scatter-brain!" exclaimed Camillo Bill. "She ain't got the sense Old Bill had—by a damn sight! Er she'd never fall fer a rank chechako like Stiles—'specially after she'd got a look at them eyes. I never seen a man yet with them cold, pale, fishy eyes that I'd trust around the first bend of a crick."

"Well, you gotta remember, Camillo, she ain't as old as Bill was," reminded Bettles. "This here Stiles ain't a bad lookin' fella, barrin' mebbe his eyes. An' he's got plenty of dust, an' spends it free. Margy's young yet. She's damn good lookin', too—an' she likes a good time."

"It ain't her looks Stiles gives a damn about," growled Swift-water Bill. "It's Old Bill's dust—you kin bet on that! Margy'll come twenty-one next week, an' the bank's guardeenship'll expire an they'll turn over Bill's dust to her. Stiles knows all about that; don't never think he don't. An' he knows that what she'll have then'll make what he got out of Dorgan's cache look like chicken feed! That's what's holdin' him here in the face of that investigation. He's takin' a chanct that that constable won't turn up nothin' on the Porcupine till after Margy gits her money."

"Yeah," Camillo agreed, "an' the way he's rushin' her, I'm expectin' any day to hear they're married."

"An' when they are," seconded Bettles, "he'll hit fer the outside as fast as God'll let him—an' take her an' Old Bill's money along with him!"

"An'," added Burr MacShane, "take it, with a girl like Margy that ain't never lived nowheres but here, without no friends down in the States, an' everything strange to her—it ain't hard to figger what'll happen. An' the hell of it is she'll be twenty-one by then, an' there ain't a damn thing anyone kin do about it. Ain't that so, John?"

BLACK JOHN nodded. "Yeah," he replied thoughtfully. "Anyone is in a hell of a fix when they ain't got no friends. I was thinkin' about a fella, one time, down on Birch Crick."

"I figgered," said Moosehide Charlie, "that Margy aimed to marry young Joe Emerson. He's a good kid, an' more her own age. But it looks like this damn Stiles had beat his time."

"Yeah, an' it's too bad," opined Camillo Bill. "If he'd git Margy they could put in a flume an' git water onto that inland claim of Joe's on Quartz Crick. That would be a damn good proposition if they could git water to it. An' that's the way Old Bill would liked to had his money used. By God, Bill was a minin' man!"

"Joe, he'll prob'ly git his flume whether he gits Margy er not," said MacShane. "Trouble is, the financin'll come mighty high."

"If he don't git Margy, the chances is he won't give a damn

about no flume," opined Bettles. "She's all he thinks about."

Black John ordered a round of drinks. "I rec'lect," he said, "when Old Bill's wife died. It was back in ninety-five—on Birch Crick."

"Ninety-six," corrected Bettles. "It was right after that snow-slide buried them Siwashes on Peabody. The slide come in December, an' Bill's wife died in January, about a month after."

"Guess yer right," Black John admitted. "Anyway, it was that winter. Old Bill, he shore done me a good turn, onct—him an' his wife. It was in the matter of a U.S. marshal that come snoopin'

along Birch Crick on the trail of someone he claimed had held up a major an' three common soldiers down around Fort Gibbon, er somewheres like that, an' robbed 'em of the army payroll."

"Did he ketch the damn miscreant?" grinned Bettles, as the other sourdoughs chuckled.

"Not if I remember right, he didn't," Black John replied gravely. "As I rec'lect the incident, this fella had be'n travelin' fast an' light to keep ahead of this marshal, an' he come to Old Bill's an' stopped in fer a rest, an' a bite to eat. Bill's wife was doin' a washin' that day, an' Bill goes out fer a couple more pails of water when he seen this marshal comin' up the crick. He hustles back an' tells the fella to curl up on the floor at the corner of the bunk, an' grabs up a big armful of dirty clothes an' throws 'em on top of him. The marshal comes along an' Bill invites him in, cordial. It's pretty steamy in the cabin, what with a tub of water b'ilin' on the stove, an' Bill's wife up to her elbows in suds in another one. The marshal he stands jest inside the door an' asks a lot of questions to which Bill gives him certain answers. There's a young girl there—Bill's girl—an' seems like she's jest a-bustin' to blat out evidence sort of contrary to what Bill's be'n tellin'. But every time she opens her mouth her ma starts talkin' fast, an' sets her to work at somethin'.

"Pretty quick Bill, he offers to guide the marshal up the crick, an' on west, where this here fella he was huntin' might of gone.

"An' after they'd be'n gone a short time, the fella crawls out from in under the clothes, sweatin' like a nigger—not so much on account of the heat, as on account of what that mouthy young-un might of said if she'd got the jump on her ma.

"It so happened that I was in funds, at the time, havin' right around forty thousan' in U.S. money on me, an' feelin' a sort of a personal interest in this fella the marshal was huntin', I offered Bill's wife a lib'ral cut out of it. But she wouldn't touch it. Claimed that what they done wasn't done on no cash basis, an' couldn't be paid fer. Claimed she'd ruther not have nothin' to do with money like that, nohow, meanin' I take it, that she preferred dust to bills. So I left there, headin' down the crick, an' east, at a pace commensurate with the len'th of my legs—an' eventually crossed onto the Yukon.

"I never seen Old Bill agin, an' never got the chanct to return the favor he done to that friendless fella on Birch Crick, that day. I heard he'd struck it lucky after that—an' later, I shore was sorry to hear he'd died."

"Yeah," agreed Bettles, "they didn't make 'em no better'n Old Bill."

"TOO DAMN bad Margy'd take up with any one like Stiles," said MacShane.

"That's the only trouble with women—they ain't got no sense," opined Swiftwater.

"Well," grinned Bettles, "I wouldn't hardly go so fer as to say it was the only trouble with 'em—but it's one of the main ones."

"Why'n hell don't one of us go right to Margy an' tell her Stiles is no good?" asked Moosehide Charlie.

"The suggestion," grinned Black John, "is a forthright one an' at first blush, would seem to have much to commend it. But considered in its broader aspect, it savors slightly of bluntness—seems somehow lackin' in finesse, as a diplomat would say."

"I don't know nothin' about that," said Swiftwater, "but I know damn well it wouldn't work. If you tell a woman anythin' agin a man, bein' nach'ly contrary to start out with, she'll stick up fer him. An' if you start augerin' about it, she'll git plumb stubborn—an' then all hell couldn't change her."

"They're like a mule," opined Burr MacShane. "It takes a damn good man to handle one."

"This here Dorgan that disappeared on the Porcupine—has he got any heirs, I wonder?" asked Black John.

"Hell, no!" Bettles replied. "He come into the country when the Yukon wasn't nothin' but a crick! I wintered with Old Paddy on the Koyukuk, way back in ninety. He don't even know if his name is Dorgan. He thinks he kin rec'lect bein' in some kind of a home where there was a hell of a lot of other kids in London. An' he rec'lects livin' with some folks named Dorgan, an' skippin' out because they was mean to him, an' from then on he follered the sea ontil he was wrecked on a whaler somewheres along the coast in the eighties, an' he's be'n knockin' around, here an' there, ever sence. What did you want to know about him fer?"

"Oh, jest by way of conversation," replied Black John. "I was really thinkin' about that good turn old Bill Rodney done me—an' how I'd never got no chanct to pay him back. His wife claimed it was a thing that couldn't be paid fer. I don't s'pose she ever heard of a deferred payment."

"What the hell you drivin' at?"

"Oh, jest sort of ramblin' on. Guess this licker's kind of loosened my tongue. Let's have another, an' then I'm goin' to supper."

II

BLACK JOHN TOOK a seat near a window in the dining-room of the hotel, and a few minutes later Stiles entered, accompanied by a young woman who glanced in his direction and, after being seated at a nearby table, leaned forward and spoke in an undertone to the man who looked his way with a smile as she talked.

"Undoubtless purveyin' a bit of ancient hist'ry," grinned the big man, to himself, as he caught the words "Birch Creek" and "outlaw." "Beats hell how a young woman's looks kin change in a few years. Cripes, back there on Birch Crick that time, she was freckled faced an' leggy—kind of ganglin' lookin'. She looks like a girl on a calendar, now."

A waitress brought his supper and, noticing that his glance strayed toward the other table, she volunteered information. "That's Tom Stiles. He's rich. Good mixer, too. Everyone likes him. That's Margy Rodney with him. She's rich, too—or will be when the bank pays over the money her old man left. They gotta give it to her next week. She'll be twenty-one, then. They jest give her so much a month now. Tom's rushin' her awful hard. She's all caked in on him, too, by the looks. She throw'd down young Joe Emerson fer him. You can't blame her. Joe's a nice kid, but he's kinda slow. Wouldn't never show her the good times Stiles will. But it's too bad some poor girl can't get him, instead of one that's rich, already. Some girls has all the luck."

Black John nodded slowly. "Yeah, some pore girl might git him, at that. But you want to remember, sister—there's a damn sight of difference in luck."

Late that evening Stiles entered the Tivoli and stepping to the bar, ordered a drink. Farther along the bar, surrounded by the little group of sourdoughs, Black John loudly ordered another round.

"Yes, sir!" he roared, apparently feeling his liquor. "It's gittin' along towards Saint One Eye's Day agin—an' you boys'll have to come on up to Halfaday an' help us celebrate!"

"Cripes—I shore had a head on me after that last celebration!" exclaimed Swiftwater Bill. "I never did remember leavin' Cush's."

"I'll say we done old Saint One Eye proud," grinned Bettles.

"Seems like I rec'lect someone gittin' pizned," said Camillo.

"It must of be'n me," opined Moosehide. "I couldn't git nothin' to set on my stummick fer a week."

"I wasn't in on that one," said Burr MacShane. "But from what I heard when the boys got back, it must of be'n a paloozer! I shore missed somethin'."

"You missed damn near dyin', if that's what you mean," grinned Moosehide.

"Yeah," MacShane laughed, "I hear the boys are pretty free with their hangin's, on Halfaday."

"You bet we are!" cried Black John, slanting a swift glance that assured him Stiles was listening. "What any man done before he come to Halfaday ain't none of our business. But onct he gits there he's got to refrain from murder, larceny, claim-jumpin', an all forms of skullduggery, er a miners' meetin'll see to it that he's provided with a damn good practical hangin'.

"As long as a man uses us right, we'll use him right. There's forty, fifty of us up there, an' I don't mind sayin' that most, if not all of us, is outlawed, one way er another. But we ain't loosin' no sleep over it. No, sir! Layin' as we do, right up agin the Alasky line, we don't live in no fear of the police of either country. If a Mounted shows up the Yukon wanteds slip acrost the line an' hole up in the Alasky Country Club till he goes back—an' vicy vercy, like if a U.S. marshal should show up on the Alasky side.

"There's plenty good claims on the crick, if a man's minded to work. An' Old Cush is right there to look after our needs an' requirements in the matter of licker an' supplies. An' on top of all that, we have a lot of fun, what with a stud game every night, an' all. I couldn't see where a man would want no better place to live than Halfaday Crick!"

"Cripes, John," grinned Bettles, "anyone would think you'd staked out a townsite up there an' was down here sellin' lots!"

"Nope. There ain't no townsites on Halfaday, an' there ain't goin' to be none. An' I ain't got nothin' to sell, nor no commercial interest in the community whatever, outside of my claim, I'm jest extollin' the virtues of Halfaday so them of you that ain't be'n there to see fer yerselves would feel free to come up an' help us celebrate Saint One Eye's Day without fear of gittin' hung, er bein' bored to death."

STILES CROSSED the room and joined half a dozen chechakos in a stud game, and shortly thereafter Black John sought his room in the hotel and busied himself with a lead pencil and a piece of wrapping paper. When he had finished, he folded the paper, slipped it beneath the door of Stiles' room which was next his own, and went to bed.

Long after midnight he heard the sound of footsteps in the hallway and the opening and closing of a door. A few minutes of silence was followed by a full hour of restless pacing back and forth in the next room, and again silence.

As he was eating breakfast, the following morning, Stiles entered the dining room and paused beside his table.

"Mind if I sit here," he asked. "It's rather lonesome eating by one's self."

"Set right down," Black John invited heartily. "I was jest thinkin' the same thing."

"Stiles is my name," began the man, by way of introduction. "I happened to be in the Tivoli last evening and, quite by accident, I overheard you speaking of Halfaday Creek."

"Yeah, I've got a claim up there, an' I was sort of invitin' the boys up to help us celebrate Saint One Eye's day."

"I don't seem to place this Saint One Eye."

"We did," grinned the big man. "Right where he belongs. In a grave. He's a fella we hung a while back. Of course, the saint part is what you might say more er less synthetical, bein' a post mortum honor conferred on the spur of the moment. I doubt if it's accepted where he's at now. Fact is, some of the boys happened to drop in on us onetime an' bein' as we're all serious minded citizens, we didn't like to pull off no drunk right out of a clear sky. So we cast about fer a reasonable excuse, like a holiday er some time like that, when a man of ordinary intelligence is s'posed to git drunk on general principles. But accordin' to Cush's calendar there wasn't no red letter day within a month er so of us. Bettles, he rec'lected how the Mexicans is hell to celebrate a saint's day every time they feel a drunk comin' on. But none of us was up on our saints an' we didn't have no list of 'em an' couldn't think up none whose day come that time a year, ontil I happened to rec'lect that it was about a year back when we hung One Eyed John Smith."

"What did you hang him for?"

"Oh, damn if I remember. It was prob'ly somethin' he done, er looked like he was goin' to do. But bein' as it was the approximate anniversary of his hangin', I proclaimed him a saint—

an' we went ahead an' celebrated his day without our conscience prickin' us, or losin' our self respect by gittin' drunk without no reasonable excuse. What I claim, when a man begins pullin' off trivial an' aimless drunks—right then's when he begins slippin'."

"I believe you mentioned that there are claims on the creek. Would it be possible for anyone—me, for instance—to stake a location up there? Or is the whole creek staked?"

"Hell, man Halfaday ain't even been scratched yet! Most any location a man's a mind to stake will pay bettern' wages."

THE MAN cleared his throat nervously and continued. "The fact is, I'm a bit fed up on Dawson. The creeks hereabouts are all staked. I did pretty well farther down the river, but my claim finally petered out and I came to Dawson, hoping to stake a new location."

"Couldn't of come to a worse place. The sourdoughs, them that was in the country before the rush, got most of the good locations. An' sence then, all the damn chechakos that could rustle the price to git here has come pourin' into Dawson with the result that they won't one in ten git their passage money back."

"That's right. That's the reason I'd like to go someplace where I'd stand a reasonable chance of making a strike, and at the same time be able to make expenses."

"Halfaday's yer crick, then!" exclaimed Black John. "Anyone kin make expenses—an' some of us is doin' quite a bit better'n that."

"I believe you mentioned, last evening, that—er—some of the men on Halfaday are—er—outlaws. I still have a little dust left from my downriver claim—only a few ounces, but I—er—wouldn't like to lose it."

"It's a more er less deplorable fact," explained Black John, "that the bulk of us is outlawed, one way er another, but I'm right here to tell you that there's more damn honesty, per capita, on Halfaday than on any other crick in the Yukon! An' you don't have to take my word fer it. Ask Corporal Downey er any other policeman. If a man refrains from crime er skullduggery, he's safer on Halfaday than he is right here in Dawson. I don't know a place in the world where a man gits what's comin' to him quicker'n he does on Halfaday!"

"I believe you mentioned that a man could procure supplies there—and that he could find an occasional stud game. I rather enjoy stud now and then, as a diversion."

"A man kin git anything he wants in the way of supplies an' diversion at Cushing's Fort—barrin' women. Women contaminates an' contankerates a crick somethin' scandulous. One shows up now an' then, but she ain't never encouraged to stay. Our main diversion is stud. We play stiff; but we play honest. We keep the game honest by accordin' a prompt an' hearty hangin' to anyone who tries to bolster up his luck with sech subterfuges as second dealin', holdin' out cards, er runnin' in a cold deck."

"Halfaday sounds like an ideal place to locate," opined Stiles, after a brief pause. "I believe I'll go there, if you can tell me how to reach it."

"Won't need to. I'll be pullin' out myself in the mornin'. You kin go along with me."

THE OTHER shifted uneasily. "I believe," he said, "that I'd rather pull out today. You see—er—quite a number of chechakos as you call them—men whose acquaintance I have made since I reached Dawson—know that I had a good claim downriver—and—er—they might jump to the conclusion, if they should see two of us pulling out together, that we were going upon a prospecting trip, they might follow us, believing that because I had made one strike, I would probably make another. It might create a stampede, and I am sure that neither you nor I would care to have a stampede of chechakos pouring in onto Halfaday."

"Hell no!" grinned Black John. "They'd be worse than them

locusts that come buzzin' in on old Pharaoh, that the Good Book tells about. You go ahead whenever yer ready an' I'll overtake you on the White. Cross over an' paddle upstream on the far side of the Yukon till you come to a sizable river that runs in from the west about eighty miles up. That's the White, an' you kin head up it a ways an' wait fer me. No one'll see us from there on. When we git to Halfaday you kin throw yer stuff into One Eyed John's cabin till you git a chanct to look around fer a location of yer own. Er you might go ahead an' work One Eyed's claim. Funny thing about that claim.

"One Eyed must of took considerable dust out of it—me an' Cush figgers right around thirty, forty thousan' dollars—but after we hung him we never found a damn ounce of it. No sir, not a damn ounce! And, we shore as hell tore up' every likely lookin' place where he could of cached it. But he was too smart fer us. He shore done a good job of cachin'. Well, I'll be stirrin' around, now," the big man concluded, pushing back from the table. "So long. Be seein' you in a couple of days on the White."

III

TEN DAYS LATER Black John strode into the barroom at Cushing's Fort closely followed by a smooth shaven man who swung a small but obviously heavy pack to the floor at his feet as he ranged himself beside the other at the bar.

"Hello, Cush!" he greeted. "Meet Tom Stiles. Tom, he got kind of bored by the hectic inactivity of Dawson an' its environs, so he decided to try his luck on Halfaday."

Old Cush carefully inserted a soiled playing card between the leaves of the Bible he had been reading, shoved the square-framed steel spectacles from nose to forehead, closed the book and returned it to the back bar from which he removed a bottle and three glasses.

"This un's on the house," he said. "Yukon wanted?"

"What?" asked Stiles.

Black John grinned. "Jest a formality, by way of openin' the conversation—like you'd say, 'It's a pleasant day,' er vicy vercy. You see, located as we are in close proximity to the international boundry, many of the itinerants who sojourn amongst us are fugitives from justice. Speakin' academically, it ain't none of our business what a man's past was. Nevertheless it has frequently militated to the malefactor's advantage to inform us whether it is the United States or the Canadian authorities he's dodgin' so, in the event that some minion of the law should show up, he could be advised of the fact an' govern himself accordin'. Cush's question was actuated, not by way of gratifying an idle curiosity, but purely in the spirit of helpful cooperation."

Cush scowled at Black John, and shifted his glance to the bottle that stood before Stiles. "Fill up an' shove it," he said. "All I says was was you a Yukon wanted? So in case Downey'd show up someone could slip you the word. Fer's I kin see, it didn't call fer no oration. But if John sees a chanct to make a couple hundred long words do the work of two short ones, he shore grabs it. It's fellas like him made 'em print dictionaries—so folks could find out what they was tryin' to say, if anyone would give a damn of would listen."

Stiles laughed, filled his glass and pushed away the bottle. "It's rather refreshing to find an educated man in this environment, though."

Cush's scowl of disapproval deepened. "So yer another of 'em, eh? What I claim eggication is made fer lawyers an' preachers, which their game is to ring in all the long words they kin lay their tongue to fer the confusal of good straight thinkin'."

"There's more truth than poetry in that," laughed Stiles, glancing about the room. "Nice place you've got here."

"It does."

"What?"

"Cush means," explained Black John, "that it admirably answers the purposes for which it was designed and constructed."

CUSH SHOOK his head in somber resignation, and eyed Stiles fishily. "Yer worst even than John. Leastwise, he does know what the little words means."

"Which reminds me," grinned Black John, "that you have not answered Cush's question. Our etymological discussion havin' momentarily diverted—"

"I would ruther stand around an' listen to a Chinee!" interrupted Cush, swallowing his liquor. "So you might's well dry up an' buy a drink."

"Fill 'em up," Stiles invited. "I'm buying this one. To return to your question, I am not wanted by any police. I'm just a prospector."

Cush shrugged. "It's all the same to me. It ain't nothin' agin a man if he ain't wanted somewheres. I was jest askin'—in case."

"I told Stiles he could throw his stuff into One Eyed John's cabin," said Black John, cramming tobacco into the bowl of his pipe and holding a match to it. A moment later he tossed the match to the floor in disgust. "Damn this pipe—it's plugged up! I'll step over to my cabin an' git another one. Got a couple of chores to do, too. Be back in half an hour an' take you over to One Eyed's place," he said to Stiles. "You kin be gittin' what you want in the way of grub from Cush. You'll be wantin' to git settled, an' yer supper out of the way so's to meet the boys when they come driftin' in fer the stud game this evenin'."

Proceeding straight to his cabin, Black John tossed his pack onto his bunk, busied himself for a few moments with pencil and paper, thrust the resultant memorandum into his pocket, stepped to the spring and removed two fruit jars filled with gold dust from the muck in the bottom and, avoiding Cush's, made his way swiftly toward One Eyed John's cabin. Just before reaching it he paused at a bend in the creek to remove a stone that completely concealed the mouth of a crevice at the base of a huge rock, placed the two jars within the aperture, and replaced the stone.

Entering the cabin he stepped to the opposite wall, removed

a section of log by pulling upon a short thong that protruded from the wall close beside one of a row of pegs obviously placed for convenience in hanging up clothing. Into the disclosed aperture he dropped the memorandum he had written, and replaced the section of log, being careful to leave the thong protruding just enough to be noticeable to one approaching the wall to hang up a garment.

RETURNING TO the fort, he found Stiles and Cush in the trading room crowding supplies into a packsack. A few minutes later he accompanied Stiles to One Eyed John's cabin and left him, returning to the saloon where Cush greeted him with a frown, as he set out bottle and glasses.

"I wouldn't know why you'd be fetchin' someone like this here Stiles to Halfaday—onlest it would be so's you'd have someone here that could understand all them big words you say."

"Merely for friendship's sake, Cush—merely for friendship's sake."

"Huh. It's the first time I ever know'd you to kick up sech a hell of a friendship with some damn chechako!"

"The friendship," explained Black John, filling his glass, "was with Old Bill Rodney."

"Bill Rodney! You mean Bill Rodney that used to be down on Birch Crick? Him that hid you in under his woman's dirty worshin' the time that marshal was on yer tail fer holdin' up them soldiers?"

"The same. One good turn deserves another, as the Good Book says."

"Cripes—he's dead! Downey was tellin' about it the last time he was up here. Claimed he struck it lucky 'fore he died, an' left right around a million to his daughter. Er mebbe it was half a million. Anyways, it was a hell of a lot. But she won't git it till she's twenty-one."

The big man nodded. "Yeah," he said, "an' that was last week.

It was on her account that I deemed it wise to remove Stiles from Dawson."

Cush sniffed audibly. "I smelt a woman in the woodpile somewheres, as the Good Book says! I s'pose she's a damn good looker, an' this here Stiles is a friend of hern that she wants hid out fer awhile! Damn if a woman can't git anthin' she wants outa you!"

"She's good lookin' all right. An' Stiles was a friend of hers. But the hidin' out idea is my own. In fact, I believe that if she knew I was responsible for his disappearance, she'd hate me. I don't like her. She's a brat. If it hadn't be'n fer her ma, that time on Birch Crick, she'd of run off at the head till that marshal would of been up to his ears in them dirty clothes, huntin' me. An' the other evenin' in the hotel dinin' room I overheard her tellin' Stiles I wasn't nothin' but an outlaw. You see, I suspect that Stiles knew she was about to come into a fortune an' was makin' a play fer it."

"Huh!" snorted Cush. "What's it any of your business if he did git it—if that's the way she done you? If some woman done me like that damn if I'd go out of my way to do her a good turn!"

"The good turn is fer Old Bill. I know he wouldn't want neither his daughter er his dust to fall into the hands of a damn skunk like Stiles. An' after all, whether I like her er not—she's Old Bill's daughter. She's young, yet, an' ain't got no sense. An' fer Bill's sake I'm givin' her a break."

"That's different," Cush opined. "This here Stiles, he claimed he didn't have but a few ounces of dust when he was buyin' them supplies. But I took notice that when his pack hit the floor in front of the bar, it thumped damn heavy fer the size of it. He was askin' me about the stud game, an' when I told him the stakes sometimes run pretty high, he never batted an eye— jest said he'd be over tonight an' set in. He's one of them cold-eyed liars that looks right at a man when he lies."

"**HE TOOK** good care that I never got a chance to handle that pack on a portage, coming' up," grinned Black John. "But from observin' the apparent amount of effort he expended in handlin' it, I jedge it to weigh somewheres between a hundred an' a hundred an' twenty-five pounds—say thirty thousan' dollars, roughly speakin'."

"Where would a damn chechako git thirty thousan' in dust?"

"Accordin' to what I heard in Dawson, Stiles an' his pardner, one Dutch Dietz, had a claim on the Porcupine. Rumor has it that an old timer by the name of Paddy Dorgan, who was s'posed to have had somewhere around thirty er forty thousan' in dust cached, disappeared suddenly, an' shortly thereafter Stiles an' Dietz parted company, an' Stiles went to Dawson. It was common knowledge around Dawson that Old Bill's daughter was about to come into her money, so Stiles decided to stick around an' make a play fer it—an' it looked to me like he was havin' good luck."

"Didn't the police do nothin' about this Dorgan?"

"Yeah, the inspector at Forty Mile sent a constable down to investigate the case. Stiles knew that, but it didn't seem to worry him none."

"Then what did he come away from Dawson fer, before the girl got her money?"

"I have reason to believe," grinned Black John, "that Stiles, in some manner, received disquietin' information concernin' the progress of that investigation on the Porcupine—information that made a hasty departure from Dawson seem advisable, if not actually imperative."

"You mean someone tipped him to lam out?"

"Paraphrasin' it succinctly an' in the vernacular—yes."

"You couldn't of jest said 'yes,' I s'pose—like anyone else would?" scowled Cush.

"I merely strove to call attention to the crudity of your style. I deem it my duty to attempt to broaden your vocabulary."

"You do, eh? Well, listen—I ain't got no vocabularies, whatever they be. If I had, they would be broad enough as they was without you sayin' all them big words. About Stiles—if the police wants him, an' Downey can't find him around Dawson, he'll figger he hit fer Halfaday, an' he'll come up here after him. What I claim, it's a damn shame if some chechako would murder a sourdough an' git away with his dust."

Black John nodded gravely. "The same thought has occurred to me."

"An' when Downey gits here," continued Cush, "Stiles would either hit out acrost the line with the dust, er else Downey would arrest him an' take him an' the dust back to Dawson. Them old timers don't hardly ever have no heirs that anyone could locate.

"It seems like a damn pity if Downey would turn over all that dust to the public administrator—an' him not able to locate no one to divide it up amongst."

Black John fixed Cush with a disapproving frown. "Are you hintin', perchance, that we should, in some questionable or underhanded manner, obtain possession of this dust an' convert it to our own use?"

"Well—no. That is—I wouldn't want we should rob his cache, er run in no markers on him, without we ketched him cheatin' first nor nothin' like that. All I says was that it's a pity if that dust gits off'n Halfaday, an' no rightful owner to claim it. What I was gittin' at—a man with eyes like Stiles is bound to cheat— give him time. An' then we could run in the markers on him, fair an' square."

"No!" thundered Black John, smiting the bar with his fist. "Here on Halfaday we have builded an' unassailable reputation for pristine rectitude that is a precious heritage which we must jealously guard—"

"Can that crap!" Cush growled. "I wouldn't know what it means, even if I would listen. An' besides, I've know'd you to run in markers before now."

"Only when I deemed the end justified the means. I'm tellin' you that if Stiles leaves Halfaday without takin' that dust with him, it'll be entirely of his own choice an' volition. We've got to watch our ethics!"

Cush shrugged. "What with all them big words—an' you doin' all the deemin', Stiles'll be lucky to git off'n Halfaday with his hide. Here comes Pot Gutted John. It's your turn to buy a drink."

IV

AS DARKNESS GATHERED the men of Halfaday drifted into the saloon for an evening's entertainment. Stiles appeared and was introduced by Black John. A stud game was organized that ran into the wee sma' hours, after which the men drifted back to their cabins, Cush locked the saloon, and Halfaday slept.

Early the following morning Black John arose and, proceeding to the rock beneath which he had cached his two jars of dust, pried away the stone, and stared into the empty aperture. He made a clicking sound with his tongue, as he shook his head slowly from side to side. "Tch, tch, tch—don't it beat hell what a damn chechako will stoop to?"

Rising to his feet he strode to One Eyed John's cabin and rapped sharply upon the door. Presently a sleepy voice bade him enter and he stepped into the room to see Stiles sitting on the edge of his bunk in his underwear, regarding him sleepily.

"What's up?" the man asked. "It seems like I just got to bed."

Seating himself Black John drummed on the table top with his finger tips. "You know," he began hesitatingly, "the boys kind of took me last night in the stud game."

The other nodded, frowning. "I noticed that your luck wasn't running so hot. But I didn't get it all. If this is a touch—there's nothing doing. You know I told you I only had a few ounces—"

"It ain't that," the big man interrupted reassuringly. "The fact is, I've got plenty of dust cached—couple of fruit jars full. My name is wrote on the inside of the covers." He noted that the man's hands tightened their grip on the edge of the bunk, and that he moistened his lips with his tongue.

"That's good," he said, in a voice that sounded a bit hollow.

"Yeah. I gen'lly keep some dust cached where it's handy. But the trouble with me is I'm so damn fergitful I can't never rec'lect where I cached it."

"What! You mean you've forgotten where you cached your dust?"

"Yeah. It's a failin' I've got. A nurse dropped me on my head one time when I was a baby, an' I ain't be'n able to remember much ever sence. That is, ma ketched her at it onct. She might of dropped me more times—we don't know. It's right unhandy—not rememberin' things. But I always write down where I've got my dust cached so I kin go an' git it when I want it."

"That's a good idea," approved Stiles weakly.

"Yeah. I don't carry this paper around with me on account I might lose it out of my pocket, er git it wet so the writin' would rub off er somethin', so I cache the paper, too."

"Oh."

"Yeah. But the trouble is I can't remember where I cached it."

"You mean you can't remember where you cached the paper that tells where you cached your dust?" the man asked, his voice stiffening perceptibly.

"Yeah. That's right."

"That's tough luck. I'm sorry. But why come to me about it? I can't do you any good. I haven't got that paper."

"It's like this," explained Black John. "Knowin' my failin', I always write out on another paper where I cached that first paper, an' I keep this last paper on my shelf in under my clock. So this mornin' when I wanted to go to my cache an' git some dust, I read the paper that's under the clock, an' it says I cached the paper that tells where my dust cache is, here in One Eyed

John's cabin. It says it's in his cache over there in the wall. There's a piece of thong sticks out beside one of them pegs where yer coat an' slicker's hangin'. If you give a pull on the thong a section of log comes out. So I guess I'll git my paper an' go to my cache."

AS HE rose from the chair Stiles leaped from the bunk, barring the way to the opposite wall. "Stay right where you are!" he commanded. "You can't go into that cache! I have some dust cached there! I examined the hole thoroughly last evening when I found it, and there was no paper in it!"

"Wasn't, eh?" asked Black John, uncertainly. "That's funny. That's where the paper said it was. Mebbe I better take a look. You might of missed it."

"Stand back!" cried the man, reaching for his rifle that stood in a nearby corner.

"This is my home temporarily. And a man's home is his castle. He can defend it with his life. That's the law!"

"It is, eh?" asked Black John, as the other jacked a shell into the chamber of the gun. "Well, here on Halfaday we figger Old Man Colt is pretty good law. If I was you, I'd drop that rifle before you git hurt. Unlest you really want to prove yer p'int by defendin' the cabin with yer life."

The man's eyes widened in sudden terror as they fixed upon the blue-black six-gun in the big man's hand—a six-gun whose muzzle centered exactly upon his midriff, at a distance of some eight feet. "Don't shoot!" he cried as the rifle clattered to the floor.

"All right. Stand over there in the corner where I kin keep an eye on you while I hunt fer my paper."

"You told me back in Dawson," quavered the man, "that you never found One Eyed John's cache! That you all figured he must have left a lot of dust—but you never could find it!"

"Did I? It's that damn nurse's fault, fer droppin' me that time. I must of fergot. What I claim, folks should pick out nurses which wouldn't go about the house droppin' babies on their head." He tugged at the thong, removed the section of log, thrust his hand within the aperture, and drew out a fruit jar full of dust. A moment later he drew out another and turned to Stiles, who stood in the corner, white and shaking. "So you keep yer dust in fruit jars, too, eh?"

"No," faltered the man, "those jars—I—I—they must be yours."

"Mine! Wait till I look!" Unscrewing the cap the big man glanced at the inside of it. "Why—damn if they ain't!" he exclaimed. "There's my name. How in hell did they git here?"

"I—I can explain that," said the other. "When I saw that thong sticking out as I went there to hang up my slicker, I pulled at it and a section of the log came out. I felt within and found a paper on which were directions to the cache beneath the big rock—"

"I thought you claimed you didn't find no paper?"

"I—I'll have to admit I—I lied about that. I did find it. And I found the two jars of dust and carried them back and placed them together with my own dust in the cache. I supposed, of course, that those jars contained the dust that One Eyed John had cached and which you never found."

AS THE men talked Black John removed twenty-three eighty-ounce caribou hide sacks of dust from the cache and placed them on the table beside the fruit jars. "Is these the few ounces of dust you claimed was all you had?" he asked.

"Yes. I—I didn't think it was anyone's business how much dust I had."

Black John nodded. "Yer right. It wasn't. But if a man's prone to lie, he ought to lie reasonable. I had yer pack gauged almost to the ounce. However, the boys won't be holdin' them lies agin you when they hang you this afternoon fer cache-robbin'."

"Hang me! Good God—man—you can't hang me!"

"Think not?"

"I mean—you can't hang a man for taking the dust from a

dead man's cache! That's not robbery. You can't rob a dead man!"

"What the hell's that got to do with it? I ain't dead. You robbed me."

"I mean—when I took that dust, I believed it had belonged to a dead man!"

"The case will be interestin' to try before a miners' meetin'," admitted Black John. "Near's I kin rec'lect the p'int ain't never be'n adjudicated on Halfaday—whether a robber who inadvertantly mixed up his robbees is guilty, er not guilty? Off hand, I'd hazard the guess that the p'int is far an' away beyond the legal erudition of most of the residents of the crick, who'll undoubtless vote 'Guilty' on the broad theory that any damn skunk that would rob a cache had ought to be hung—no matter whose cache it was. In fact, the odds in favor of an acquittal is far too infinitesimal to be figgered by any known system of mathematics."

"But I tell you the law considers the intent! I had no intent whatever of committing a robbery when I took that dust."

"How about yer intent when you told me, a while back, that you didn't find no paper in the cache, an' couldn't do me no good in findin' my dust—when you thought I'd fergot where I'd cached it?"

"I—I'd have turned over the dust. I was only having some fun with you."

"Our ideas of humor is dissimilar. But we'll pass that over."

"The crime, if any," persisted Stiles, "was consummated when I committed the overt act of removing the dust from the cache. And I maintain that, at that time, I had no intent of robbing any living man."

BLACK JOHN grinned. "Cush ought to be around to hear that. But I realize that there's a modicum of truth in the assumption. It constitutes what might be deemed a mitigatin' an' extenuatin' circumstance—not mitigatin' or extenuatin' enough to carry any weight with a miners' meetin', but by an unprejudiced an' un-

biased judge, the argument might be considered. I hesitate to
be a party to hangin' any man who claims he hadn't done nothin'
contrary to the dictates of his own conscience, if any. So rather
than subject you to trial by miners' meetin' which would amount
to certain death, I'm constrained to let you go back to Dawson—
if you'll start right now. We don't want no such hair-splittin'
character on Halfaday."

"But," faltered the man, "I—I can't go back to Dawson."

"Shore you kin. It's easy—jest foller Halfaday down to the
White, an' the White down to the Yukon, an' then down the
Yukon."

"I mean—I don't dare show up in Dawson."

"Why not? Hell, you was there till you come up here!"

"I know. But I have reason to believe that the police suspect
me of being implicated in a—a—a murder and robbery on the
Porcupine."

Black John shrugged. "It ain't none of our business what a
man done before he come to Halfaday. Are you guilty?"

"Well—in a way—I—I suppose I am implicated. The fact
is, my partner did kill this man and took his dust."

"If it was yer pardner done it, what are you afraid of?"

"The police would involve me—guilty knowledge, or accessory after the fact, or something."

"Might even prove you was an accessory durin' the fact,"
suggested Black John. "That is, if yer pardner should squawk."

"And he's going to do just that! He'll lie like the devil to put
the crime onto me. I found a note under my door the night before
I joined you at the breakfast table—the night before I left Dawson.
It was from Dietz, my partner. He wrote that a constable had
found the body and had arrested him, and that he was going to
squawk to save his own neck. He said the constable was bringing him upriver and that they would reach Forty Mile the next
day. Said he'd managed to slip the note to an Indian he had
bribed to deliver it to me so I'd have a chance to skip out."

"Mebbe it wasn't yer pardner wrote it," suggested Black John. "It might of be'n someone with a sense of humor like yourn, that done it fer a joke."

"It would be a hell of a joke! But it wasn't a joke. Dietz couldn't write. He printed out his words, and misspelled most of 'em. It was from him, all right. I could tell that at a glance."

"Well, in that case I guess you can't go back to Dawson," admitted the big man. "This here dust in them pokes couldn't, by no chanct, be part of what yer pardner got out of the dead man's cache, could it? I mean the man that was murdered an' robbed."

Stiles winced at the words. "Yes—that's part of it."

"How much did you git?"

"There were thirty-five sacks. I took twenty-seven of them. Dietz is a dumb Dutchman. I let him keep eight sacks. I spent four sacks in Dawson—making a play for a million."

Black John nodded grimly. "Yeah, I seen that. The Rodney girl is the daughter of an old friend of mine."

"She told me you were an outlaw."

"That's right. A lot of us is on Halfaday, Stiles."

"I—I suppose I'm an' outlaw, too—now."

"Yeah. An' as long as you can't go back to Dawson, the only thing fer you to do is cross over into Alasky, an' hit fer the Tanana country."

"But—how far is it?"

"It's a hell of a ways. But you won't be the first that's tried it."

"Those others—did they get through?"

"I wouldn't know about that. It would be owin' to their luck."

"But—I couldn't possibly make it! Why, that dust alone weighs a hundred and fifteen pounds!"

BLACK JOHN shrugged. "It's a long trip—an' a rough country. Of course, it ain't none of my business what you take in yer pack. But if it was me, I wouldn't tackle it without a good hundred an' fifty pounds of solid grub."

"But—the dust!" cried the man, his eyes on the little caribou sacks. "That would make two hundred and sixty-five pounds! I can't even lift that much—let alone carry it! What can I do?"

Again the big man shrugged. "It's your problem—not mine."

"It's a hold-up," cried Stiles, his voice breaking shrilly. "I'll be damned if I'll stand for it! You're forcing me to leave the dust behind!"

"I ain't forcin' you to do nothin'. There's the pack of grub you fetched from Cush's. An' there's the dust. Take yer pick—either one—er both."

"Suppose I refuse to leave Halfaday?"

"In that case, we'll be goin' on over to Cush's an' I'll call a miners' meetin', an' we'll try you fer robbin' my cache."

"Listen!" cried the man, in a panicky voice. "You're all outlaws, up here, I'm an outlaw—why not let me stay here with you?"

"What you don't seem to grasp, Stiles, is the fact that there's a hell of a lot of difference in outlaws. There's been quite a few of your kind show'd up on Halfaday from time to time. The bulk of 'em is buried there in the graveyard back of the saloon. A few moved on—but not many. I'm givin' you yer choice—you kin remain here an' jine the vast majority. Er you kin pack yer sack an' take yer chances with the few. An'—you've got jest five minutes to make up yer mind."

"I—I've heard how you hang men on Halfaday. I wouldn't have a show, if I stayed." Hastily he began stowing the supplies into his packsack. "Which way is the line?" he asked jerkily as he swung the pack to his back. Black John pointed to a gulch that led upward into the hills, and with a last longing glance at the little pile of sacks, Stiles stepped from the room and headed up the gulch.

When he had gone, Black John picked up the jars and the little sacks and proceeding to his own cabin, slipped them under his bunk. Then he removed his packs and threw himself down on his blankets to make up for lost sleep.

V

ONE DAY A month later, Corporal Downey stepped through the doorway of Cushing's saloon to find the proprietor and Black John shaking dice for the drinks. As the officer approached the bar, Cush spun a glass toward him, and Black John shoved the bottle. "Chasin' some damn miscreant, no doubt," he grinned.

"Yeah," replied the officer, filling his glass. "Fellow by the name of Stiles. You may have noticed him, John, when you were in Dawson a few weeks ago. He was runnin' around with Margy Rodney quite a bit."

Black John nodded. "Yeah, I rec'lect him. What do you want him fer?"

"Murder an' robbery down on the Porcupine. Him an' his pardner murdered a prospector name of Dorgan. A constable from Forty Mile brought in the pardner, a dumb Dutchman named Dietz, an' he puts the blame on Stiles. Stiles hung around Dawson about a month after he knew the constable had gone to the Porcupine. Then suddenly he disappeared. He must have got wind, somehow, that the constable had broke the case."

"Yeah, he must of, at that," agreed Black John. "He showed up here about a month ago, an' hung around fer a night an' a day, an' then pulled out."

"Pulled out! Where to?"

"Alasky, I s'pose. That's where most of 'em goes that don't stay here on the crick."

"Did he have any dust with him?"

"Claimed he didn't have only a few ounces. Couldn't of had no hell of a lot, an' back-packed enough grub to take him to the Tanana country."

"I doubt if a man can back-pack enough grub to take him

to the Tanana—if he didn't pack an ounce of dust."

"It seems like a reasonable doubt, at that," Black John admitted. "It's a hell of a big country—an' no trails."

"Accordin' to the man, Dietz, that the constable brought in from the Porcupine, Stiles took the bulk of Dorgan's dust—right around thirty thousan' dollars worth. That would run better than a hundred pounds. He prob'ly cached it somewheres. Not that it makes much difference. Dorgan didn't have any heirs."

"Any news in Dawson sence I was there?" asked Black John.

"No, nothin' I kin think of," Downey replied. "Oh, yes—you know Margy Rodney, don't you, Old Bill's girl? Well, she come into her money, five, six weeks ago, an' last week she an' young Joe Emerson over on Quartz Crick got married. That was jest a day er so after the news got out that Stiles was wanted fer murder. Joe's a good kid, an' with Margy's money back of him he can run a flume in to his claim. They say he'll clean up big. It's a mighty good thing she didn't marry that damn Stiles! It looked fer a while like she was goin' to. She sure is lucky!"

Black John nodded thoughtfully. "Yeah," he agreed, "she shore is. I thought a lot of Old Bill. He done me a good turn onct. I'm glad no harm come to his girl an' his money. Seem like, mebbe, Old Bill kin kind of rest easier in his grave."

EVIL COMPANIONS

BLACK JOHN SMITH rotated the pan, clawed out the coarser gravel, and continued the rotating motion until, with the deftness of long practice, he flirted out the last of the water and sand and examined the thin scattering of yellow grains that remained in the bottom of the pan. Carefully transferring them to a little moosehide sack, he tossed the pan onto the gravel bar, dipped a bucket of water from the creek, walked to the tent pitched a few feet up the bank, lighted a small fire, and suspended the tea pail above the flames on a stick whose end was weighted with a stone. He sliced a liberal portion of bacon into a frying pan and in another pan mixed a bannock.

The sun dipped behind the rim rocks and the only sounds were the monotonous gurgle of the water among the rocks of a riffle, and the tapping of a woodpecker on a dead spruce. As he waited for his water to heat two figures suddenly appeared on the skyline of the opposite rim and stood limned against the western glow. They were pack-laden figures and as Black John looked one raised his arm and pointed to the thin spiral of smoke that rose from the little campfire. The other focused a glass and for several moments Black John felt himself the object of careful scrutiny. Deliberately he raked coals aside with a stick and nested his bannock pan among them. When he glanced upward again the figures were gone, and a few moments later the sound of snapping twigs and the rattle of a small avalanche of stones told him the two were negotiating the steep descent to the creek bed.

They crossed at the riffles, stepped to the fire, and swung the packs from their shoulders. Black John nodded a greeting as he noted that the pack of the larger man, while small of bulk, thudded heavily upon the ground, and that the other pack was lean and surmounted by a blanket roll.

"Had supper?" he asked, glancing up into the faces covered by a three weeks' stubble of beard.

"No. An' by God, bo, we're hungry—if anyone should drive up in a hack an' ask you! I hope you've got plenty."

"Oh shore. I ain't got no fresh meat, but I'll slice up some more bacon an' mix up another batch of bannock. You kin git to work on that tea, an' I'll bile up another pail. Got to use yer own dishes. I've only got the one set."

THE TWO seated themselves on the ground as one of them rummaged in the lean pack. "About all we've got left is the damn dishes," he said. "We're lost. Et the last of our grub last night, an' ain't seen nothin' bigger'n a woodpecker all day. You located here?"

"No, jest prospectin'. Been snipin' the bars on the say-so of a Siwash who claimed he washed out four an' six bits to the pan up here a month ago. If he did he must have got it all. I ain't been able to do no better'n two bits, at the most."

"What crick is this?"

"Damn if I know. Prob'ly ain't got no name."

"How could a Siwash tell you about it then?" asked the larger man, a note of suspicion in his voice.

"He claimed the crick run into the Sixtymile jest above the big bend, an' this un does. Trouble with a damn Siwash, you can't never tell what they'll call a crick. They're liable to count one that ain't nothin' but a trickle, er even they might count a dry wash. This here's the first decent side crick that runs in above the big bend."

"You say this crick runs into the Sixtymile? How fer below here?"

"About five er six mile."

"Hell, we crossed what we figgered was the Sixtymile a couple of weeks ago on a raft an' got into a country so damn rough we got lost. We crossed the Yukon at Dawson an' hit out acrost country prospectin'."

"How'd you make out?"

"Not so hot," answered the larger man. "'Bout like yer doin' here—on some of the cricks we panned. We need grub. How fer's the nearest tradin' post?"

"Ogilvie's the clostest," Black John replied. "It's jest acrost the Yukon from the mouth of the Sixtymile."

"How fer from here?"

"About thirty mile, I reckon. You could run it in a day with a canoe."

"Yeah, but we ain't got no canoe. How about you goin' down an' fetchin' the grub up to us? We'll pay you fer yer time, an' the rent of the canoe, besides. We kin wait here till you git back. We'll pay you fer what grub we eat while yer gone, too."

"Well," Black John replied, apparently weighing the offer in his mind, "I might, at that. I ain't takin' out no hell of a lot here. How about one of you fellas goin' along. Downstream ain't so bad, travelin' light. But comin' back up with a load there's goin' to be some considerable portagin' to do around rapids. Two'd be a lot better'n one on the poles an' paddles, too."

The men exchanged glances and the larger one shook his head. "We ain't neither one of us in no shape to make the trip," he said. "Fact is, we're plumb wore out packin' up an' down them damn hills fer the past three weeks. You've got grub enough here to last us till you git back. You'd ought to make it in four days if it only takes you one to git there. We'll pay you three ounces a day—one fer yer time, one fer the canoe, an' one fer the grub we eat. That's fair enough. Them four days' rest ort to put us back in shape."

"Well, of course, if a man's wore out he ain't in no shape to make a trip. I'll go down to Ogilvie an' fetch up yer grub. I'll be pullin' out early tomorrow."

Shortly after daylight the following morning, Black John pocketed the poke of dust the larger of the two handed him and stepping into his canoe, pushed off down the creek. As he rounded the first bend he grinned to himself. "Wonder what kind of prospectin' them two's been up to? Looks like they've got a hell of a lot of dust—an' no pan nor shovel."

II

EARLY THAT EVENING Black John slanted the canoe across the Yukon and beached it before the trading post at Ogilvie. He entered the building to find Corporal Downey the center of a group of half a dozen angry prospectors.

"What I claim," growled one, "any fellow that would blast a man down to shet his mouth after robbin' him had ought to be strung up to the first handy tree!"

"You bet! It wasn't no question of self-defense, neither!" exclaimed another. "There wasn't a gun in the shack, accordin' to the way I heer'd it."

"By God, he better not show up around here!" cried a third. "We'll shore save the territory the expense of a trial."

"Better let the law handle him," advised Corporal Downey. "Lynchin's murder in this country."

"That ain't the way the law looks at it where I come from," the man retorted. "We've pulled off quite a few lynchin's, back home, an' no one ever got convicted of murder on account of 'em."

"It ain't," reminded Downey, "the law where a man came from he's got to worry about—it's the law where he's at."

"Ain't the police got nothin' to go on, at all?" queried another. "Didn't the one that done it leave nothin' to go by? Er didn't anyone see no strangers hangin' around?"

"We ain't got a thing," Downey replied. "Not even a foot track er a fingerprint. We've questioned everyone on Ophir an' no one seen any strangers on the crick. The man's pardner come back from huntin' about eleven, that night, an' found him layin' on the floor of their shack with a bullet through his head, an' the dust gone—twenty-five hundred ounces. It was their spring clean-up which they was goin' to take to Dawson the next day. The man was still breathin' an' they hustled him down to the hospital, hopin' he'd come to long enough to tell somethin'. But he died without regainin' consciousness. It's prob'ly a two-man job. One went in the shack while the other acted as lookout. That's only my guess. We don't know. But we're doin' everythin' we can. We're patrollin' the river an' all the important cricks, checkin' up on everyone we don't know. We've notified White-horse an' Forty Mile to stop everyone goin' up er down from Dawson. But it's one of them cases where the police didn't git no breaks. We generally git somethin' to go on, even if it ain't much. Most of the damn crooks ain't very wide between the ears an' they make a mistake somewhere along the line, either committin' the crime, er in the get-away. But it looks like this case is different."

"Mebbe his pardner done it," suggested a man.

"No chance," Downey replied. "We checked that angle. The pardner was off huntin' with a couple of fellas from the next claim. When they got back these others stopped in their shack an' the pardner went on to his own, an' he was back in less'n ten minutes all out of breath from runnin', an' told about findin' his pardner layin' on the floor with blood oozin' out of his forehead. They all run back there an' it was jest like he said, an' the blood had thickened around the edges. He'd been shot anyways an hour or so before—prob'ly longer."

SO EXCITED and angry had the men been that no one had noticed Black John's entry into the trading room. When he spoke from the edge of the crowd all turned to face him. "Looks like a swell murder you've got on yer hands, Downey, from what I've heard. When did it come off?"

"Hello, John!" greeted the officer. "I'll say it's a swell murder— an' a damn dirty one!

"It happened about three weeks ago. An' we ain't no nearer a solution of it than we was the day it was committed. These two pardners had jest finished their clean-up an' was goin' to start fer the outside the next day. They was fambly men, too. I'd shore like to lay my hands on the one that done it."

"Yeah," Black John agreed, "it's too damn bad to have a venture like that got away with. A damn cuss like that ain't no one to have runnin' loose on the cricks."

"I'll say he ain't!" exclaimed a miner heartily. "As long as he's loose there ain't no one safe!"

"Jest come down from Halfaday, John?" Downey asked.

"No, I been prospectin' over acrost the river fer about a week. A Siwash told me about a crick. But he must of lied."

"I'm headin' fer Halfaday, now," said the officer. "It may be that whoever done it hit for there."

"It's possible," the big man admitted. "A hell of a lot of riff-raff comes stringin' in on us, much as we try to keep the crick moral. Go on up, Downey, an' help yerself to any strangers you find. If you don't have no luck you better hang around Cush's till I git there. Like I said, the crick I'm prospectin' don't look like much, an' I'll be hittin' back fer Halfaday in a day er so. I'll sort of keep my eyes open an' if I find out anythin' I'll let you know."

"Much obliged, John. But in a case like this where we ain't got a damn bit of evidence to go on, I don't know how the hell we're ever goin' to get a conviction even if we should arrest the right party—unless he'd talk. An' he ain't likely to."

"By God, if we git holt of him he'll talk!" growled a prospector, and the others heartily indorsed the sentiment, as Black John made his purchases and carried them to his canoe.

III

ON THE EVENING of the fourth day thereafter he nosed the canoe against the bank of the creek and the two who were waiting helped to unload her. "Git a good rest?" he asked, as he joined the men at supper.

"Yeah, we sure did," answered the larger of the two who apparently did the talking for both. "We mostly jest laid around, but we done a little pannin', off an' on. Found it like you said. It's about like them other cricks we tried. A man would have to work like hell to make wages. What's the news along the river?"

"Oh, nothin' much. The steamboat woodpile at Five Fingers burnt up. There's a kind of a flurry on Henderson Crick. Someone shot a prospector an' got away with a clean-up him an' his pardner was goin' to take into Dawson the next day. The talk at Ogilvie is that whoever done it got twenty-five hundred ounces, accordin' to the man's pardner. He was off huntin' that day, an' when he got back to the shack he found his pardner layin' on the floor with a bullet through his head, an' the dust gone.

"They took him to the hospital in Dawson, hopin' he'd be able to tell who done it when he got better. But he never come to—lived four, five days an' then died."

"Where was this robbery pulled off at?"

"On Ophir—way up near the head of the crick."

"Ain't they got no idee who done it?"

"Nope. The police is workin' on the case, though. They're watchin' the river at Whitehorse an' Forty Mile, an' they've got patrols out checkin' up on all strangers. Coons, the trader, said a policeman name of Corporal Downey had gone up to Halfaday Crick to see if the one that done it had hit fer there. But he hadn't, 'cause this Downey come back through Ogilvie while I was there, an' he said there wasn't no newcomers on Halfaday."

"What do you know about Halfaday Crick?" asked the larger man, eyeing him sharply.

"I don't know nothin'—except it's a damn good place fer honest men to stay away from. They claim they're all outlaws, up there. I've heard that it lays right up agin the Alasky line, so if the police shows up huntin' anyone he kin slip acrost the line an' lay low till the police goes back. It's claimed that no police except this here Downey dares to show up there—an' he don't never have no luck. Them outlaws stick together. The police ain't got no show."

"Do you know where Halfaday Crick is? Know how to get there?"

"Accordin' to what I've heard, it's up the White. It runs into White River somewheres clost to the line."

"How far's the White River from here?"

"Well—let's see. It runs into the Yukon about eighty mile above Dawson from the west—that's this side of the Yukon. From what I hear, this Halfaday Crick runs into the White about a hundred an' twenty-five mile from the mouth."

"How'd you like to go there?" the man asked abruptly, after a moment of silence.

BLACK JOHN snorted into the cup he held to his lips, slopping hot tea onto his trousers as he shot the other a startled glance. "Who—me! Go to Halfaday Crick? Not by damn sight!"

"Why not?"

"What—go up there amongst all them outlaws?"

The other grinned. "Hell—they won't bother you as long as you don't bother them!"

"They won't never bother me, then—'cause I shore as hell ain't goin' to bother them!"

"That's what you think," replied the man, and Black John noted a sinister gleam in his gray-green eyes, though his lips still smiled. "But the fact is we're headin' fer Halfaday Crick an' we need someone to help with our packin'.'."

"Cripes!" exclaimed Black John. "There ain't much packin' to do. We kin load the stuff in my canoe in the mornin', an' drop down to the Yukon. Then you kin git a canoe of yer own an' hit on up the big river, an' on up the White till you come to Halfaday. I don't mind helpin' you boys down to the river. But like I said—I wouldn't go to Halfaday fer no money!"

"An' like I said," replied the man, a flinty note in his voice, "mebbe you think you won't, but you will. An' we ain't goin' by the Yukon, neither. We're goin' overland from here an' yer goin' to help with the packin', whether you want to, er not. I might's well tell you that we're the lads that knocked off that guy on Ophir an' lifted the twenty-five hundred ounces of dust.

"You ain't goin' to tell no one till we git to Halfaday. After that you kin talk yer fool head off, fer all we care. Onct we git there we'll be safe. Twenty-five hundred ounces is a hundred an' sixty pound—a damn heavy pack fer anyone that ain't use' to packin'. I've been luggin' it around these damn mountains fer three weeks—an' believe me, I know! We didn't dast take the river fer it, so we hit out fer Halfaday overland—an' got lost. Yer a big man, an' prob'ly a damn sight more use' to packin' than I be. If you ain't, you will be by the time you git to Halfaday, 'cause yer sure as hell goin' to pack that dust! Me an' Shorty here'll handle the rest of the stuff. We'll pay you an ounce a day."

"You can't make no one work, if he don't want to," protested Black John. "This here's a free country!"

"That's right," agreed the other, drawing a six-gun from the front of his shirt and balancing it on his palm, "an' we're givin' you the chanct to do yer own decidin'. You kin either help us pack this stuff to Halfaday, er git the same thing that damn fool on Ophir got. We cooled him so he couldn't squawk. You know too much, now, to turn you loose before we git to Halfaday—an' dead man tells no tales."

"It's—it's kidnappin'," protested Black John. "It's agin the law! An' if you shoot me, it's murder!"

"Yeah? So what? You said that bird we shot died. They can't hang us no higher fer two murders than one, kin they? We ain't got nothin' to lose by knockin' you off, have we? En' we'd have a hell of a lot to lose if we turned you loose with what you know. You better look at it reasonable. An ounce a day's better'n feedin' the fish on the bottom of this crick with a rock tied to yer neck!"

BLACK JOHN nodded, after a short silence. "It looks like you've got me, boys," he admitted. "But if I was you I'd never take all that dust up amongst them outlaws. They'll prob'ly rob you."

The man laughed. "Rob us! Not if my old friend Black John Smith has anythin' to say, they won't!"

"Black John Smith!" exclaimed the other, his eyes widening. "You mean the Black John Smith that's claimed to be king of Halfaday Crick? The one that's boss of all them outlaws?"

"That's the one."

"Do you know him? Be you a friend of his'n?"

"Hell—yes! Many's the deal we've pulled off together. Me

an' Black John is one, two, three. I saved his life, one time. It was up a gulch that runs into the Forty Mile. We'd jest knocked off a prospector an' was dividin' his dust when his pardner showed up an' I seen him jest as he draw'd a bead on Black John, an' I jerks out Old Sally, here, an' lets him have it before he could pull the trigger. Rob us—hell! I'd jest like to see anyone try an' rob me whilst Black John was around! He's beat 'em to it—you bet!"

"Well, he might, at that. You see, I didn't know about you savin' his life. Them outlaws prob'ly won't harm me none, seein' I'm with you—that is, if you'll say a good word fer me."

"You don't need to worry about them outlaws. Hell, Black John would hang any of 'em that bothered you, if I'd tell him to! We're jest like brothers—me an' Black John. You stick with us, an' we'll see you through. Ain't that so, Shorty?"

"Sure we will," agreed the other. "Any friend of ourn is a friend of Black John Smith's. You don't need to worry none."

Black John heaved a sigh of resignation. "All right. I'll go. I don't like the idee—but it looks like you boys has got me. An' remember, you promised to say a good word for me to Black John. It's jest like my old gran'ma used to say; 'shun evil companions, boy,' she'd say. An' I be'n shunnin' 'em all my life, but it shore looks like I've fell in with 'em, now."

IN THE morning they broke camp and the larger of the two turned to Black John. "Which way'll we go?" he asked. "We've be'n wanderin' around these damn mountains till we don't know up from down! An' see that you don't make no mistakes," he added, significantly patting his shirt front. "Any shenannigan out of you—like steerin' us back to the Yukon, an' out goes yer light. An' remember this—if we're picked up by the police, it's you that'll be packin' the dust. An' there's two of us to swear it was you knocked that guy off. So you better be thinkin' that one over—in case you might have any funny ideas in yer head."

"Don't you boys worry none," Black John replied. "I'll git this

dust to Halfaday fer you. From then on, you'll have to look out
fer it yerselves. I won't be responsible fer what happens amongst
them outlaws."

"That's all right," grinned the man. "Onct we git to Halfaday
with it, we're okay. Jest leave them outlaws to me. I kin handle
'em."

"I'm shore glad of that. I'd hate to see you boys lose yer dust
through any fault of mine. We'll git goin', now. This here crick
we're on must head over somewheres near the White, by the
way she runs. We'll load the stuff in the canoe an' shove up as
fer as we kin. There'll prob'ly be a lot of portages. But it'll be
easier an' quicker than hittin' out acrost country. It might be we
kin portage acrost to the White, an' then shove on up to Halfaday. It's accordin' to where this crick heads."

The three worked the loaded canoe up the creek, poling,
paddling, track-lining, and portaging until on the evening of
the third day they ran out of water, the stream forking into two
branches neither of which would float the canoe.

"Well," said Black John, as they camped, "looks like the crick's
petered out on us. In the mornin' I'll slip on ahead an' see what
I kin find. It can't be so damn fer to the White from here."

"I'll go 'long," said the larger man meaningly. "Jest in case."

"Oh, shore—come on along. Shorty kin stay with the stuff.
I hope we're clost enough to carry the canoe acrost. I shore ain't
got no appetite fer packin' them hundred an' sixty pound of dust
up an' down these damn mountains."

IN THE morning, accompanied by the larger man, Black John
ascended the ridge against the base of which the two branches
of the creek rose. From its crest they could see a valley of considerable width lying beyond a lower ridge. A mile of rough
going brought them to the rim of the valley through which
wound a sizeable stream.

"Is that the White?" the man asked.

"Damn if I know," Black John replied. "It won't take long to find out." He pointed to several thin plumes of smoke that rose above the scrub spruce on the bank of the stream.

"It might be the police," suggested the man.

"Most likely a bunch of Siwashes. The police don't travel in bands, in this country. One smoke would do fer all the police you'd ever find together. Mostly they travel alone."

Descending into the valley Black John led the way to the encampment of half a dozen tepees. An old Indian greeted them with a smile and Black John spoke to him at length in his own language, the Indian replying in the same tongue.

"He says," translated Black John, "that this here's Ladue Crick, an' that it runs into the White about thirty miles below here. An' he says that Halfaday is the next big crick that runs into the White from this side—he figgers right around a hundred mile up."

"You mean we've got to run down this crick fer thirty mile, then up the White a hundred mile before we come to Halfaday?"

"That's what he claims."

"S'pose we'd run onto the police on the White?"

"We ain't apt to. You know I told you Corporal Downey jest come back from Halfaday. An' accordin' to the talk, he's the only policeman that dares to show up there. There wouldn't be no sense in him turnin' right around an' goin' up there agin."

"Guess that's right," the man admitted. "An' canoe travel beats back-packin' all to hell. Even that damn grub pack gits heavy, along to'rds night. But the three of us can't make out in that little canoe of yourn, what with all the stuff we've got."

Black John talked with the Indian and the three stepped to the bank of the creek and inspected a large canoe that lay drawn up among several smaller ones.

"He says he'll trade the big one fer a little one, if it's in good shape, if we give him two ounces to boot."

"Okay," the man said, "an' see if you can't hire a few of 'em to help pack the stuff acrost. To hell with doublin' back acrost them ridges."

The deal was made and by mid-afternoon the three embarked in the big canoe.

"How come you kin talk Siwash lingo if you don't know the country no better'n what you do?" asked the larger man, a note of suspicion in his voice, as they camped that evening at the junction with the White. "I be'n studyin' about that ever sence you an' him was talkin'."

Black John grinned. "Hell, if you'd be'n married to a klooch fer five years you could talk their lingo, too, couldn't you? Them Siwashes come from the Birch Crick country. They jest come back from a trip to the coast. Siwashes likes to move around the country."

IV

ON THE SIXTH day thereafter they drew ashore and inspected the mouth of a considerable stream that flowed into the White from the west.

"Accordin' to that Siwash this here aught to be Halfaday," opined Black John. "We must of come about a hundred mile sense we hit the White."

"Well, it seems like two hundred!" Shorty exclaimed. "What with all the damn portagin' around rapids, an' polin,' an' haulin' on that line! Tellin' you about me, I'm gittin' fed up with this here upriver travelin'. It ain't so bad goin' down."

"Button yeı lip!" growled the larger man. "It's be'n a damn sight easier'n back-packin' through the mountains. It can't be so fer from here to that there Cushing's Fort, Cuter Malone told us about. We'd ought to make it in a day er so."

Black John frowned and glanced apprehensively up the creek. "Listen, fellas," he said, a note of pleading in his voice, "how about payin' me off here, an' lettin' me go back? There ain't no tellin' what them damn outlaws might take a notion to do. I've heard how they hang folks up here, jest fer fun."

"That's damn nonsense!" retorted the larger man. "Didn't I

tell you I'm a friend of Black John Smith's? Well, on Halfaday, what Black John says goes—an' don't you fergit it. Any friend of mine's a friend of his'n, right from the start.

"You couldn't go back down the White nohow, without a canoe. An' we're takin' this one clean to the fort."

"I would ruther walk back along the bank than go up there amongst them outlaws," Black John replied. "But if you won't pay me off, I s'pose I'll have to go on. I've got twenty-two ounces comin', an' right around thirty ounces on me, besides. I'd shore hate to have them outlaws rob me!"

"They won't bother yer damn dust!" replied the larger man impatiently. "An' you ain't goin' to git paid off till we git to Cushing's Fort! So if you've got that through yer skull we'll pile into the canoe an' shove on up the crick."

TOWARD EVENING, as they rounded a bend Shorty, who was paddling the bow, uttered a sharp exclamation. "Look—there's a cabin!"

Holding the craft against the bank all three inspected the log cabin that stood in the center of a tiny clearing across the creek from a willow flat.

"There ain't no smoke," said the larger man, "an' there ain't no canoe on the bank. Looks like no one lives there."

"Yeah," agreed Black John, "it does look kind of deserted. But mebbe the fella's gone up to the fort, er somethin'."

"We kin damn soon find out."

"Yeah, an' if it's empty, by God, I vote we camp there tonight!" cried Shorty. "I'm tireder'n hell. An' besides, it looks like rain."

"Might be a good idee, at that," agreed the larger man.

"I shore hope it won't make none of them outlaws mad," said Black John timidly. "Mebbe we better shove on up a ways an' set up the tent."

"To hell with the tent! Like Shorty says, it's cloudin' up, an' I'd rather be in under a good tight roof, an' a dry floor in under me, than in a tent, if it's goin' to storm. Shove off an' we'll look the shack over."

The place had apparently been abandoned. The footpath to the creek was overgrown with coarse grass, and the spring hole was silted in. Pushing open the door, the three entered the cabin and inspected the interior. They found a stove, a built-in bunk, a rude table, and two short benches which had served as chairs. A worn pair of overalls hung dejectedly from a nail driven into the wall, and strewn about the floor were several torn magazines, three discarded socks, a tin can, and several empty whiskey bottles.

"Roof looks tight, except where she leaks over there by the winder," said the larger man, pointing to a stain on the floor. "Guess we'll fetch the stuff in an' camp here tonight. Good thing we got here when we did. It's thunderin' off to the south. Prob'ly be rainin' like hell 'fore long."

THE CANOE was unloaded and overturned on the bank, and its contents carried into the cabin. Shorty started a fire with kindlings piled near the stove, and Black John picked up the ax and stepped outside. "I'll lay in some dry wood," he said. "We'll need it in the mornin'." A few minutes later he returned. "Look what I found!" he exclaimed, holding aloft a quart bottle of whiskey.

"Where the hell did you find that?" asked the larger man, taking the bottle, removing the cork, and sniffing the contents. "Smells good," he added, licking his lips expectantly. "Was there only the one bottle? I ain't had a drink in a month!"

"Yeah, that's all there was," Black John replied. "It was layin' in a cache. Looks like someone had fergot it."

"A cache?"

"Yeah—damn good cache, too. Right at the bottom of the rock wall. I was goin' along there huntin' dry wood an' I ketched my toe on a rock an' it throw'd me down. It moved the rock a little an' I seen a hole in under it, an' I shoved it away, an' there laid this bottle kind of down in a corner of the hole."

"Let's go take a look," suggested the larger man. "There might be more. Hell—what's one quart, amongst the three of us! I feel a drunk comin' on."

"Mebbe," said Black John, "we better put it back where I found it. I'd hate to make them outlaws mad at us. They might hang us, er somethin'."

"Hang hell! Where's this cache? Come on, let's look fer some more hooch!"

Black John led the way to an aperture at the foot of the rock wall. Dropping to his knees the larger man thrust in his arm and explored every corner and crevice. "Nothin' in there," he announced disappointedly, and picking up the flat rock fragment that lay at his feet, fitted it into place. "Some cache!" he said, eyeing the neatly fitted rock. "I don't see how you could of ketched yer toe in it."

"It wasn't layin' like that," Black John explained. "It was shoved kind of off to one side an' cocked up a little so my toe ketched under the edge. Cripes, if it hadn't laid like that I'd never even know'd it was there!"

"No one would," agreed the man. "By the looks of the ground no one's be'n around here in quite a while. Whoever used it last must of left in a hurry er he'd of put the top on right—an' he wouldn't of fergot that bottle of hooch, neither. Well—if that's all we got, it's all we got. We'll go back to the cabin an' h'ist one."

Lining up the three tin cups on the table the man poured each half full. The two picked theirs up greedily, but Black John shook his head. "You boys go ahead with the licker," he said. "I ain't much of a hand to drink, nohow. Seems like I can't never git used to the taste of it—an' it don't set good on my stummick, neither. Besides," he added, with an uneasy glance toward the door, "if that there bottle should belong to one of them outlaws, he might git mad as hell if anyone drunk it up on him. An' if he should come along here, damn if I want any licker smellin' on my breath! You boys go ahead, if you want to risk it—but not me!"

"Suits us!" laughed the larger man. "A pint apiece ain't so bad fer a starter. We ought to fetch the fort tomorrow an' we kin git all we want. Here's how!" Holding the tin cup to his lips the man drank slowly and with evident relish, as Black John picked up the water pail and stepped to the door.

"I'll git supper," he said, "an' you boys kin go ahead with yer drinkin'."

THE TIN cups were large and the half-cups of raw liquor took immediate effect upon empty stomachs that had had no liquor for a month. As Black John prepared the meal the other two drank, diluting the subsequent drinks with water to make them last longer. By the time supper was ready both were showing the effect of their drinking. The larger man waved the food aside.

"T'hell with eatin'," he said. "A man kin eat any time. Shove it back on the stove till we kill this bottle."

Black John eyed them solicitously and shifted his glance uneasily to the packsack containing the dust. "You boys is gitting kind of drunk," he said. "S'pose some of them outlaws comes along an' sees that packsack with all that dust in it. You ain't in no shape to stand 'em off if they wanted to rob you. An' I shore as hell ain't a-goin' to fight no outlaws! I'm a-goin' to take my thirty ounces an' shove 'em in that cache, an' then if the outlaws comes they won't find 'em."

"Fergit the outlaws! Hell, didn't I tell you Black John was a friend of mine?"

"Yeah, but there's other outlaws besides Black John. What if some of them other ones comes along? He mightn't be along with 'em. An' they mightn't believe you was a friend of his'n. Even if they did, they might jest take the dust an' keep on goin'. Cripes, fer that much dust they might quit Halfaday fer good!"

The larger man stared owlishly into the face of the speaker, blinking as though having difficulty in focusing his eyes. "B'God you might be right, at that," he said, thickly. "Yessir, that ain't a bad idee. If that dust was in that hole an' that rock on top of it, all the outlaws on the crick could pile in on us, an' to hell with 'em! Fetch the dust along an' we'll cache it along with yer thirty ounces. 'T'aint a bad idee—one feller stayin' sober. He kin kind of think of things."

The dust was cached, the rock fitted snugly over the hole, and the three returned to the cabin. Thunder muttered in the distance, and the southern horizon was aglow with almost continuous flashes of heat lightning. The night was sultry, and in the cabin the two men sipped their whiskey and water as Black John ate his supper.

"Y'know," the big man said, pouring a liberal portion of liquor from the depleted bottle into his tin cup and filling it with water, "I be'n kinda thinkin' about the set-up, here on Halfaday, an' damn if it don't look purty good."

"How do you mean?" asked Shorty, guzzling some liquor.

THE OTHER winked with an elaborate contortion of the face. "How'd you boys like it if I was king of Halfaday Crick?"

"But—how about this here Black John?" Shorty asked.

"Oh, Black John's all right, in a way. Trouble is, he ain't got no brains. Ain't got no hell of a lot of guts, neither—when you come right down to it. Cuter Malone claims if someone with plenty of guts an' brains would git in on Halfaday an' knock Black John off an' take holt of things, there'd be a million in it fer him. Cuter, he'd like fer to make some kind of a hook-up with Halfaday. He'd slip us the word when there was a good haul to be made on some crick—jest like he slipped me the word about them two chechakos on Ophir—an' then we could take a bunch of the boys from here an' slip down an' do the job. Then we'd slip back here again—an' the damn police couldn't never ketch up with us."

"Why ain't Cuter hooked up with Black John, then?" Shorty wanted to know.

"Black John won't have no truck with him. He hates Cuter 'cause he knows Cuter's got more brains than him, an' he's afraid he'd be outguessin' him all the time. It hadn't ought to be so hard to knock Black John off, if we watched our chanct."

"But I thought you claimed he was a friend of yourn," said Black John, pausing with a forkful of food in mid-air.

"Oh sure—me an' Black John is friends all right—but when it comes right down to business, friendship don't count. Hell, when I'm king of Halfaday, I'll put you two boys in the way of gittin' rich."

"I wouldn't like fer to be no outlaw," said Black John fearfully. "There's too damn many police."

"Police—hell!" sneered the other. "Didn't I jest git through tellin' you that the police can't do nothin' up here? Cripes, if the Mounted shows up all we got to do is step acrost the line an' thumb our nose at 'em. An' God knows there ain't no U.S. marshal goin' to bother us!"

"Yeah—but I wouldn't want nothin' to do with it," insisted Black John. "I'm scairt of outlaws the way it is, an' if I had to be scairt of the police, too, I would be in a hell of a fix."

"Cripes—you wouldn't be afraid of outlaws if you was one! Us outlaws hangs together."

"Yeah—that's what I'd be afraid of."

"I mean, we stick together. We're all pals, one with another."

"You mean, like you knockin' Black John off so's you kin be king of Halfaday Crick?"

"That's different. That's what you might call politics."

"Yeah? Well, I wouldn't care fer no politics, nor neither to be no outlaw." He shoved back from the table, wiping his mouth with a huge red bandana, as his glance strayed to the stove. "By God," he exclaimed, "I plumb fergot the firewood! When I found that there bottle I fetched it in here an' never thought no more about the wood. That thunder's gittin' closter. I'll git the wood before the rain starts."

Putting on his hat he stepped out into the night, but instead of going for wood, he passed around the corner of the cabin and stood close beside the window he had managed to raise a few inches while the others were busy with their cups. A moment later the larger man stepped to the door, glanced about, and returned to the table.

"Listen," he said, leaning forward and leering into the other's face, "that big boob ain't no good to us from now on. We kin pole on up to the fort from here without his help. I'm goin' to pay him off."

"Pay him off!" exclaimed Shorty. "I thought you told me we wouldn't never pay him off. You figgered to string him along till we got to the fort, then make him fork over them thirty ounces he's got an' we'd buy drinks fer the boys with 'em, an' kick him off the crick."

"Yeah, that's what I figgered. But I changed my mind. Fact is, this licker got to talkin'. I shot off my mouth too free a few minutes ago. He knows too much."

"Hell, s'pose he should run to the police with what he knows about that Ophir Crick job? We're on Halfaday, now. We're safe!"

"It ain't the Ophir job I was thinkin' about. He'll be sore as hell if we take his thirty ounces, an' don't pay him what we owe him, to boot. S'pose he'd pass the word to Black John that we was up here to knock him off? Why, ten minutes after he'd got through talkin', me an' you would be danglin' limp from one of Cushing's rafters!"

"Why not jest kick him out now without payin' him off? Scairt as he is of them outlaws he won't dast to show up at the fort to tell 'em nothin'. He'll hit back down the crick, hell bent fer election."

THE OTHER tapped the front of his shirt significantly. "I'm payin' him off in lead—not gold. We passed a snye a little ways back that led off into that willer flat. We'll be a damn sight safer, with what he knows, when he's sunk in the muck at the bottom of that snye with a rock wired to his neck. If we turned him loose it would take him quite a while to starve to death, an' he might run onto someone in the meantime an' shoot off his mouth."

Shorty nodded, slowly, and slopped some more liquor into his cup. "Yeah, I s'pose yer right," he admitted, "but, damn if I like all this murderin'."

"They can't hang us no higher fer knockin' off two men than one."

"No, but every time we knock someone off, we stand jest that much more chanct of gittin' caught."

"Listen, dope! It's only the ones that makes mistakes that gits caught! I didn't leave a damn thing fer the police to go on down there on Ophir, did I? An' I ain't leavin' nothin' here, neither. I don't make mistakes!"

Shorty shrugged. "Okay," he said, gulping his drink. "Up there over the stove is a piece of wire the guy had fer a dryin' rack. We kin use that to wire the rock to his neck." He reached for the bottle but the other snatched it up and held it between his eyes and the lantern.

"No, you don't!" he growled. "There's only two drinks left, an' I aim to git my share." He finished his drink and divided the remaining liquor equally between the two cups. "Good thing the big boob didn't want none of this hooch," he said. "This here is only a teaser. I could drink another quart, right now." They diluted the liquor with water and for ten minutes guzzled in silence, during which the larger man drew the six-gun from beneath his shirt and several times leveled it at the open doorway, squinting along the barrel. "I'll let him have it when he comes in with the wood," he grinned. "There's one guy that ought to minded his gran'ma."

The thunder had become louder and brilliant flashes of lightning illuminated with dazzling distinctness the spruce spires beyond the clearing. A few big raindrops splashed on the door sill, then the heavens seemed suddenly to open and the rain descended in torrents with a low roar broken at short intervals by deafening crashes of thunder that came simultaneously with the vivid lightning flashes.

Shorty giggled inanely. "If he don't git back here with that wood purty quick he'll git drownded before we kin sink him in that snye."

"Eh?" The larger man drained the last drop from his cup and fixed his gaze on the doorway, beyond which the lightning flashes showed a gray smother of falling water. "B'God, that's right! Where is he?"

"Prob'ly ducked in under some overhangin' rock to keep dry. The rain come so sudden he couldn't make the cabin. It'll let up, purty quick. Them thunderstorms don't never last long. He'll show up when it's over. Keep yer gun handy—an' fer Pete's sake, don't miss! We don't want the big boob workin' on us with a len'th of stove wood in this little room. We wouldn't have a show!"

THE FLASHES of lightning became wider spaced, and the thunder followed at longer intervals. The rain tapered off into a mere drizzle and ceased altogether as the thunder rolled and reverberated to the northward.

"He ought to be back, by now," Shorty said. "Mebbe he skipped out on us."

"Skipped out! Where in hell could he go—without no grub, an' not even a rifle?"

Shorty shrugged. "Scairt as he is of them outlaws, mebbe he'd rather take a chanct of starvin' to death than go on to the fort."

"The cache!" cried the other, leaping to his feet and snatching his pistol from the table. "Hey, grab the lantern an' come on!"

Hastening across the rain-soaked clearing by the dim light of the kerosene lantern, the two made their way to the cache where both stood for a long moment gazing in stunned silence at the displaced rock cover and the yawning empty hole. Then suddenly the man burst into a tirade of obscene objurgation.

"By God, he can't git away with it! The damn lousy thief! He can't rob us like that!"

"Yeah—but he did," stated the matter-of-fact Shorty.

"He's got the dust—but he ain't got away with it—by a damn sight! Where kin he go—without no grub? By God, he'll never git off this crick! You know what Cuter Malone said—Black John don't stand fer no crime on Halfaday! They hang men here fer cache robbin'!"

"Yeah—but they ketch 'em first."

"They'll ketch him, all right! If we offer Black John a cut on them twenty-five hundred ounces, he'll have every man on Halfaday huntin' him. He can't git nowheres afoot!"

"Mebbe he ain't afoot," suggested Shorty.

With a bellow of rage the larger man headed back across the clearing closely followed by Shorty. At the bank of the creek both gave vent to expressions of relief as they saw the canoe lying on the bank as they had left it. "That's a break, anyway," he said. "If the damn fool had of took the canoe we'd be in a hell of a fix. The way it is we'll hit out hell bent fer the fort in the mornin' an' set all Halfaday on his trail."

"How about shovin' on tonight?"

"We couldn't do nothin' on a black night like this. We'd smash the canoe, er tip over, er somethin'. Besides, time we got there the fort would be closed. They wouldn't start out to hunt him in the dark, nohow—an' he ain't goin' to git fer tonight. I'll bet he's holed up within' half a mile of here, right now—the double-crossin' coot! The damn rain worshed out his tracks er we might trail him by lantern light. Come on, we'll roll in an' git an early start in the mornin'. That damn hooch has lost its kick. I'm soberer'n hell, right now."

V

THE FOLLOWING MORNING Black John stepped into Cushing's Saloon soon after the proprietor had opened the door. "Hello, Cush!" he greeted as he approached the bar where Old Cush was already setting out a bottle and two glasses. "Any excitement along the crick?"

The somber one peered over the tops of his square rimmed spectacles. "No. Downey's here. Been hangin' 'round three, four days.

"The Yukon wanted is holed up over to the Country Club. Downey claimed you told him to wait till you come."

"Yeah. Where's he at?"

Cush jerked his thumb toward the ceiling. "Upstairs. Didn't git to bed till kinda late. Been killin' time nights playin' stud with the Alasky wanteds. Do any good on that crick?"

"Nope. Either the Siwash lied er I never found the right crick. No newcomers showed up last night, eh?"

"No. It rained like hell an' come off black dark."

Black John nodded. "Yeah, I got ketched in it."

Footsteps sounded on the stairs and the big man turned to greet Corporal Downey who appeared in the doorway of the trading room. "Hi, Downey! Step up an' jine us. Cush is buyin' one."

Downey advanced to the bar. "Not before breakfast for me, thanks. Did you find out anything?"

"Found out there's damn little dust to be got out of the crick I was prospectin'. Wait till I git holt of that damn Siwash!"

"I mean about that murder an' robbery on Ophir I was tellin' you about down to Ogilvie."

"Oh—that! Seems like I do rec'lect you sayin' somethin' about a robbery on some crick. Couple of fellas got held up fer their spring clean-up, wasn't it? One of 'em got knocked off, er somethin'?"

"That's right. An' when I told you I was headin' fer Halfaday you told me to stick around till you showed up an' you'd let me know if you run onto anything."

"Did I? I been kinda fergitful ever sence a nurse dropped me on my head one time when I was a baby." Corporal Downey chuckled and the big man regarded him with a frown. "What's so damn humorous about that?"

"Oh, jest the thought of you bein' lugged around by a nurse struck me kind of funny."

"By Cripes, one could do it yet—if she showed up!" exclaimed Cush. "A nurse, er any other woman! John kin look out fer hisself with anyone that wears pants, but jest let—"

"Why Cush—how you talk!" grinned the big man. "How would I know if she wore—"

"You know damn well what I mean! I never seen the man yet that could git the best of you—nor the woman that couldn't!"

"It seems to me," laughed Downey, "that John's managed to take care of himself, so far."

"Yeah, he's been lucky. But you wait! Some day some woman's goin' to take him fer plenty. I've had four of 'em, an' I know!"

"So you didn't find out anything that would interest me, eh?" Downey said. "I'll be pullin' out, then. That's one case that don't look like it's goin' to be broke."

"I wouldn't be in no hurry, if I was you," advised Black John. "You know damn well, Downey, that whatever a man done before he come to Halfaday ain't none of our business. An' you know that up here we don't neither help nor hinder the police. I seem to rec'lect, sence you mentioned it, that you claimed the murder an' robbery on Ophir was a damn dirty one—that the fellas that was robbed was jest about to start outside takin' their dust back to their families. But even at that, if any man on Halfaday know'd the one that done it was on the crick he wouldn't lead you to him—me least of all. However, neither will we interfere with you stickin' around an' tryin' to locate the damn miscreant fer yerself. If I was you I'd come on over to my place fer breakfast, an' then slip in here the back way an' go on upstairs an' lay kinda clost to that stovepipe hole there in the ceilin' so you kin listen to what's said here in the saloon, an' git a good view of anyone standin' at the bar. Like I said, if you was to hear anythin' to yer advantage there ain't a man on Halfaday would interfere with yer makin' an arrest. Come on along to my cabin. I set the coffee pot on, an' it might b'ile over." As the officer followed, Black John turned to Cush. "If anyone should show up an' inquire fer me, personal, send someone after me, an' I'll come."

ALONG TOWARD mid-forenoon Old Cush carefully folded the two-month old newspapers he had been reading and shoved his spectacles from nose to forehead as a large man strode abruptly into the room, closely followed by a short one.

"Is this Cushing's Fort?" demanded the large man, as he halted before the bar and elevated a foot to the brass rail.

"Yeah, this is the place," Cush replied, shoving out a bottle and three glasses. "Have one on the house."

The two filled their glasses, gulped down the liquor, and refilled them from the bottle.

"We've been robbed!" exclaimed the short man.

"Yeah?" Cush uttered, with professional indifference. "Lots of folks has, one time an' another."

"We was robbed on Halfaday!" supplemented the larger man. "Last night—in a cabin, five, six mile down the crick!"

"Does it set on the left hand side, goin' down, right acrost from a willer flat?"

"That's the one!"

"That's Olson's old shack. It's claimed to be onlucky."

"I'll say it is! A big boob we hired fer a packer robbed our cache of twenty-five hundred ounces in dust."

At a table across the room, One Armed John and Pot Gutted

John halted their cribbage game. "Twenty-five hundred ounces!" boomed Pot Gutted John. "By Cripes, pardner, I wouldn't call no one a boob which he could git away with twenty-five hundred ounces!"

"I was down past Olson's old shack day before yesterday, fishin'," said One Armed John, "an' there wasn't no one livin' there then."

"We come in last night," explained the larger man. "We was headin' fer here, an' about dark we come to this cabin an' it looked like rain, so we camped there fer the night. This damn packer claimed he was goin' fer wood ahead of the rain—an' he never come back! When the rain let up we went an' looked in our cache an' the dust was gone!"

As Old Cush listened he noted the bulge in the front of the man's shirt—a bulge that suggested the outline of a heavy revolver. He glanced at his own Colt that lay ready to hand beneath the bar. "That's tough luck," he opined. "We aim to keep Halfaday moral. What a man done before he come here ain't none of our business—but after he gits here, he better watch his step. We've hung men fer cache robbin'—an' we'll hang others fer the same thing. But first off, we allus make shore a robbery has been pulled off. You look like chechakos to me. An' I don't mind tellin' you that twenty-five hundred ounces is a hell of a lot of dust fer a couple of chechakos to have."

The larger man downed his second drink and refilled his glass. "Listen, brother," he said, leaning his forearms upon the bar, "I know all about you boys, up here. Cuter Malone, down to the Klondike Palace, in Dawson, give us the lowdown. He told us all about you boys bein' outlaws—an' that suits us fine. We're outlaws, too. Cuter claims the police don't dast to show up here—all but a corporal named Downey, an' he don't never have no luck. So, jest between us five, here in the saloon, I'll wise you up how a couple of chechakos come to have that much dust. I kin see how you might doubt it, if we had to dig them ounces—but we' didn't. An' I ain't sayin' I'd tell you this if we didn't need yer help to git it back. But it's a cinch you won't help us if you don't believe we had 'em. But we did; we robbed a couple of guys—that's how we got 'em."

Cush appeared unimpressed. "That's easy to say," he shrugged.

"But we did, I tell you! Did you hear about a robbery down on Ophir?"

CUSH NODDED slowly. "Seems like I did hear tell of one. Some fella got shot, didn't he?"

"That's right. Well, we're the boys that pulled off that job! Cuter Malone slipped us the word that these two chechakos had made a good clean-up an' was goin' outside, so we went up there an' waited till one of 'em went off huntin', an' then we slipped into the shack an' I blasted the other one down, an' we got away with the dust—twenty-five hundred ounces. What's more, we didn't leave a damn thing fer the police to go on! When we do a job we do it right! We don't leave no witnesses to identify us if we was to git picked up. Hell, the police is right now runnin' around in circles down along the Yukon without knowin' who to hunt fer!"

"Yeah," Cush agreed, "that might be a good way. But sometimes them police swings a damn wide circle."

"But," scoffed the man, "what good does it do 'em, if they don't know who they're huntin' fer?"

"Yeah—there's that angle, too," Cush admitted.

"Well—do we git help from you boys, er don't we?" the man demanded. "Are you goin' to let that damn boob git away with a robbery on Halfaday?"

"You claim he pulled off this robbery last night?" asked Cush. "Did he have a canoe, an' plenty of grub along?"

"No. He's afoot. An' he didn't have a damn ounce of grub! All he had was our dust, a hundred an' sixty pound of it, an' about thirty ounces he claimed he had of his own."

"Chances is he won't git far, then," Cush opined.

"No, but at that, there ain't no use standin' around here gassin'! Let's be gittin' out after him! You boys knows the country. It hadn't ought to take long to locate him. Where's this Black John Smith Cuter told us about? I'll bet he'd git the boys out—from what Cuter said!"

"Black John? He's prob'ly over to his cabin." He raised his voice with a glance across the room. "Hey, One Arm! Slip over to Black John's an' tell him a couple of fellas is here askin' fer him!"

A FEW moments later a shadow darkened the doorway and Black John stepped into the room and advanced toward the bar. At sight of him Shorty made a strange gurgling sound in his throat and clutched at the bar for support. The larger man stared into the newcomer's face with eyes that seemed to bulge from their sockets. His mouth sagged open and a rope of thick spittle drooled onto his chin. He wiped it away with the back of his hand.

"Who—who the hell are you?" he uttered thickly.

"Smith is the name. Black John, by common repute. Are you the parties that sent fer me?"

"We—I—I—asked—" the man's voice broke, and seizing a glass from the bar he downed its contents at a gulp.

"Was there somethin' special you wanted to see me about?" persisted Black John in a suave, smooth voice. "Speak up—what's on yer mind? You shore ain't afraid of us outlaws, up here, are you? You ain't been talkin' like you was fer the past week er so. If I rec'lect right, you claimed Black John Smith was a friend of yourn."

"I—I was only kiddin'," faltered the man, managing to summon a sickly grin.

"Oh, that's all right. I didn't believe you, nohow. You was kiddin', too, I s'pose when you told how you was goin' to knock Black John off an' git to be king of Halfaday Crick an' then hook up with Cuter Malone?"

"Yeah—sure—I—I was only kiddin'."

"An' after I stepped out of the cabin, last night, to git the wood—you was only kiddin' when you told Shorty how you was goin' to pay me off in lead, instead of gold? How you was goin' to blast me down when I stepped through the doorway with the wood, an' then sink me in the muck of that snye with a rock wired to my neck? An' all the while you was practicin' drawn' down on that doorway with yer six-gun—that was only kiddin', too, I s'pose?"

"Yeah—sure—sure it was."

"Yer quite a kidder, ain't you? You shore like yer little jokes. But some folks might think you've got a perverted sense of humor."

"Where's our dust?" the man asked. "We'll—we'll cut you in on it."

"Dust? What dust?"

The man stiffened at the words. "What dust! Why the twenty-five hundred ounces you've been packin' fer us over them portages fer the last ten days, er so!"

"Don't you never quit kiddin'?" Black John asked.

"Kiddin'! There ain't no kiddin' about that dust! An' you know damn well there ain't!"

"I don't know what yer talkin' about," Black John answered.

"What did you skip out fer, last night?" cried the man. "You skipped out with our dust—that's what you done! You know'd that cache was there, an' you steered us to it—an' when we put our dust in, you robbed us!"

"Tch, tch, tch, still kiddin', eh? I'll tell you why I come away from there, last night. It was because I didn't want to be paid off in lead, instead of gold. You see, I didn't know you so well, then. I didn't realize you was only kiddin'."

SUDDEN INSANE rage seized the man. "Damn you!" he cried in a high, shrill voice. "You can't git away with it! I killed one guy fer that dust, an' by God, I'll kill another—if it's the last thing I ever do!" His hand flew into the front of his shirt and came out with the six-gun.

"Drop that!" The words rang crisp and clear from above the man's head. He glanced upward—squarely into the muzzle of Corporal Downey's service revolver that protruded through the stovepipe hole in the ceiling. He jerked his eyes downward to encounter another revolver in the hand of Black John, while Old Cush reached across the bar and shoved a .45 against his ribs. His own pistol clattered sharply against the brass rail as it dropped from his nerveless hand.

Two minutes later Corporal Downey was snapping handcuffs about the wrists of the unholy pair. "Yer under arrest," he was saying, "fer the murder of one James Chaffee, on Ophir Crick, an' fer the robbery of him an' his pardner. It's my duty to warn you that anything you say may be used against you." He paused, and added with a grin, "But there ain't much you could say that would hurt yer case none—after the talkin' you've done here before these witnesses. An' you claimed you was the guy that don't make mistakes!"

The larger man shook his manacled fists at Black John in a frenzy of fury. "Damn you," he cried, "this is a trap! You steered the police up here to git us!"

"Ye're in error," corrected Black John. "Downey told me at Ogilvie, he was comin' up here. I didn't have nothin' to do with his comin'. On Halfaday, we don't neither help nor hinder the police."

"You told us Downey had been here—not that he was comin' up here!" cried the man.

"Did I? Cripes—I must of fergot whether he said he was comin' er goin'! It's owin' to a nurse which she kep' droppin' me around on my head when I was a baby. I ain't been able to re-member good, ever sence."

CORPORAL DOWNEY regarded Black John thoughtfully. "I

don't s'pose there's any use askin' you whether you got that dust or not?" he said. "An' if you did, I s'pose you've fergot where you put it—on account of that nurse?"

"Well, Downey, seein' you put it up to me kind of blunt, I'll have to tell you. You know I couldn't lie to a policeman. As a matter of fact, I did remove that dust from that cache. Deemin' it to have been the emolument of a foul crime, I didn't want it cached nowheres along the crick where it might offer a temptation fer some weak brother to perpetrate a sim'lar crime. I fetched it to my cabin. Cush will keep these two damn malefactors covered while you come over an' git it."

In his cabin Black John turned over the pack containing the twenty-five hundred ounces of dust. The officer grasped his hand and shook it warmly. "Good work, John!

"I sure appreciate yer doin' this for me! I'd never gathered in them damn cusses in the world, if it hadn't been for your help."

"Cripes, Downey—don't git me wrong! I didn't do nothin' toward helpin' to ketch them men. I wouldn't help no policeman under no circumstances, whatever. Of course, turnin' over this dust to you is different. I'm glad it's goin' back to its rightful owners. It's too bad one of 'em had to git knocked off—but I'll bet his share'll come in handy to his family. I rec'lect you told me, one time, that I never at no time turned over no considerable amount of stolen dust to you—"

"I said no such thing," interrupted Downey, "an' you know it! What I did say was that you had never turned over to me any dust that had been stolen from any big outfit. An'," he added, with just the suspicion of a grin, "I doubt if you ever will!"

"W-e-l-l," drawled Black John gravely, "I s'pose, accordin' to law, Downey, even a policeman is entitled to a reasonable doubt."

MURDER ON HALFADAY

BLACK JOHN SMITH cast the dice and shoved the leather box across the bar toward Old Cush, proprietor of Cushing's Fort, the combined trading post and saloon that served the little community of outlawed men that had sprung up on Halfaday Creek close against the Yukon-Alaska border. "Beat them four fours in one," he announced, "er else buy a drink."

"Four fours!" Cush exclaimed, bending forward to scrutinize the little cubes through his square-framed, steel-rimmed spectacles. "By God, when them dice rolled out I only seen three fours!"

"You mebbe wasn't countin' this one," suggested Black John, indicating a dice that lay close to the outer edge of the bar. "Yer eyesight's goin' back on you, er mebbe it's owin' to the darkness in here. It was cloudin' up pretty black in the west when I come in. I look fer a storm."

"Yeah," growled Cush, "it's gittin' dark all right—a damn sight too dark to shake dice with you till I git the lamp lit! That there dice by yer thumb was a five when it rolled out!"

"Prob'ly shrunk a mite, owin' to the dampness," grinned the big man, "'cause it's a four now."

"Huh," Cush grunted. "After this you keep yer thumbs to home when you roll out them dice." He gathered the cubes, rolled them out onto the bar and glanced sourly at the three sizes that stared him in the face. "That would of beat you, by rights. Dark as it's gittin', I can't keep an eye on the dice an' yer thumbs too." Picking up the dice he returned the box to the back bar and set out a bottle and two glasses. "Cripes, listen to that wind! Never seen it git so dark this time of the forenoon! I shore hope we don't git one of them tycoons like the paper told about some army transport run into over there in the Philippines."

"I assume," grinned Black John, "that you refer to a typhoon."

"Typhoon!" scoffed Cush. "What the hell's a 'phoon'? Them Philippyne Islands is nigger country an' everyone knows a nigger is a coon. It's tycoon, jest like I said it."

"Or possibly a monsoon," suggested Black John, filling his empty glass from the bottle.

"An' the way some folks talks they could be a baboon," Cush retorted, and glanced wide-eyed toward the open doorway. "Cripes sakes—look out there! That was the tarpaper off'n the kitchen roof that went by! An' look at them trees—bent damn near double!"

Both hastened to the doorway and peered out at the storm. Black clouds raced before the wind, obscuring the mountain peaks. The conical spires of tall spruce trees lashed wildly against the background of flying clouds, and now and again a tough stem snapped, sounding above the hoarse roar of the wind like the crack of a rifle. Ten minutes later the wind subsided as suddenly as it had sprung up and the tossing spires were all but obscured in a torrent of drenching rain.

The young Indian woman who did Cush's cooking called from the doorway of the trading room, "De wat'ter she com' in t'rough de top!"

"Yeah," Cush replied, "an' if this rain keeps up like it's comin' down now it won't be long 'fore the crick'll come b'ilin' up through the floor, an' we'll all go floatin' down to the Yukon like old Noer in his ark. Spread a tarp over what stuff you kin an' I'll fix the roof when it lets up."

A half hour later the rain ceased and the sun came out bright and clear. An inspection showed that nearly half the tarpaper had been blown from the roof of the kitchen while the pole and sod roof of the main building remained intact.

"Git out a roll of tarpaper an' I'll help you patch it," said Black John. "We ought to git her fixed in an hour."

"Better let her dry out a little first," opined Cush. "We got plenty of light now—I'll shake you fer the drinks."

CUSH WON the round in straight horses, set out bottle and glasses, and entered a charge against Black John in his day book, with a pointed comment to the effect that some folks could win at dice without the benefit of either thumbs or darkness.

An hour later with the repair job well under way, one Alexander Burr, according to the name can, burst into the little clearing that surrounded the fort and called to the two on the kitchen roof, "Hey, Black John! Cush! Aaron Hamilton's deader'n hell! When the storm let up I went over to his claim an' found him layin' there right where his flume had blow'd over on him an' smashed his head in!"

"The incident," opined Black John, removing a handful of roofing nails from his mouth, and laying aside his hammer, "calls fer a drink."

Following him from the roof, Cush took his place behind the bar and set out the bottle and glasses.

"It's too damn bad about pore Aaron," lamented Burr, swallowing his liquor. "Jest when he'd struck it lucky, too."

"Yeah," Black John agreed. "He was in here the other night an' showed me some test pannin's out of his dump. Claimed he'd jest finished his flume so he'd have plenty of water to sluice out with."

"That's right," Burr said. "What with his claim up that dry wash he had to build a dam further up to ketch the snow water an' run it down through his flume. I loaned him two thousan' dollars to put in the dam an' flume. He was a good friend of mine."

"Yeah," said Cush, "an' accordin' to Hamilton you was chargin' him four hundred dollars interest on it. That's twenty percent."

"I'd of loaned him what he needed fer his dam an' flume at ten percent—an' called it a good investment," Black John said.

"It is a good investment," Burr agreed, "an' that's jest what I charged him. Ten percent fer one thousan' makes twenty percent fer two thousan', don't it? I had thirty-five thousan' in cash layin' idle in Cush s safe."

"You wasn't, perchanct, a banker—back where you come from, was you?" queried Black John.

"Who—me? Hell, no! That thirty-five thousan' come out of a bank, all right," replied the man, with an elaborate wink. "But I used a gun instead of a check to draw it out with. What made you think I might be a banker?"

"Yer aptitude fer figures suggested the thought. No offense, I trust. I wouldn't like to insult no one."

"Oh, that's all right. Every man to his own grift. I s'pose we'd ort to go down an' bury pore Aaron, seein' it's come off hot after the storm."

"Why, shore," Black John agreed, "some stranger might come along an' conclude we wasn't tidy if he seen Aaron layin' there. What I claim, there's nothin' that'll give a crick a bad name quicker'n someone stumblin' over corpses along it. We'll fetch Aaron up here an' bury him in the graveyard. We always welcome the chanct to add a D in amongst all them M's an' H's."

"What's that about D's, an' M's an' H's?"

"Check letters," Cush replied, swallowing his liquor.

"Yeah," Black John explained, "we burn them letters into the slab when we bury 'em. D is fer died natural. So fer we ain't had so many of them. The M's an' H's is fer murdered an' hung, respectively."

"I was wonderin' about them letters the other day when I come through the graveyard," Burr said.

"We figgered the system would have a salutary effect on prospective murderers. It's to be hoped, from your angle, the information didn't come too late."

"What? All I mean is—it seemed like there was a hell of a lot of H's."

"Yeah. You'll find a correspondin' H fer every M, so far. Them surplus H's has accrued on account of our habit of hangin' folks fer various other forms of skullduggery than murder."

"You mean, you'd hang a man on Halfaday if he didn't murder no one?"

"Oh, shore. We don't aim to be what you might say 'loose' with our hangin's. We try each case on its merits, an' if we deem the offense of sufficient importance we hang the defendant. It's be'n our experience that hangin' is an effective remedy fer a lot of crimes. It enables us to maintain a high average of morality along the crick."

"But—it ain't legal!" exclaimed Burr.

BLACK JOHN grinned. "Well, of course, if a man's a stickler fer legality, he might have a kick comin'. But the fact is, before a man's actually hung, he ain't got no case—an' afterwards it's too late to do anythin' about it. At that," he added pointedly, "our hangin's is as legal as usin' a gun instead of a check-book for the purpose of drawin' money out of a bank."

One Armed John stepped through the doorway and approached the bar. "That was a hell of a storm we had!" he exclaimed. "The wind blow'd all the tarpaper off'n my roof, an' then the damn rain come an' my shack leaked till I might's well live in a river! I laid in a hundred pound sack of flour jest last week, an' the damn thing's all dough, right now!"

"Why don't you shove her in the oven an' bake her, then?" grinned Black John.

"You mean, sack an' all? What would a man do with a hundred pound loaf of bread?"

"It shore ought to stay by him if he left the sack on fer a crust," laughed the big man.

"I got to git a couple rolls of tarpaper an' a new sack of flour," grumbled One Armed John. "Seems like if it ain't one thing, it's somethin' worst!"

"You'll need the tarpaper, all right," said Cush. "But you'll find yer flour ain't hurt none. The water won't soak in very deep. Wait till she drys out an' you'll see that there'll only be a little of it crusted agin the sack. The rest'll be good as ever."

"It ain't goin' to rain no more today," opined Black John, "so you don't need to be in no hurry about that tarpaper. We've got a job of buryin' to do."

"Buryin'? Who's dead?"

"Aaron Hamilton."

"Aaron Hamilton! Cripes, he was alive yesterday! I seen him. Said he was goin' down to Pot Gut's this mornin' an' help him set up a win'lass."

"Folks is always alive the day before they die," reminded Black John.

"What did he die of?"

"That," replied Black John, "will be fer Cush an' the jury to say. He's the coroner."

"Coroner!" exclaimed Burr. "What the hell's a coroner got to do with it. Cripes, anyone kin see how he got killed—layin' right there where his flume blow'd down on him!"

"On Halfaday," replied Black John, "we always do things accordin' to our interpretation of the law—as you was warned when you come here. If a man would die of the mumps on Halfaday we'd hold an inquest on him an' Cush would record his demise, so in case the public administrator would want to turn over his property to his heirs, he'd have legal proof of his death."

"But Aaron didn't have no heirs," explained Burr. "Him an' I was friends, an' he told me there wasn't no one in the world that was kin to him, that he know'd of."

"ANOTHER REASON," continued Black John, ignoring the interruption, "is that it's common repute along the Yukon that some of us up here on Halfaday is outlawed, fer one reason er another. As a result of this rumor, we're inclined to be looked askance at by the pious, an' regarded with suspicion by the uninformed. As a matter of fact, owin' to our strict observance of law an' order, an' our settled habit of nippin' incipient evil in the bud, our record fer rectitude prob'ly ain't equalled nowheres in the world. We figger our morals is worth a hell of a lot to us, in the long run, an' we don't like to do nothin' to jeopardize 'em. On Halfaday every man who refrains from murder, larceny, claim-jumpin', an' general skullduggery has the right to expect to die in a normal an' satisfactory manner."

"Gittin' killed by a flume is normal an' satisfactory enough, ain't it?"

"Oh, shore! A bit onexpected, an' mebbe a trifle abrupt—but perfectly normal an' satisfactory. We'll go ahead, now, with the inquest so we'll have the record fer the public administrator er the police."

"Police! What's the police got to do with it?"

"Oh, like if Downey should come along an' make inquiries regardin' the whereabouts of this Aaron Hamilton. It wouldn't be enough that we should disclose them whereabouts to be a certain grave. We must be prepared to show that his arrival there was satisfactory to the law in all its ramifications."

"How would the police know he was Aaron Hamilton?" demanded Burr. "He draw'd that name out of the name can, same as I done."

"Familiarity with the Good Book," replied Black John, "would acquaint you with the fact that a rose would smell as sweet by any other name. So if One Armed will go up the crick an' collect Long John, an' Short John, I'll drift down an' pick up Pot Gutted John, an' Long Nosed John, an' Red John which, includin' me, is the citizens of Halfaday Cush has app'inted to serve as the jury to set on Aaron's corpse. We'll all meet at Hamilton's claim at three o'clock, sharp. You kin stick around here, Alec, an' come down with Cush. We'll be needin' you fer a material witness, bein' as you're the one that found the deceased."

"Looks like damn nonsense—holdin' an inquish on a man killed by a flume," growled Burr.

"Yeah? Well, mebbe it'll look different to you by the time it's over," retorted Black John dryly as he turned and disappeared through the doorway.

II

PROCEEDING DOWN THE creek, Black John paused at the mouth of a dry wash that emptied its spring flood waters into Halfaday. A short distance up this gulch Aaron Hamilton had staked his claim. Black John's interest centered upon two sets of footprints in the sand of a bar that stretched across the mouth of the wash. Both sets had been made by the same pair of boots, those leading into the wash being normally spaced, while those heading out were widely spaced and dug more deeply into the sand. Both sets had been made since the rain.

"That jibes with what Alec told about goin' up to Aaron's after the storm," he muttered, "an' by the looks of them outcomin' tracks he shore was in a hell of a hurry to git up to Cush's to report what he found."

ON HIS way to round up his jurors the big man halted to scrutinize another sandbar a quarter of a mile down the creek, and proceeded on to Pot Gutted John's claim. He found the fat one profanely removing bits of glass from the frame of his shattered window.

"It's a hell of a note," growled Pot Gutted John, "when a spruce top can't find nowheres else to light except right plumb through a man's winder! An' not only that, the butt of it knocked hell out of my stove, an' the damn wind ripped half the tarpaper off'n my roof, an' the rain soaked my bed!"

"It's ondoubtless the hand of fate reachin' out to chastize you fer some past malfeasance," grinned Black John.

"I don't know what yer drivin' at," replied the other, "but what I claim—it's a hell of a note!"

"At that, you got off fairly lucky," Black John said. "Come on along an' we'll swing down an' pick up Red John, an' Long Nosed John an' go up the crick an' set on a corpse."

"A corpse! Whose?"

"Aaron Hamilton's."

"Aaron Hamilton! Cripes sake, he was down here till jest a little before the storm hit! He helped me set my win'lass, there. When them clouds begun gittin' blacker an' blacker he hit out fer his shack, claimin' he'd hung his blankets out to air, an' he wanted to git 'em in before they got rained on. Then that hell of a wind blow'd up, an' I figgered he wouldn't have time to make it to his claim before it hit. Where's he at? An' how come he's dead?"

"Accordin' to Alec Burr he's layin' up there in under his flume which Alec claims must of blow'd down on him. The coroner's jury will pass on the manner of his death."

"He must of gone like hell to make it ahead of the wind," said Pot Gutted John. "But if that's where he is, he must of. Too damn bad. I kinda liked Aaron. He had a good thing up there, too. Borried some money off'n Burr an' put in a dam an' flume. He was tellin' me only this mornin', how his test pannin's showed he's struck it lucky. Wouldn't be s'prised an' he had one of the best propositions on the crick. It jest goes to show gold's where you find it. No one else ever give that dry wash a second look. Too damn bad it couldn't of be'n Alec Burr instead of Aaron the storm ketched—what with him gougin' Aaron fer interest, an' all. I shore could enjoy settin' on his corpse, but I never could take no pleasure settin' on a friend—no matter what he died of."

"Yer sentiment does you credit," replied Black John gravely. "It shows yer heart's in the right place. But cheer up, Pot Gut. Things might turn out better'n you think."

"How do you mean, John?"

The big man ignored the question. "Come on, we've got to git holt of Long Nose, an' Red John an' git back up to Aaron's claim by three o'clock. We don't want to keep the boys waitin'."

"Yeah—let's git it over with. I got a winder to fix, an' my roof, an' my stove. Wait till I hang out my blankets to dry an' we'll go."

Both Long Nosed John and Red John grumbled about having to serve on a jury when they had repairs to make on their shacks—for the storm had wrought much havoc on Halfaday.

As they proceeded up the creek Black John steered them wide of the sandbar he had stopped to scrutinize a quarter of a mile below the mouth of Hamilton's dry wash.

III

THE MEN FROM up the creek were waiting when the four reached Hamilton's claim. Cush swore in his jury as its members gravely inspected the body which lay, face downward, beneath the wrecked section of flume which at that point had been elevated some twelve or fourteen feet to bridge the mouth of a small side gully. The ground for several yards about was strewn with broken props and braces, and one of the main stringers, a six-inch log, hewn square, lay close beside the dead man's head, the back of which had been bashed in and the hair matted with clotted blood.

"All right, Cush," said Black John, "there's yer corpse. It's up to you to decide whether he's dead er not, an' then up to the jury to say how he come to his death."

"He's deader'n hell," pronounced Cush, wangling a corner from a plug of tobacco with his teeth. "An' any damn fool kin see how the wind blow'd his flume down on him, an' smashed his head."

"That's right," agreed Burr, as the others nodded. "It's jest like I told you. He shore got a tough break—jest whan he'd struck it lucky, too!"

"Yeah," Black John seconded, "he shore did. An' now it's over an' done with, I'm sockin' in my stakes an' takin' over this claim— jest in case the public administrator don't find no heirs."

"No you don't!" cried Burr. "This claim belongs to me." Producing a paper from his pocket, he handed it to Black John. The document, duly executed and signed by Aaron Hamilton, provided that in the event of Hamilton's death before the two thousand dollar loan, together with all accrued interest at the rate of twenty percent, had been paid in full, the claim was to become the property of Alexander Burr.

Black John read the paper aloud and handed it back to Burr. "It looks like the claim's yourn," he admitted. "I ain't no lawyer, but as fer as I kin see, the document is draw'd up all fair an' regular.

"But," and here he paused and allowed his glance to travel over the faces of the little assembly, "it raises one p'int that it might be well fer the jury to contemplate before renderin' a verdick."

"What's that?" demanded Burr truculently.

"Why, merely that it furnishes you a damn good motive fer knockin' him off. After you found out he'd struck it lucky, the claim would be worth a damn sight more to you than them two thousan' dollars he borrowed."

"What d'you mean—knockin' him off!" cried Burr. "Didn't Cush jest say how any damn fool could see the wind blow'd his flume down on him an' smashed his head?"

"Yeah," Black John agreed, "but I ain't a damn fool. So I don't see it that way. An' besides, bein' coroner, Cush's job is to determine the fact of death. The manner of its accomplishment is up to the jury."

"You couldn't git no rights to this claim by sockin' in yer stakes till it had went through the hands of the public administrator," opined Cush, eying Black John.

The big man grinned. "That's so, come to think about it, I couldn't. But the gesture served its purpose. It brought out a real party in interest, as a lawyer would say."

"Well—there lays Aaron. An' there's the busted flume," interrupted Burr impatiently. "Let's git this monkey business over with. The jury kin see how it happened, can't they?"

"I'm hopin' they can," Black John replied. "I'd hate to see a murder got away with on Halfaday."

"That's the second time you've practically accused me of killin' pore Aaron!" Burr exclaimed angrily. "Jest because I was the one that found him ain't no sign I killed him, is it?"

"No, I wouldn't hardly go so fer as to say that findin' a corpse was tantamount to murder. But there's other little things— straws, as the Good Book says, that shows which way the wind blows."

"It blow'd from the west," volunteered One Armed John. "That there tarpaper off'n my roof went sailin' off east of the shack."

"I was referrin'," grinned Black John, "to wind in general, an' to figurative straws—like this blood on the back of Hamilton's head. You all rec'lect, I s'pose, that the wind had quit before the rain started. An' you all know that it rained like holy hell. It seems to me that if Hamilton had laid there all durin' the rain, with the back of his head exposed like it is, the blood would have be'n washed out of his hair."

All stared down at the clotted blood, and several of the jurors nodded. Burr spoke up quickly.

"The blood that come first—right after he was hit by the flume, prob'ly did worsh off. What I claim, he kep' right on bleedin' after the rain quit. It didn't last no more'n half an hour, at the most."

Black John nodded thoughtfully. "The p'int seems well taken," he admitted, "an' in view of the absence of expert medical opinion, can't be refuted."

"An' besides that," added Long Nosed John, "we can't prove he didn't keep right on bleedin' after the rain quit."

"But there's the matter of the blankets," continued Black John. "Accordin' to Pot Gut, Aaron knocked off work on the windlass when it clouded up, an' hustled up the crick to take in his blankets before they got wet. Pot Gut claims he figgered Aaron didn't have time to make it back here to his shack before the wind hit—"

"Anyone kin see he did make it, though," Burr interrupted. "He shore as hell got here in time to git killed, didn't he?"

"That fact seems incontrovertible," admitted Black John. "But about them blankets. If Aaron got back here before the wind hit, why didn't he take his blankets in? That was the chore he come up here to do—why didn't he do it? You kin all see that there's no blankets in his shack. An' you kin all see them four rain-soaked blankets layin' over there amongst them bushes where the wind blow'd 'em."

"He prob'ly didn't have time to," explained Burr glibly. "What it looks like to me, Aaron musta got here jest about the time the wind hit, an' before he had time to git his blankets in he seen his flume startin' to wabble, an' he fergot about the blankets an' run over here to try an' brace the flume so it wouldn't go down, an' got ketched under it when it fell."

"Sounds reasonable, at that," agreed Red John. "A man would let his blankets git a wettin' if he thought he could save his flume."

"You might be right agin, Alec," Black John admitted. "But there's another p'int. When I stooped down a few minutes ago to examine the corpse I noticed that the ground under it is wet—soaked jest like the rest of the ground that was rained on. It is admitted that the wind come before the rain. Then why ain't the ground under Aaron dry—like the ground under this piece of board, fer instance?" Stooping, he lifted a broken board and pointed to the bone-dry ground beneath it.

"By God, that's right!" exclaimed Pot Gutted John, stooping to slip a hand beneath the body. "It's wet as hell in under Aaron!"

Burr stared for a moment at the dry patch of ground that had been covered by the board, then pointed to the body.

"'Course it would be wet in under him!" he exclaimed. "Anyone kin see the ground's sidlin' where he lays. The water run down under him whilst he laid there an' wet the ground. It's level where that board laid. The water couldn't git in under it."

"Might be," admitted Black John. "We can't prove it didn't." The others, eying the slight pitch upon which the body lay, nodded agreement.

"Looks like the house of straw yer tryin' to build ain't holdin' up very good," taunted Burr, vastly encouraged by the nods of the jurors.

"It does seem a mite shaky, don't it?" grinned Black John. "But speakin' of straws, Alec, you'll rec'lect how it tells in the Good Book about it's bein' the last straw that broke the camel's back. It looks like a pretty fair lawyer might of be'n wasted when you turned to bank robbin', an' prospectin', an' usury, an' murder—"

"Hold on there! You ain't—"

"Mebbe," interrupted Black John, "you kin explain this one. You'll note that the timber that lays right clost to Aaron's head is a squared timber. If that's what killed him the wound in his skull would be either sharply cut, like if a corner hit him; or it would be flat, if the side of the timber smashed his skull. But it ain't neither one. If you'll examine the wound you'll find it was made by a rounded object—like a baseball bat."

Short John stooped and gingerly explored the wound with his fingers. "That's right," he agreed. "His skull was stove in with somethin' roundish."

"An' you'll further note," continued Black John, "that there's plenty of pieces layin' around here—broken pieces of props an' braces—that could easily have be'n used by anyone slippin' around behind Aaron, to bash his head in."

THE JURORS nodded agreement and glanced at Burr who replied with a sneering grin. "Why shore—look at all them pieces of props an' braces! They're strung all over the place where the wind blow'd 'em when the flume tipped over. Strong as the wind was, any one of 'em, flyin' through the air, could of ketched Aaron in the back of the head an' killed him. Jest because he happened to drop right beside that squared stringer ain't no sign it was the stringer that killed him."

Again the jurors nodded agreement, and Black John grinned. "You know all the answers, don't you, Alec?" He paused and allowed his gaze to travel slowly over the faces of the others. "An' as fer you boys, there couldn't no one accuse you of bein' observant, 'cause not a damn one of you noticed any of these things I've p'inted out. But I will say fer you that yer an open-minded bunch. You don't jump at no hasty conclusions. You'll listen to reason, no matter how faulty the reasonin' may be. Yer willin' to give a damn low lived murderin' skunk all the breaks he's got comin'—"

"What d'you mean—damn murderin' skunk?" interrupted

Burr, glaring angrily at the big man.

"You."

"Listen here—that's the fourth time you've accused me of murderin' pore Aaron. An' you ain't produced a damn bit of evidence to prove it! What I claim—you've either got to shet up, er make yer crack good. A man ain't got no right to git called a murderer onlest you kin prove he is one."

"There's ondoubtless somethin' in what you say," grinned Black John, "if a man could figger it out. I'll admit these here little items I p'inted out to the boys, taken separately, wouldn't be considered evidence enough to hang a man on—even on Halfaday. But considered collectively, they're corroborative evidence. Like I said a while back, they're the straws that show which way the wind blows.

"I've got one more little item to p'int out, an' then we'll be goin' back to Cush's an' call a miners' meetin' an' git on with the hangin'—that is, if the boys is convinced that a meetin' is called fer.

"Of course, you'll be give a chanct to explain it away, like you've explained away all the other p'ints. Mebbe you kin. Yer agile-minded an' glib-tongued, like a lawyer. But there's an old sayin' to the effect that any lawyer that ondertakes to try his own case has a damn fool fer a client.

"In the meantime, Cush, as coroner, orders you placed under arrest, an' he app'ints Long John an' Red John as custodians of yer person—they to produce you without fail at the miners' meetin'."

"Hold on there!" Burr cried. "You can't arrest me on no sech flimsy evidence as you've produced! I won't stand fer it!"

"You ain't arrested fer murder," Black John replied. "We're holdin' you temporarily on a skullduggery charge—an' the evidence ain't flimsy. By yer own admission, backed by the terms of that paper Aaron made out, yer guilty of charging twenty percent interest instead of the statutory twelve percent. That constitutes the crime of usury in the first degree an' automatically entitles you to be held under a skullduggery charge.

"Cush further orders Pot Gut to remove the corpse's boots an' fetch 'em along. An' now he adjourns this here inquest, *sine die* an' *pro tem,* to reconvene on a certain sandbar a quarter of a mile down the crick. We will now proceed to the meetin' place, an' if Long John an' Red John loses their prisoner in transit, may God have mercy on their souls, which is all there'll be left when I git through with 'em."

THE PARTY proceeded down the creek, and at the sandbar where he had paused on the way to Pot Gutted John's, Black John halted the procession and pointed to some tracks in the sand—the unmistakable tracks of Aaron Hamilton's boots, which Pot Gutted John held in his hand, coming from the direction of Pot Gutted John's claim. The tracks had been made *after the rain.*

Black John stared down at the footprints. "Pot Gut claimed he didn't believe Aaron had time to git to his shack before the wind hit—an' he didn't. He holed up somewheres between here an' Pot Gut's till the rain quit. Then he went on to his claim. These tracks prove conclusively that he was alive after the rain quit. There wasn't no wind after the rain started. His flume was already down when he got there." He paused and fixed his eyes on Burr, whose face had gone pasty white as little beads of cold sweat gathered on his forehead. "Explain them tracks away, if you can!" he roared. "They're the last straw, Alec, that I was tellin' you about. There ain't only one answer to this one—an' you know it as well as I do! It's a coil of rope—an' a murderer danglin' from a rafter. It's another M an' another H fer the graveyard, not a D!"

HANGED BY A THREAD

BLACK JOHN SMITH paused as his canoe rounded a bend in the ascent of Halfaday Creek and eyed the canoe drawn up on the bank. He glanced toward the small log cabin in the center of the tiny clearing, from the stovepipe of which a thin plume of smoke was rising. A few moments later he landed, drew his canoe up beside the other, and walking across the clearing, tapped on the door of the cabin. The door opened and Black John was confronted by a small man with thin sandy hair and a sallow complexion. There was a furtive look in the faded blue eyes and an apologetic note in the thin voice.

"Hello, Mister! If this here's your house I'll git right out. It didn't look like no one lived here, so I lit. I figgered mebbe I could stay here whilst I looked around a little. My name's Ezekial Towler, an' I come up here to the Klondike to dig me some gold."

The big man grinned. "You can stay here as long as you like. This is Olson's old shack, an' it's held to be onlucky."

"Unlucky?" the pale blue eyes glanced about the bare interior. "I figgered I was lucky to find a house here. It looks like it's comin' up a rain." Even as he spoke a muttering of thunder sounded from the hills, and the first big drops of a shower pattered down. "Come inside," he invited. "I'm cookin' me a mess of vittles."

The big man seated himself upon a rude bench. "Ain't you got nothin' but flank meat?" he asked, as the other turned to the stove and forked over a slab of meat that was sizzling in a frying pan.

"This here's moose meat," the man explained. "I boughten it off'n a man down the river a ways. Give a dollar a pound fer ten pound of it. It's tough meat, but it stays by a man."

"Dollar a pound fer that damn stuff!" Black John exclaimed. "Hell, that's dog feed—onless a man was starvin'! Was it an old cuss you bought it from? Lives in a run-down outfit that used to be a tradin' post at the head of a rapids, about thirty miles down the White?"

"Yes, I guess that might be him. It might be an old tradin' post. It was at the up end of a rapids. It might be thirty mile, an' it might be the White."

"That's old-man Hizer. Used to have a pretty good outfit, but he drunk it up. Makes a kind of a livin' now, sellin' hooch to Siwashes, an' cheatin' chechakos like you."

"I'm a Hoosier," the man corrected. "I come from Indiany. I read about all the gold there is up here in the Klondike, so I come up to git me some of it. They claim it's mixed in with the gravel along cricks."

"Yeah—that's right," the big man grinned. "Kind of a thin mixture, though. Throw that damn flank cut out the door, an' I'll fetch you in a chunk of meat you can chaw. Me an' Cush got kind of low on meat so I went down the crick an' knocked over a yearlin' moose." Pulling down his hat, he stepped out into the rain and returned a few moments later with a front quarter which he deposited on the floor. "You can have this," he said. "Cut off a hunk an' throw it in the pan."

The man eyed the meat hungrily. "How much is it?" he asked.

"Not a damn cent. I ain't runnin' a butcher shop."

"I'm sure obliged to you," the man said, forking the sizzling flank cut from the pan and flinging it out through the doorway. "What might yer name be? You ain't spoke it."

"It might be most anything," the big man grinned, "but to

all intents an' purposes, it's John Smith—Black John, to be exact. This is Halfaday Crick—mebbe you've heard me mentioned."

THE MAN shook his head. "No. I'm a stranger in these parts. Down to a place called Whitehorse I asked the man in the store where a fella could dig him some gold, an' he says 'out on some crick.' So I asked him where these cricks was, an' he looked at me kind of funny an' he says 'out in the hills, of course. An' you better not waste yer time on no crick along the big river,' he says, ''cause they're all staked. The further back you go the better off you'll be.' So I boughten a canoe an' some grub an' paddled down the Yukon till I seen where this other river run into it, an' I headed up it, an' kep' on a-goin', an' a-goin'. I passed quite a few cricks, but kep' on, figgerin' I'd git to some crick that was so fur away no one else would be there. This here crick looked good, so I come up it. Then I seen this house, so I know'd someone had be'n here. An' then you come along. Do you live on this crick, too?"

"Yeah—me an' forty, fifty others."

"Oh, pshaw! Then I guess I'll have to move on. But I'm tired

of paddlin' an' shovin' up a river. I'd like to begin diggin' out gold aa' git back. This here Klondike's a bigger place than what I figgered."

"Yeah, there's plenty room fer a man to move around," Black John agreed. "An' you ain't nowheres near the Klondike, neither. The Klondike's eighty miles down the Yukon from where you turned up the White."

"You mean," the man cried, "that I've got to go clean back to the Yukon, an' then eighty mile further down it, an' besides that, paddle up some other river an' find some other crick?"

"Not necessarily," Black John grinned. "Fact is, there wouldn't be no p'int in goin' to the Klondike. Everything's staked, down there. There's forty thousan' chechakos in Dawson an' that many more out in the hills. If I was you I'd try my luck, right here. Most of the boys on the crick is takin' out better'n wages, an' some of 'em's doin' a lot better'n that."

"They claim it gits pretty cold up here in winter," the man said. "I figger I'd like to dig me out what gold I could carry—say a hundred pound er so, an' git back before the cold weather starts. A hundred pound of gold would run into money."

"Yeah. Well, if I was you, Zeke, I'd stick where you are till I kind of got the hang of things." He paused, and glanced toward the two packsacks that were ranged against the wall. "Besides you ain't got no hell of a lot of grub."

"I figgered it would be enough to last whilst I dug out what gold I wanted," the man replied. "But—what about the man that owns this house? An' why did you say it's unlucky?"

"Olson, the man that built this shack is dead, an' the boys figure the place is onlucky because everyone else that's lived here sence has met up with bad luck—one way an' another."

"You mean they couldn't find no gold here? That this claim ain't no good?"

"No one's ever worked it long enough to know whether it's any good, er not. It might be a damn good claim. You see, we hung Olson—an' what with gittin' hung, er shot, er drowned, all the subsequent tenants added to the belief that the place is onlucky."

"What did you hang Olson fer?"

"I disremember. It was quite a while back, an' don't make no difference, now. It was ondoubtless fer somethin' he done. You see, we don't want no crime on Halfaday, so when someone commits a murder, or a theft, er robs a cache, er—"

"I ain't got no cash to speak of. I had more'n a thousan' dollars when I started but I ain't got only thirty-one dollars left."

Black John grinned. "That ain't the kind of cache I meant."

"What other kind is there? You folks talk funny, up here—chechako, an' cash that ain't money. I ain't never heard tell of them words before."

"A chechako is a greenhorn—someone new to the country. An' a cache is where a man hides his dust. Like when you begin takin' out dust, you can either deposit it in Cush's safe, er cache it. You can slip along the rim-wall there, an' find some likely lookin' hole er crevice, an' then put yer dust in it, an' plug the hole up with a likely lookin' rock. Then no one can find it. But as I was goin' on to say, when someone commits murder er any other crime er skulduggery, we call a miners' meetin' an' if he's found guilty, we hang him."

"That's a good way," the man admitted. "No one would like to git hung. I would rather put my dust in some hole than put it in someone's safe. But if there's a safe up here there must be a store er somethin' where a man could git grub."

"Oh shore. Cush has got a store an' saloon up the crick about six miles. The boys does their tradin' there, an' likewise their drinkin' an' stud playin'."

"That's handy, all right. I like to play stud. I guess I'll stay here, if you think I could dig out some gold. This house is better'n a tent to live in."

"Okay. Well the rain's let up, so I'll be shovin' on. So long, Zeke. You can get up to the fort in yer canoe—er foller the foot trail."

"Fort! You got a army here?"

"No, tradin' posts is called forts in this country. Come on up, when you get time."

II

SEVERAL DAYS LATER the man showed up at Cushing's Fort, the combined trading post and saloon that served the little band of outlawed men that had collected on Halfaday Creek, close against the Yukon-Alaska border. Stepping to the bar he hoisted a foot to the battered brass rail. Old Cush, the somber-faced proprietor, closed his well-thumbed Bible, placed it on the back bar, and set out a bottle and two glasses. "Have one on the house," he invited.

"Don't care if I do," the man said, pouring a drink, as his

SKULLDUGGERY ON HALFADAY CREEK

faded blue eyes took in the details of the room. He pointed toward the back bar. "That's a Bible, ain't it?"

"Yup."

"Kinda funny book to be readin' in a saloon."

"Good's any."

"My name's Ezekial Towler."

"Good's any."

"Where'll I find Mister Smith?"

"I couldn't say."

"He must live around here somewheres, don't he?"

"He might."

"The one I mean is John Smith. Don't you know any John Smith?"

"Couple dozen."

"You mean there's a couple dozen John Smiths here on the crick?"

"Yup. Got so damn thick we invented the name can."

The man shook his head. "Name can," he repeated. "You folks sure talks funny up here."

"We say common words—all except Black John. He likes to—"

"Black John—that's the man I mean! Big fella with black whiskers. Where'll I find him?"

"I couldn't say."

A shadow darkened the doorway and a hearty voice boomed out. "Well, damned if it ain't Zeke! How you comin' down on Olson's old claim?"

"Oh, here you be! I was jest askin' where I could find you. But the bartender, here, said he didn't know."

"That's right. I come an' go." He advanced to the bar as old Cush shoved a glass toward him.

Towler grinned. "He ain't very gabby. Most bartenders sort of likes to talk to folks, an' barbers, too."

"Well—as a comprehensive conversationalist, Cush—"

"What did I tell you?" Cush grunted. "If there's any big words to be said, John'll say 'em—an' if there wasn't he'd make some up."

Black John filled his glass and eyed the little man. "You say you was inquirin' fer me, Zeke? What can I do fer you?"

"It's about that there claim. Do I have to buy it, er what? An' how do I find out where the gold's at? I seen the hole where someone had be'n diggin', but there was a lot of water in it. So I got my bucket an' tied a rope on it an' put in all day dippin' the water out. Then when she was empty I looked in the bottom, but I couldn't see no gold there. It was kinda dark by then, though, so I figgered to wait till mornin'. But in the mornin' damn if it hadn't filled up with water again—an' it hadn't rained none neither."

BLACK JOHN laughed. "You've got a hell of a lot to learn, Zeke—like all the other chechakos. This here minin' is a business, an' there's a lot of savvy to it. You don't have to buy Olson's claim. All you do is record it. It's be'n abandoned an' relocated a dozen times. Cush, here, he'll record it fer you till someone goes to Dawson. An' you can't do no shaft minin' in the summer time in a crick bottom. That there water you bailed out is seepage—it comes in through the gravel an' fills up the shaft damn near as fast as a man could empty it. You've got to wait fer winter. The ground freezes then, an' there can't no water seep in."

"You mean you can't do no minin' except in winter!"

"No shaft minin'—an' that's the only real minin'. The gold mostly lays right down against bedrock."

"What's bedrock? An' how kin you dig if the ground's froze?"

"Bedrock underlays every crick an' river bed. The gravel, an' the gold along with it, has be'n washed down onto the bedrock an' covers it—an' the gold bein' heavier naturally works to the bottom. An' the way to dig in winter is to build a fire in yer shaft an' thaw out the gravel. Then throw out what's thawed onto a dump, an' build yer fire agin—an' so on, till you hit bedrock. Then sink another shaft. In the spring when the dumps thaws out, you sluice out yer dump an' pick the gold out of the gravel."

"Sounds like hard work. I never done much hard work."

"Never mind—you will—before you git that hundred pounds of gold you was tellin' me you wanted."

"I don't like cold weather, neither."

"I'd recommend Floridy then," Black John said dryly.

"But—they ain't no gold in Floridy."

"Well, of course—that's a drawback, too."

"How fer down is this here bedrock? I never seen no gold in the bottom of that hole—an' it's six, seven foot deep."

"Bedrock's anywheres from right on the surface to fifty, sixty foot down—an' mebbe more. You can't never tell till you git there."

"An' you mean miners don't do nothin' all summer but jest set around an' wait fer winter to come?"

"No. There's no surcease from toil fer us minin' men. In summer there's wood to be cut an' piled handy to be hauled in to keep the shaft fires goin', an' sluices to be built, an' then if a man's got any time left he generally prospects some new crick, er takes a pan an' snipes the bars, er shovels around in the grass roots back off the crick. 'Gold's where you find it,' the sayin' is. An' it's true. Sometimes a man makes a hell of a strike practically right on the surface—gold that ain't had time to work on down deep, or somethin'. An' here's somethin' else—you spoke of not seein' any gold in the bottom of that shaft. Well, even on a good location you don't see the gold in the gravel—except now an' then a nugget. You wash off the lighter stuff in a sluice er pan, claw out the coarse gravel, an' pick the gold off the bottom—an' it's fine particles—not big hunks."

"How kin you dig somethin' you can't see?"

"Come on an' I'll show you about pannin'," Black John said. "Wait till I get a pan an' a shovel. There's a bar down the crick aways that shows colors. I can show you quicker'n I can tell you."

<h1 style="text-align:center">III</h1>

IT WAS ALONG in June when the Missouri Kid showed up on Halfaday. Black John and Cush were shaking dice in the saloon when a young man in a broad-brimmed Stetson hat, baby blue silk shirt open at the throat, flaming red silk scarf loosely knotted about his neck, and the ivory butt of a six-gun protruding from an elaborately stamped leather holster, breezed in and ranged himself beside the big man at the bar.

"Two to one you're Black John Smith! Just the man I came up here to see!" he announced, flipping a twenty-dollar gold piece onto the bar. "Put up the box, and have a drink on me."

"No takers," Black John replied, eyeing the man's get-up. "An' I trust the sight justified the trip."

Old Cush ignored the coin, set out another glass, and shoved the bottle toward the newcomer. "The first un's on the house," he announced somberly.

"Okay," grinned the man, pouring his drink. "An' then we'll start in on the yellow boy, there. An' don't be afraid to drink her up. There's plenty more where that came from."

"Ondoubtless a man of wealth," Black John observed, filling his own glass.

"Well, maybe not what you'd call wealth. But I've got a little bag of those heavy boys, an' a roll of bills—an' some dust, too. An' we might as well get acquainted right on the start. I'm the Missouri Kid—straight from the bad lands of Montana."

"What was the trouble? Wasn't them lands bad enough to suit you?"

"It ain't that. There's too damn many people huntin' me, back there. So I come far, an' I come fast. I belonged to the Kelly gang, an' we was reckoned bad hombres.

"Best gang of horse rustlers in the whole damn west. An' if Ed Kelly had listened to me we'd be okay yet. Long as we stuck to our racket we done swell—cuttin' out bunches of horses, doctorin' the brands, an' foggin' 'em over acrost the line, or over to Dakota an' sellin' 'em to farmers. But Ed he got cocky, an' nothin' would do but we had to take a bank. I told him—'Ed,' I says, 'we better stick to the horse game.' But he wouldn't listen, an' he'd talked the other boys into it, too. So one day we rode into Fort Benton an' knocks off the bank. There was six of us, an' we run into a posse on Big Sandy an' they got Joe Thorne. Then on Eagle Crick we run into another one, an' they knocked off Slim Becker an' Bad Bill. I an' the two Kelly boys got away, an' we cached the stuff at the Three Buttes, an' scattered, fig-gerin' that if another posse would try to cut us off from the bad lands, three wasn't enough to shoot it out with 'em, nohow, an' we'd stand a better show of givin' 'em the slip that way than if we was all together.

"I was ridin' down Black Coulee an' I got to figgerin' what if the Kelly boys would slip back to the Three Buttes an' grab off that money we cached—where the hell would I be? So I doubled back an' beat 'em to it. Then I hit north an' crossed the line an' sold my horse an' saddle to a rancher, an' got me some store clothes so I wouldn't look like me—like if the damn sheriff had put out a hot dodger—an' caught the C.P.R. for Vancouver.

"Then I heard about this country an' how they was shovelin' out gold along the cricks, so I bought me a ticket on the boat, figgerin' that if there was so damn much gold up here a man ort to be able to gather some with a six-gun instead of a shovel. An' besides, I figger the further I am from the bad lands when Ed Kelly slips back to that cache, the better off I'll be. He's a bad egg when he's on the prod, an' he might figger I double-crossed him, or somethin'."

"Yeah, he might, at that," Black John agreed.

"Sure he would! Well, on the boat was a bunch of steers that a fella name of Jack Dalton was fetchin' in. I had my outfit in my warbag, so I hired out to him to help drive 'em from Haines. He's goin' to butcher 'em down on the big river an' float the beef down to Dawson in a scow. Jack he was tellin' me about Halfaday Crick, an' how you was all outlaws up here. So when we got to the mouth of it, I quit him an' he paid me off in dust. That's the place fer me, I figgered—so I come up to throw in with you boys."

"Yeah?"

"Sure! Anything you want to pull off, you can count me in. This time, a year from now, you'll wonder how the hell you ever got along without me. I'm a bad man—me. An' you've got Jack Dalton to thank that I'm here."

"Yeah," Black John agreed. "I'll shore as hell thank him when I see him."

"He said he figgered you'd find me the means to an end."

"We-e-e-e-l-l, I wouldn't hardly know which end of what you'd be the means to—onless it was the end of a rope."

"What do you mean?"

"Meanin' that what a man done before he come to Halfaday ain't none of our business. But after he gits here he's got to refrain from any kind of crime whatever, er git hung. We don't want the police runnin' in on us, so we aim to keep Halfaday moral."

The other nodded, and winked. "Oh, sure—I get you. Don't pull nothin' on the crick, eh? Okay, pardner. You can trust me. I ain't a guy that would go back on a friend. When yer ready to pull off somethin' just slip me the word an' I'll be in on it. In the meanwhile, where the hell am I goin' to stay?"

"There's a cabin down the crick a ways you can hole up in. One Eyed John lived there till we hung him. Jest throw yer stuff in an' make yerself to home."

WHEN, AFTER a few more drinks, the man disappeared, Cush

scowled across the bar at Black John.

"Don't it beat hell—the kind of folks that comes to Halfaday! Cripes, of all the brash, mouthy, no-'count sons of guns that ever hit the crick, he takes the cake! 'You kin trust me,' he says—an' he jest got through tellin' us how he robbed his pal's cache!

"What the hell did you tell him about One Eye's cabin fer? We don't want no sech ornery cuss on the crick, nohow."

"He's here, whether we want him er not. An' it's better to have him close by where we can sort of keep an eye on him. I surmise that his sojourn amongst us won't be onduly prolonged."

"Yeah—an' besides that, mebbe he won't stay no hell of a while. When he finds out you don't figger to pull no holdups, he'll prob'ly move on to Dawson, er somewhere's an' try to pull off somethin' on his own hook."

"Yeah—an' if he does he'll be duck soup fer Downey. He ain't no wider between the ears than what he is dry behind 'em. But he claims to have a bag of them twenties, an' some bills an' dust besides, an' he seems willin' to spend 'em. I wouldn't favor his departure ontil we'd had a chanct to work on that pile. Fellas like him generally thinks they can play stud."

"Yeah, but even a damn fool like him could have a run of luck."

"It would have to be phenominal luck. I know his kind. They bet 'em high, wide, an' han'some. But in the long run, brains is worth more than guts in a stud game."

IV

A MONTH PASSED uneventfully. On Halfaday men chopped and piled wood against the coming winter, smoked supplies of meat and fish, and prospected likely looking creeks. In the evenings they drifted into Cushing's Fort to drink, and talk, and sit in the stud game that ran far into the night.

As Black John had predicted, the Missouri Kid was a steady loser in this game, while Zeke Towler, a cautious, silent player, generally won. The loud mouthed, bragging Kid was heartily disliked by the men of Halfaday, while Towler, a quiet, industrious man, was generally accepted. Men passing up and down the creek noted that he was always busy with pan and shovel on Olson's old claim. Occasionally they stopped for a chat, and his answers to their queries as to how he was doing were always the same, "I'm doin' all right. Diggin' out quite a lot of gold." When they advised him to lay in a supply of wood, he replied that he didn't figure to winter here. He didn't like cold weather, and he aimed to dig what gold he wanted and go back to Indiany.

The Missouri Kid neither cut wood, nor hunted, nor prospected. He hung around Cush's saloon spending his money, drinking with all and sundry, practicing with his six-gun, and throwing occasional hints to Black John that it was about time to start something.

One morning the big man sauntered into the saloon to find Cush alone. "Them damn chechakos," he announced with a grin, as Cush set out bottle, glasses and dice box, "you can't tell 'em nothin'. They've got to learn everything the hard way."

"Meanin' the Missouri Kid?" Cush asked, rattling the dice in the box.

"No. He won't never learn nothin', no way. Meanin' Zeke Towler. He won't cut no wood, nor lay in no meat. Jest keeps peckin' away at the grass roots day in an' day out. Claims he aims to dig a hundred pound of dust agin fall—the damn fool!"

"Yeah. He'll do well if he gits a hundred ounces, let alone a hundred pound of dust, summer minin'."

"Who got a hundred pound of dust summer minin'?" asked the Missouri Kid, stepping into the room and advancing to the bar.

"Zeke Towler," Black John replied.

The Kid laughed. "Hell—he ought to—the way he works all

the time! I wouldn't work like he does for a thousan' pounds of dust. There's a damn sight easier ways to get it than workin' for it. Ain't that so, John?"

"W-e-e-e-l-l, some folks seems to go on that theory. Personally, I'm of the opinion that honest toil is the best, in the long run."

The Kid laughed and winked. "Oh sure. But say, John, ain't it about time we was puliin' somethin' off? I'm about broke. Everything goin' out, an' nothin' comin' in, as the fella says." He turned to Cush. "Put up the box an' have one on me. Might as well spend her while she lasts. There'll be plenty more when we get goin'. Ain't that so, John?"

"Easy come, easy go, eh? Well, when a man gits down to the bottom of his pile his luck generally changes—one way er another."

The Missouri Kid downed his drink and headed for the door. "I got to go down to Pot Gutted John's place. He killed a moose yesterday an' promised to sell me some meat if I'd come down an' get it. See you later."

A few minutes after his departure One Armed John burst into the room, his eyes wide with excitement. "Hey, Jake Zilkey's deader'n hell over to his shack!"

"Jake Zilkey!" Cush exclaimed.

"Yeah. You know Jake. Works that crick that runs into the White about a mile above where Halfaday runs in. Owl Crick, Jake calls it, on account of he claims there's owls there."

"Oh, shore, I know him," Cush said. "He's a sourdough. What the hell would he die of?"

"Looks like it was somethin' sudden. He's layin' there in front of his shack. He might of got shot, er somethin'."

"Shot!" Black John exclaimed. "Didn't you look to see?"

"Hell, no! I never stopped to claw him over. I seen him layin' there, an' hollered at him, an' when he didn't holler back er move, I throw'd a rock at him an' when it bounced off'n his head without him movin' I figgered he was dead, so I come to let you know."

"The chances is," grinned Black John, "that he was jest takin' him a little nap, an' your rock finished him off. If the coroner so finds we'll have to hang you."

"Aw hell, John—that rock never killed him. It wasn't no bigger'n a hen's egg, an' I never throw'd it very hard."

Cush scowled. "Here it is—hot weather, an' the flies an' mosquitoes thicker'n hell—an' you've got to find a corpse!"

"It ain't my fault if it's hot, an' the flies is bad. I didn't find him a-purpose. Hell, I'd rather not! Corpses allus scares me!"

"You ort to be satisfied findin' 'em on Halfaday, without goin' to hell an' gone up some other crick," Cush growled.

"Well, Cripes, Cush—if a man's fishin' an' finds a corpse, he can't help what crick it's on!"

Black John grinned. "The matter calls fer an investigation. Me an' Cush'll go over there an' look around a little."

"What the hell do I have to go fer?" Cush growled.

"You're the coroner, ain't you?"

"Yeah, but anything we done wouldn't be legal less'n there was a coroner's jury to set on him."

"There's a modicum of truth in what you say, except fer the fact that there's exceptions to every rule. Take a case like this— if Jake was murdered, it might be that someone on Halfaday done it, an' if so, it's our duty to locate the culprit an' string him up. In a case of this kind the fewer that knows about it the better. If we was to take a reg'lar six man jury over there, some of 'em might let a word slip here er there that would put the murderer on his guard. The secret is safe with jest the three of us. You won't say nothin', an' I won't—an' One Arm better not, because blabbin' out information is hangable under our skulduggery law. You're the coroner, an' I'll constitute a *de facto* jury, an' our findin's will be perfectly legal—'specially as I'll sign five more names to the verdict after it's rendered—jest to keep the record straight."

Cush grunted and reached for his hat. "Damned if you can't make anything you want to do sound legal as hell—whether it is er not! One Arm kin tend bar. I s'pose I've got to go."

"Shore, Cush—it's yer bounden duty. What I claim—if the law was founded more on common sense, an' less on theory there'd be a damn sight fewer lawyers—an' a damn sight more jestice in the world."

"Chances is," Cush grumbled, "I won't git no fee out of this here case. Jake must of had quite a bit of dust cached some-wheres, 'cause he never deposited none in the safe here—an' he wouldn't trust no bank. Claims one busted one time down where he come from an' his dad lost all his money. But if the one that knocked him off found the cache, then we won't git nothin' out of it—an' if he didn't, chances is, we can't find it, neither. Jake was a sourdough an' his cache would be hard to find."

Black John grinned. "I deplore the mercenary attitude with which you approach a civic duty."

"Yeah? Well, you kin explore it an' be damned—whatever them words means! But if we was to find his cache, you'd grab off your half quicker'n a cat could lick her whiskers. Come on, let's git goin'. Hot as it is, Jake ain't gittin' no fresher as time goes on."

THE TWO struck out across country, and arriving at the cabin on Owl Creek, found the body lying as One Armed John had described it, face downward before the door. It took but a moment to determine that the man had been shot through the heart and had died almost instantly. The bullet had passed through the body, and diligent search failed to find it lodged in the cabin, nor could the two find any ejected shell case, nor any footprints that the murderer might have left. Back against the rimwall they did find what had evidently been the man's cache—but the cache was empty.

When they returned to the cabin Black John turned to Cush. "It is the verdict of the duly empanelled coroner's jury that the deceased, to wit, Jake Zilkie, er alias Jake Zilkie, as the case may be, come to his death by means of a gunshot wound, said shot havin' be'n fired by the hand of a party onknown. So you can go ahead now, an' dig the grave an' we'll bury him."

"Me dig the grave! What the hell's the matter with you helpin'?"

Black John regarded the other with a look of pained surprise. "Why, hell, Cush—I jest rendered the verdict ter you, didn't I? You don't expect me to do all your work for you, do you? After all, it's you that's the coroner—not me. An' besides, there ain't only one shovel here, an' I want to do a little more lookin' around. We can bury him there in the sand where the diggin's easy. Holler when you git the grave dug, an' I'll help with the corpse."

V

A WEEK AFTER the investigation of the Owl Creek affair, Black John was paddling down Halfaday in search of a moose. At Olson's old cabin he landed and glanced about him expecting to see Towler at work with shovel and pan as was his custom. But the man was nowhere to be seen, nor did he receive any answer to his repeated shouts. The door of the cabin stood slightly ajar, and no smoke rose from the stovepipe.

Stepping into the room, Black John emitted a low whistle as he surveyed the interior. Towler's blankets and cooking utensils were gone, and the floor was liberally sprinkled with porcupine droppings. "Be'n gone anyways, three, four days, by the looks," he muttered, and turning abruptly, made his way to the rimwall where the man's cache had been. The cache was empty.

Leaving his canoe, he made his way back to the fort by the footpath to find Cush alone in the saloon, a copy of the Police Gazette spread out on the bar.

"How long is it sence Zeke Towler was in here?" he asked casually, as Cush folded the paper, and set out bottle and glasses.

"Why—damn if I know—four, five days, mebbe. Why?"

"I swung down by Olson's to see if I could pick up a moose, an' Zeke wasn't around there. His stuff's gone. Looks like he'd pulled out."

"I kinda figgered he would," Cush said. "He didn't cut no wood, nor put up no meat. Claimed he didn't have no appetite fer cold weather."

"Yeah—but he claimed he was goin' to get a hundred pounds of dust before he pulled out, too."

"That's right. Well, Zeke was a hard worker."

"Yeah, but you know damn well no chechako—nor no sourdough neither, fer that matter—could dig out no hundred pounds of dust out of Olson's claim in one summer. An' I happen to know that ten days ago he didn't have no more'n a hundred an' fifty ounces in his cache—an' he won most of that playin' stud."

"How do you know what he had?"

"Well, I happened to look in his cache one day when I was down that way. All the folks that lights in Olson's shack use that cache. It's a natural—looks like no one could find it, onct they plug it up with that stone that I leave layin' there. I jest glanced in the cache to sort of check up on how he was doin'."

"He prob'ly seen he couldn't never git that hundred pound of dust, an' quit," Cush opined.

"Mebbe. An' then agin, mebbe he got his hundred pound of dust."

"How the hell could he of got it in ten days?"

"Out of Jake Zilkie's cache. It's my good guess that it was Towler who knocked Zilkie off. It ain't so very far acrost to Owl Crick from Olson's."

Old Cush swallowed his liquor and refilled his glass. "I don't figger he done it," he said.

"Don't figger he done it! Then what the hell did he pull out fer?"

"Every time a man pulls out he ain't murdered someone."

"No. But look at it reasonable. Zeke was closter to Zilkie's than anyone else on the crick. He prob'ly got acquainted with him an' seen how he had a damn good thing there on Owl Crick. He didn't aim to winter here because he don't like cold weather. But he'd set his heart on hittin' outside with a hundred pounds of dust. He wouldn't have to work very long to see that he'd never take that much out of Olson's claim before winter. So what does he do? He piddles along peckin' amongst the grass roots an' claimin' he's doin' all right, till he can locate Jake's cache. Then he knocks Jake off an' hits fer the outside with his hundred pounds of dust—Jake must have had at least that much dust in his cache—mebbe twict as much. It's plain as the nose on a man's face—if he uses his powers of deduction."

Cush nodded somberly. "Uh-huh. You better throw that drink into you. Yer one behind. I don't claim to have no powers of reduction. But I don't need none. I know who pulled off that Owl Crick job."

Black John downed his drink and rasped the dregs from his throat. "You know who murdered Jake Zilkie! Why the hell ain't you mentioned it?"

"I didn't know till last night. An' if you git up early an' go on a moose hunt I shore as hell ain't goin' to foller you all over the crick to tell you. I know'd you'd be in here sometime today. But I didn't figger you'd come in barkin' up the wrong tree. Them there powers of production you claim you've got had ort to told you a quiet, hard workin' cuss like Zeke Towler wouldn't pull off no trick like that, when there's a loud mouthed, lazy, lyin', thievin', drunken, no 'count son of a gun right in under yer nose."

"You mean the Missouri Kid?"

"I don't mean no one else."

"How do you know he done it?"

"Stands to reason. An' besides, he's packin' the evidence around with him. You rec'lect how he claimed he was about broke awhile back, an' was wantin' you to pull off somethin'. An' you rec'lect he ain't never spend no dust—jest them yaller gold pieces an' bills. Well last night he come in an' called fer a drink an' when he come to pay fer it, instead of throwin' out a gold piece, er a bill, he tossed a poke of dust onto the bar."

"That don't prove nothin'. You remember he told us that Jack Dalton paid him off in dust fer drivin' in them cattle."

"Yeah. But this here poke had a good eighty ounces in it— right around thirteen hundred dollars. An' you know damn well Jack Dalton never paid him no eighty ounces to drive them cattle in, by a damn sight. An' what's more the Kid ain't done no winnin' in the stud game, neither—only losin'."

"That's right," Black John admitted.

"Yeah, an' that ain't all. This here poke was sewed with sinew. No damn chechako would sew a poke with sinew, an' a sourdough would. An' on top of that I know this here poke belonged to Jake Zilkie."

"How do you know that?"

"It's like this—one time Jake come in here an' he'd bust a button off'n his shirt, an' he wanted some stout thread to sew it on with. I went to the storeroom to git him a spool an' found out I'd run plumb out of thread. Then I happened to think about a sewin' basket that's be'n kickin' around ever sence my fourth wife died that had a lot of stuff in it like scissors, an' needles, an' thimbles, an' thread, so I hunted it up, an' the only spool of stout thread was blue colored. About half the thread was gone off'n it, an' I rec'lect how she was makin' some kind of a rag rug out of a old blue suit I had, an' when she couldn't git no stout blue thread she got some dye an' dyed a spool of white. So I give Jake what was left of the spool, an' a needle, an' he set right there by the stove an' sewed his button on, an' stuck the spool in his pocket.

"Well, this here poke the Kid tossed on the bar had ripped a little ways down from the top—an' it had be'n mended with *blue* thread. An' there ain't another damn bit of heavy blue thread on Halfaday, an' mebbe not none in the hull Yukon, 'cause the only stout blue thread I ever seen was that there spool my wife dyed.

"An' the way it turned out it's a good thing she done it, even if I did give her hell fer cuttin' up that there blue suit, which it wasn't more'n half wore out yet. An' besides that, it proves that if a man would keep his eyes open, it's better'n havin' them there powers of percussion, or whatever that big word is you claimed you had."

Black John grinned. "The evidence that you've adduced may well portend catastrophic repercussions fer the individual under suspicion."

"The wronger you be the more big words you string together to cover it up. When are we goin' to hang the Missouri Kid?"

"We'll hang him when a miners' meetin' finds he's guilty," Black John replied. "If what you've told me is true, an' I have no doubt it is, it looks mighty bad for him. But just to make sure, I'm goin' to do a little investigatin' on my own hook. I'll take the Kid on a moose hunt—an' by the time we git back, I'll know damn well whether he's guilty er not. Meanwhile, you might have One Armed John notify the boys to be here tomorrow at noon sharp fer a miners' meetin'. I'd hate like hell to hang a man fer somethin' he didn't do. So far, we ain't made no mistakes with our hangin's."

"Huh," snorted Cash. "It wouldn't be no mistake to hang that damn cuss, whether he done it er not."

"Well, takin' it by an' large, I believe yer right. But after all, Cush, a hangin' is a specific matter."

"It's a damn good way to git shet of some ornery cuss like him—if that's what you mean."

VI

BLACK JOHN FOUND the Missouri Kid at One Eyed John's cabin intently studying the backs of a deck of cards. He looked up with a grin, as the big man stepped into the room.

"Hello, John!" he greeted. "Just the man I wanted to see. I'm goin' to let you in on somethin'. You know I've be'n havin' a rotten run of luck—so I decided to do somethin' about it."

"There ain't much a man can do, when the cards is runnin' agin him."

"That's what you think. But did you ever hear of markers?"

"Seems to me I have—in a vague sort of way."

"Well there ain't nothin' vague about this. Look here—see anything wrong with these cards?"

Black John eyed the pasteboards and shook his head. "Can't say as I do."

"All right—now take this ace, an' hold it sort of slantways to the light—see there in the corner that little thumbnail mark? Well every ace an' king in the deck has got that mark on it. If a man knows where the aces an' kings are it gives him edge enough to win in any game—an' I'm lettin' you in on it. We'll trim them suckers like nobody's business from now on. Pretty slick, ain't it?"

The big man grinned. "It's all right—except that about the third pot you won damn near every man at the table would be onto them marks, an' we'd call a miners' meetin' an' hang you higher'n hell fer skulduggery. That tricks's so old it stunk in George Washington's time. Fergit it. We've got more important business on hand. S'pose me an' you slip out in the hills, an' sort of talk over a certain proposition. I run out of meat, an' we might git us a moose."

The man brightened. "Figger on pullin' off somethin', eh? You bet I'll go! Wait till I get my rifle. An' how about blankets an' grub? How long will we be gone?"

"We'll be back tomorrow noon. An' never mind blankets an' grub. We'll hole up in some cabin tonight. Any of the boys would be glad to put us up."

They found no moose during the afternoon, and along toward dusk they descended into the little valley of Owl Creek. The Kid who was a step or two in advance pointed up the creek.

"There's a cabin!" he exclaimed.

"Yeah, that's right," the big man replied, his eyes on the other's profile.

"I don't see no light. Maybe the fella ain't home."

"Mebbe he ain't," replied Black John dryly. "We'll go on up an' see."

They reached the cabin and paused before the closed door, the Missouri Kid standing upon the exact spot where the body of Jake Zilkie had lain. But though the big man's eyes never left the Kid's face, he could detect no slightest change of expression—nor any indication of nervousness. Instead, the Kid's eyes met his own. "Should we go on in," he asked, "or wait here till the fella shows up?"

"Might's well go in. It might be quite a while before he comes."

Entering the cabin, Black John lighted the lamp while the Kid kindled a fire in the stove. "Pretty good layout he's got here," the Kid observed, as he filled the tea kettle from the water pail.

"Yeah. Doin' right well fer himself, too," Black John replied, his eyes on the other's face.

They prepared supper from Zilkie's ample food supply and ate it in silence. Not by so much as the batting of an eye did the Kid intimate that he had ever seen the place before, much less that he had made it the scene of a cold blooded murder. Black John was frankly puzzled. Either the Kid had nerves of steel, or he was entirely innocent of the crime—an alternative that was entirely out of the question in view of Cush's statement that he had seen a poke of Zilkie's in his possession.

Supper over the two washed and dried the dishes, and Black John filled and lighted his pipe. As the Kid rolled a cigarette, he asked, "What was this proposition you wanted to talk over?"

The big man blew a cloud of smoke from his lungs. "The proposition I've got in mind involves a murder an' robbery."

The younger man winced slightly. "I don't like that word, 'murder'," he said. "You see, I knocked off one of them posse men, an' they're callin' it murder, back there in Montana."

"Yeah. We've got the same name fer it here on Halfaday, too. What did you do it fer, Kid?"

"It was him or me for it. He come ridin' out of a coulee jest as I—"

"I ain't referrin' to the Montana killin'. That ain't none of our business. But it is our business when someone commits a murder an' robbery on Halfaday an' its immediate vicinity."

The other looked startled. "What do you mean?" he asked, just the slightest suspicion of a tremor in his voice.

"Meanin' that you might as well come clean. A man was murdered an' robbed—an' you done the job. There ain't no use in denyin' it. You tossed a poke onto Cush's bar last night that belonged to the dead man. Cush knew that poke. It's mended near the top with blue thread. You've prob'ly got it in yer pocket, right now."

The color drained slowly from the Kid's cheeks. His cigarette dropped unheeded to the floor, and slowly he reached into his pocket, and withdrew the little sack and stared at it. Then he moistened his lips with his tongue. "I robbed his cache, all right," he said in a dull voice, his eyes on the blue stitching. "But I didn't kill him, by a damn sight."

"No? Who did?"

"No one did. He ain't dead. Listen—I know'd he had around a hundred pounds of dust in his cache, so I hung around an' watched my chanct, an' copped it."

"An' what was he doin' all that time?"

"He wasn't there. I watched him throw his blankets an' some grub in his canoe an' pull out. Then, after he'd gone I got the dust. I'd located his cache before—hung around an' watched him go to it to put some dust in. He ain't dead, I tell you. He's off somewheres."

Black John grinned. "Have it yer own way. But you're goin' to have a hell of a time makin' a miners' meetin' believe it. Fact is, One Armed John found the body layin' in front of the door, an' me an' Cush investigated the matter, an' seen where he'd be'n shot through the heart, an' buried him. We found the empty cache, too—over in the rimwall."

"By God, I never killed him! If he come back an' someone else killed him, that ain't my fault. I'll own up to the robbery. You've got the goods on me. It. wouldn't do no good to deny it. But I never killed him. I was broke, what with spendin' my dough, an' the rotten luck I've had at stud. So when you kep' holdin' off about dopin' out some job we could pull, I figgered I'd pull one of my own."

"The venture was ill advised," Black John said. "We'll roll in now. Git over on the bunk, there, an' I'll tie you up. We'll be gittin' an early start in the mornin'. The miners' meetin' is called fer noon."

After securing the man, hand and foot, Black John examined several shirts that depended from nails driven into the log wall, selected one which, together with a partly used spool of blue thread, he placed in his packsack, and with the sack for a pillow stretched out on the floor and was soon sound asleep.

VII

THE RETURN TO Halfaday was made next morning without incident. At One Eyed John's cabin they stopped and the Kid removed twenty-two little moosehide sacks of dust which Black John placed in his sack for evidence.

Promptly on the stroke of twelve Black John rapped on the

bar for silence. "Miners' meetin' called fer the purpose of tryin' one, to wit, alias the Missouri Kid fer murder an' robbery. Bein' as Cush will testify to the fact that the prisoner paid fer a drink last night out of the murdered man's poke, an' I later seen it in his possession, coupled with the fact that he admitted the robbery to me, but denied the murder, we will try him on the robbery charge first. Follerin' his conviction we can try him fer murder, jest to keep the record clear.

"First off, I'll call One Armed John, who found Jake Zilkie layin' dead in front of his door there on Owl Crick."

"Jake Zilkie! Owl Crick!" cried the prisoner. "By God, I—"

"Shut up!" roared Black John, banging his fist on the bar. "After the evidence is in you'll be give the chanct to try an' lie out of it—which attempt ain't likely to meet with no success. But in the meanwhile you keep yer trap shet." He turned and faced the assembled men. "As I was sayin', I'll call One Armed John." He was interrupted by a commotion near the door as a man burst into the room. The man was Zeke Towler, and as he elbowed his way through the closely packed crowd he yelled, "My cache has be'n robbed! I be'n on a moose hunt—an' when I got back, jest now—my cache is empty, an' every damn ounce of dust is gone!"

Hardly had he reached the open space before the bar than the prisoner pointed at him. "There! I told you damn fools that I never killed him. An' you wouldn't believe me!"

A tense silence followed the words—a silence broken by mutterings from the puzzled men. A great light broke upon Black John as he thumped the bar. "Silence!" he shouted. "The first man that utters a word gits fined a round of drinks. This here's a miners' meetin'—an' by God we've had interruptions enough already!" He turned to Towler. "We called this miners' meetin' to try the Missouri Kid fer murder an' robbery," he explained.

"He ain't guilty of murder," Towler grinned, "'cause I ain't dead. But someone's guilty of robbery, all right—an' it's prob'ly him. If he's the one that done it you kin go ahead an' hang him jest the same. You told me yerself that cache robbin' was hangable, on Halfaday."

"That's correct," the big man agreed. "We will now proceed with the evidence."

Old Cush leaned forward across the bar. "But hell, John—what's the use wastin' time with evidence? We've got the dust—an' he already admitted robbin' the cache. But—what's this here Zeke got to do with it?"

Black John regarded him with a fishy eye. "Corroborative evidence never hurt no case. The Missouri Kid looks like a man who would lie on slight provocation. How do we know he ain't lyin' about robbin' that cache? Anyway, if you'll shut up, we'll proceed with the evidence."

"But—"

"Listen, Cush, this here's the second time you've interrupted these proceedin's. Yer hereby fined a round of drinks fer contempt of a miners' meetin'! The drinks will be had after the hangin'. An' I might add here that everyone except the witness under examination, had better keep his eyes an' ears open, an' his mouth shet, under penalty of a like fine." He turned to Towler. "You say that this man robbed yer cache?"

"Someone did—an' Cush claims he admitted it."

"That's right."

"Well—let's hang him, then. Anyone that would rob a cache ort to git hung."

"An' that's right, too," Black John said. "I'm glad you feel that way about it. I'll swear you in as a witness. D'you swear to tell the truth, the whole truth—er any part of it—s'elpe God?"

"Sure."

"Now can you tell us how much dust was stole out of yer cache?"

"It was better'n eighteen hundred ounces. There was twenty-three sacks, an' they'd run right around eighty ounces apiece."

"Around thirty thousan' dollars, eh?"

"Yeah—somewheres around there."

"How long you be'n on Halfaday, Zeke?"

"I got here along in the early spiring."

"An' I believe you was tellin' me an' Cush at the time, that you was about broke. Is that right?"

"Yeah—I was damn near broke. I only had thirty-one dollars left."

"Yer known as a hard worker, Zeke. I s'pose you took this here dust out of yer claim—Olson's old claim?"

"That's right."

"Summer mined it? Wasn't bothered with seepage, eh?"

"No. I didn't sink no reg'lar shaft. Jest went in shallow, here an' there—back from the crick."

"Grass root dust, eh? That claim of Olson's turned out to be a heap better'n most of us thought—to net thirty thousan' in three, four months summer minin'. An' you put this here dust you dug out of the grass roots in twenty-three sacks, eh?"

"Yes."

"Could you identify them sacks?"

"Sure."

"An you had 'em in yer cache—left 'em there when you went on this here moose hunt?"

"That's right. They was right there when I left."

Black John removed the sacks from his packsack and placed them on the bar. "Is these the ones?"

"Sure! Them's mine, all right! I'd know 'em anywhere!" the man cried, glancing at the pile of little sacks.

"Made 'em yerself, I s'pose?"

"That's right."

Black John stooped and examined the sacks minutely. "What did you sew 'em with?" he asked.

"Why—thread, of course. What would a man sew 'em with?"

"I notice a couple of 'em's mended where they got ripped a little. I s'pose you mended 'em?"

"Sure I did."

"I notice they're mended with a different kind of thread than was used to make 'em." He paused and regarded the man benignly. "You see, Zeke, we want to be dead sure of this identification. We'd hate to hang a man on flimsy evidence. Do you rec'lect what color thread you done the mendin' with?"

The man hesitated. "Well—no—I don't jest remember. Sometimes I've had white thread, an' sometimes black. I can't say which I used."

"That's right—a man wouldn't. But you'd know, of course," Black John added with a smile, "that it wouldn't be no off-color thread—like red, er yaller, er blue?"

"Oh, sure," the man grinned. "I'd know that. I ain't never had no colored thread except black an' white."

The big man paused. "Well, that's about all we need in the way of evidence—what with the prisoner's own admission that he robbed the cache. There's jest one thing, Zeke—we hang men on Halfaday fer cache robbery. But onct in a while—when there ain't no complications, like murder—if the victim of the robbery so recommends, we use a little leniency—like lettin' the robber off with a lesser sentence. How do you feel about it, takin' the prisoner's age an' all into consideration? Would you care to ask fer leniency?"

The man shook his head. "No, I wouldn't. What I claim a damn cache robber ort to git hung. If you let him off, he'll sure as hell rob someone else sometime."

Black John nodded. "Okay," he said—and turned to the puzzled men who, knowing that Zilkie was the man who had been murdered and robbed, had listened to the examination in bewilderment. "An' now, boys, I'll sort of sum up the evidence an' see what it adds up to.

"In order to obtain a comprehensive view of this case we've

got to go back a few years to the time Cush's fourth wife was makin' a rag rug. She hunted in all the stores an' couldn't find no stout blue thread, this rug she was makin' bein' that color. So she got a spool of white thread an' dyed it blue. She finished the rug an' had quite a bit of the blue thread left over on the spool. This spool Cush fell heir to along with the rest of her belongin's. I'll jest p'int out here that it's lucky it was Cush's fourth wife that made that rug. If it had be'n any one of the first three Cush wouldn't have had that thread, because one of 'em run out on him takin' all her belongin's with her—an' he run out on the other two, an' bein' an honorable man, he took only his own stuff an' what cash they had on hand."

"Hey!" Cush cried. "Like hell I—"

"Shet up!" Black John roared, banging the bar with his fist. "Yer fined another round of drinks fer further contempt of miners' meetin'." He again faced the assembly. "So you see how a trivial incident might have important results, an' how true the old sayin' is—about a man's life hangin' by a thread.

"But to go on—one day Jake Zilkie come here to Cush's fer supplies, amongst which he wanted a spool of heavy thread. Cush was out of heavy thread, but he happened to rec'lect this here spool of blue thread that had be'n kickin' around fer years in a basket along with some scissors an' thimbles an' what not, that his fourth wife had, so he went an' got it an' give it to Jake. An' Jake set down right here in this room an' sewed a button on his shirt with it." Reaching into his packsack, Black John withdrew a shirt, and the spool of blue thread which he placed upon the bar. "We'll call them sacks of dust Exhibit A, an' these here items is Exhibits B an' C respectively. Anyone so desirin' can see that this here top button is sewed on with *blue* thread—the rest of 'em bein' sewed on with black. I will add that I got the shirt an' the thread in Jake Zilkie's cabin last night, which fact can be swore to by alias the Missouri Kid who is on trial here, but who is ondoubtless sech a damn liar that his corroboration would be disregarded. We have thus established the fact that Jake Zilkie had in his possession a spool of heavy blue thread.

"Now to diverge a bit. We all rec'lect that when Zeke Towler hit the crick this spring he told us he was about broke. An' we all know that Zeke's be'n a sort of likable cuss that worked his claim, an' minded his own business, an' plays a pretty fair game of stud. We know his winnin's has be'n fairly steady—but not large. Yet we all heard him swear only a few minutes ago that someone had robbed his cache of some thirty thousan' dollars in dust. We heard him swear that he'd dug this here dust out of Olson's old claim—panned it out of the grass roots, summer minin'. We also heard him swear that them twenty-three sacks of dust, to wit, Exhibit A, there on the bar is the ones that was stole from his cache. An' we heard him swear that he made the sacks himself, sewin' 'em with thread—an' mendin' several of 'em that had ripped with either white er black thread, he couldn't rec'lect which. An' we heard him swear that he couldn't have used any other colored thread, like red, yaller, er blue—because he never had any thread of them colors.

"Now I'll call yer attention to the fact that these sacks is sewed with sinew—not with thread. An' that Jake Zilkie was a sourdough an' would use sinew. Also the ones that was ripped a little are mended with blue thread—a thread that we know Jake possessed, but which Zeke jest got through swearin' he never had none of. An' on top of that, we all know that not even the twelve apostles, workin' three shifts, couldn't shovel no thirty thousan' dollars in dust out of Olson's old claim in one summer—so it's safe to assume Zeke couldn't neither.

"We also heard Zeke state it as his honest opinion that a cache robber ort to get hung, because if you let him off he'd shore as hell rob some other cache sometime.

"Of course we all know that there might conceivably be some sort of mitigatin' circumstance that would let a man off with a lesser punishment—but combinin' murder with robbery ain't no mitigatin' circumstance on Halfaday—by a damn sight!

"Now we ain't no reg'lar court of law. We're a miners' meetin'. An' we aim to arrive at jestice, rather than at legal jugglin'. There's nothin' in our code of procedure that would prevent us from freein' a prisoner an' hangin' a witness, providin' the prisoner was innocent of the crime for which he's bein' tried, an' the witness was guilty of that specific crime. In this instance bein' the murder an' robbery of one, to wit, Jake Zilkie, er alias Jake Zilkie, as the case may be. You've all heard the evidence an' are convinced beyond a reasonable doubt that this here witness, to wit, Zeke Towler, er alias Zeke Towler, is guilty of this murder an' robbery. All in favor of hangin' the damn skunk signify by sayin' 'Aye'."

A chorus of lusty "Ayes" filled the room.

"Contrary: 'No'."

Silence greeted the word as all eyes fixed upon Towler, who gripped the bar with trembling hands, his face a pasty white. "Okay," Black John said. "An' bein' as the verdick includes two crimes—murder an' robbery—both of which is hangable on Halfaday, it is hereby decreed that the hangin' shall run concurrently.

"An' while Pot Gut is adjustin' the noose, I'll take occasion to couple a warnin' with a bit of advice." He turned sharply upon the Missouri Kid. "Yer lucky. To state it plainly, an' without mincin' words, yer a damn, no-account, loud mouthed, braggin', lyin' thief—as you well know. Technically, under our code, we'd be justified in hangin' you along with Zeke fer the crime of cache robbin'. But under the circumstances, it is the verdick of this meetin' that yer theft of the dust out of Zeke's cache, constitutes a tort, rather than a crime, as you inadvertently provided the evidence that convicted Jake's murderer. But that ain't sayin' that you can continue to abide amongst us. On the contrary, you will be provided with a packsack full of grub, an' be given three hours to git off of Halfaday—an' all the rest of yer life to stay off. It is now three o'clock. At one minute past six, yer very presence on the crick will constitute the crime of vicarious skulduggery, an' you'll be hung forthwith. So if I was you I'd lift 'em high an' space 'em wide. That's all. Meetin' adjourned."

LATE IN the afternoon, with Towler's name duly burned into a new slab in the little graveyard behind the fort, old Cush removed the twenty-three little sacks from the safe. "We might's well divide this here dust up betwixt us," he said, eyeing Black John across the bar. "No use botherin' the public administrator with it. Chances is there won't no one'll ever claim it. It's our fee fer the trouble we've be'n put to."

The big man shook his head, and reaching into his pocket, withdrew a crumpled letter which he tossed onto the bar. "Read that. I found it in Jake's cabin. It's from his sister, back in Sauk Centre, Minnesota. She's a school teacher, an' she's beggin' him to come home. Their mother's ailin'—an' seems like they ain't none too well fixed. Jest shove them sacks back in the safe, Cush—an' the letter along with 'em—an' the first time Downey comes along, we'll turn 'em over to him to send down to these folks."

"Why shore!" Cush agreed heartily. "I wouldn't touch a damn ounce of that dust, bein' as it rightly belongs to them wimmin. By God, John, I allus claimed you was honest—sometimes."

ALL IN THE DAY'S WORK

"**ANY MAN,**" **SAID** Black John, shaking the leather dice box and rolling the five dice onto the bar, "is a damn fool that'll set up all night playin' stud an' take a drink every time he wins a pot. Beat them three fours in one. I feel like hell, this mornin', an' my mouth tastes like I'd et a skunk with the fur on."

Old Cush gathered the dice and cast them. "There's three sixes, to top them three fours, an' here's four deuces right back at you. It wouldn't of hurt you none last night if you'd only took a drink when you won a pot, but towards mornin' you was takin' one every time anyone won one. What's more, it ain't mornin'— it's way past noon, an' I bet you ain't had nothin' to eat."

"Yeah, I fried me up a chunk of moose an' drunk a pot of tea. I'll be all right soon's I git it climatized with three, four drinks of licker. Yer four deuces is good. Set out the bottle."

"Even when yer stummick's gone back on you, you kin think up big words," growled Cush. "Here's comes One Armed John. Drink up, an' I'll buy one. That makes three you've had," he added, as he made the proper entry in his day book.

"Yeah, I'm jest beginnin' to feel like the same fella I used to be, an' not some damn invalid."

One Armed John crossed the floor, rested his stump on the bar, and picking up the bottle, filled the glass Old Cush slid toward him.

"You know them two chechakos," he said, "them two that come in last fall an' took up claims on that feeder that run in about five mile above here—them two that you nicknamed Raymond an'—an' some other fella, 'cause they was such good friends an' stuck so close together fer the few days they hung around the fort. You said they put you in mind of them two fellas it told about in the Bible."

"Yeah—Damon an' Pythias was what I called 'em," said Black John.

"Them's the ones," replied One Armed John. "Only their names is Bill an' Jack—"

"An' besides," interjected Old Cush, "I don't rec'lect no sech names in the Bible as Damon an' Pythias, nohow."

"They come in way along to'ards the middle—further along than you've got."

"I'm damn near through Deuteromadary, er whatever you call it," defended Cush, "an' if it hadn't of been that I got coaxed into that stud game last night, I'd of been way along into Joshua by now."

"These two is way past that," grinned Black John. "At the rate you're goin', Cush, you won't be ketchin' up with them two till a year from next Chris'mas. But layin' aside theological discussions—"

"You must be feelin' better," grunted Cush. "Them two words would have anyone stopped." He turned to One Armed John. "You was sayin' somethin' about them two chechakos up that feeder?"

"Yeah, it looks like they've went to war."

"Went to war!" exclaimed Old Cush. "Where to?"

"Fightin' each other—what I mean! Fightin' with rifles."

"What about?" asked Cush.

ONE ARMED John shrugged. "How the hell would I know? If I see a couple of fellas layin' in the bresh each side of a feeder peckin' at one another with moose rifles, they could be fightin' about any thing they want to, fer all I give a damn. I heard the

shootin' an' snuck up an' peeked over the rim till I seen what was goin' on, an' then I come away from there, before I lose my other arm."

"By the way," grinned Black John, "I don't believe we ever heard how you lost the left one."

"A married woman's husban' shot it with a shotgun in a fit of anger. I think he was shootin' at me—an' it wasn't a bad shot, at that, the way I was dodgin'. Afterwards a doctor cut it off. But I don't aim to lose this other one."

"When was it these chechakos was fightin'?" asked Black John.

"Fer all I know, they're at it yet. I know you don't favor no gun-play along the crick, so I come on down as fast as I could leg it. It was mebbe an hour an' a half ago I was there."

Black John turned to Cush. "Guess we better go up an' investigate," he said. "If one of them damn fools kills the other, er visy versy, the police might git wind of it, an' come hornin' in on us."

Cush regarded One Armed John sourly. "You tend bar till I

git back," he ordered. "An' don't go pilferin' no dust out of the till, er you'll lose yer other arm in a fit of anger."

II

AN HOUR LATER, as the two left the valley of Halfaday and turned up the feeder, Old Cush scowled. "A hell of a lot of chechakos could be shootin' at one another before I would give a damn," he said. "But like you say—the quicker we git up there an' bury one an' hang the other the better it'll be on account of the police."

Black John grinned. "It might not be that bad," he ventured. "Mebbe they couldn't hit one another, or run out of shells, or somethin'. I don't hear no shootin', now. An' their shack ain't over a mile from here."

"Mebbe they each got the other one, an' we kin bury 'em both," said Cush, hopefully. "They be'n workin' all winter an' they probably sluiced out enough to pay fer the diggin', if we kin find their cache. We don't need to go down very deep—what with the ground not thawed out yet."

"Yer gittin' plumb blood-thirsty," laughed Black John. "Suppose someone was to miss them fellas, an' the police should come up huntin' 'em?"

"Who in hell would miss a chechako?" snorted Cush. "The way they're pilin' into the Yukon, if half of 'em was to turn up missin' it would be a good thing fer the country."

"There's more truth than po'try to that. But these two was only young fellas. I doubt if they was on the run. They prob'ly worked on up the White, an' jest happened to turn up Halfaday, an' then on up this feeder. They seemed to be nice enough kids—an' they shore minded their own business."

"I'll say they did," replied Cush. "They bought their winter's supplies last fall an' packed the hull works up here on the first snow, an' they ain't be'n off'n this feeder sence. They never even showed up fer the Chris'mas jamboree. What I claim, if they ain't on the run, why the hell wouldn't they show up at the fort, now an' then?"

"Most likely it's because they're chechakos, an' don't know no better. Older heads would know that it ain't so good fer two men to hole up like that in a shack fer the whole winter. One man kin do it, er three men—but there's damn few two men that kin. There's somethin' about a two-man camp that does things to a man—in here." Black John tapped his forehead significantly. "It's all right if they git out now an' then, an' mix with some others. But what with the winters as long, an' cold, an' dark as they be—with workin' hours short, an' loafin' hours long—there's too much time fer thinkin', I guess. An' no two men ever think exactly alike, so no matter how good friends they be to start out with, arguments develops, an' arguments leads to hard feelin's, an' hard feelin's to fights—an' anything kin happen."

"Yer right, at that, John," agreed Cush. "There's only one worse combination—that's two men an' a woman."

"Huh," growled Black John, "fetch a woman into any situation, an' hell's goin' to pop—no matter what the mixture is."

THE TWO paused and listened to the sound of footfalls rapidly pounding the trail.

"They ain't both dead," said Cush. "An' seems like this one is in a hell of a hurry."

"Yeah—like a man leavin' the scene of a crime." Black John swung the barrel of his rifle into the crook of his elbow, his thumb caressing its hammer, just as a figure broke suddenly around a shoulder of rock where the rim bent sharply to the creek, and came to an abrupt halt at sight of the two men in the trail not ten yards in front of him.

"Help! I need help! It's my pardner!" The figure was that of a young man, his cleanly shaven face paper white, and his eyes wide with horror.

"Is he dead?" Black John's voice sounded cool and hard, in

sharp contrast to the hysterical tone of the other.

"No. It's his leg. He's shot!"

"Done it hisself, I s'pose?"

"No. I did it."

"Accident, eh?"

"No, not an accident—not exactly. I—I was shooting at him—trying to kill him. But come on—please! We can talk later. I've got the bleeding stopped, but we've got to do something. He's in his bunk in the shack. I carried him there. It's only half a mile or so. I was hurrying for a doctor."

Black John smiled bleakly. "You'd of had a hell of a long hurry," he said. "The nearest doctors are in Dawson."

"But—isn't there a doctor at the fort? No one who knows anything about medicine?"

Black John shook his head. "A man with a shot leg don't need no medicine," he said gruffly. "Go on ahead an' we'll foller. There's three of us here. If what we kin do won't save him, he'll die."

"And I'll be a—a murderer!" The young man's voice broke hysterically on the word, and his eyes shifted wildly from one face to the other.

"That won't bother you fer long," said Black John dryly. "We hang 'em quick, on Halfaday. Git goin', an' we'll see what we kin do."

The young man led the way swiftly, and the others followed, reaching the shack a few minutes later. One glance at its interior told Black John the story. It was a commodious cabin, as cabins go—well built of straight evenly matched logs, skillfully notched at the corners, and smoothly chinked with moss and mud. The floor was of puncheons, carefully surfaced with an ax, and the door was of planks split from spruce logs, dressed also with an ax, and ingeniously pegged together. The three windows were of glass, and Black John's gaze focused on one pane, punctured by two small round holes from which radiated a network of tiny cracks.

Noting the glance, the chechako explained. "Those windows, we found them in an abandoned cabin a few miles from here. We intended to return them when we were through with them, or pay the owner."

Black John nodded. "Yer welcome to the winders," he said. "The owner ain't payable. His stay on Halfaday was more or less transient—like most folks' stay that comes to the crick. Them two holes in the glass was made by a couple of bullets. One of 'em killed a man. It was a murder. Corporal Downey figured it out from them two holes. The murderer got hung."

The chechako winced at the words, as Black John followed them with an order: "Build up a fire in the stove an' set on a couple of pails of water."

AS THE man hastened to obey, Black John crossed the room and glanced down at the unconscious man on the bunk. He was an unkempt man, a scraggly beard of half winter's growth offsetting the extreme pallor of his face. His clothing was dirty and neglected in the matter of buttons and small repairs. And a stale, slightly sour odor rose from the blankets of the bunk. Dirt was ground into the skin of his hands and showed in broad bands of black beneath his fingernails. Unwashed dishes cluttered a small table, shoved back against the wall, while discarded garments protruded from beneath the bunk and littered the floor which showed no evidence of having been scrubbed or swept for weeks.

In sharp contrast was the other half of the cabin. Upon a similar small table against the wall, clean dishes were arranged beside a neat pile of magazines. The bunk was smoothly made up with clean, well aired blankets, and the floor was freshly scrubbed and swept. Unused garments and gear hung from pegs driven into the wall, or were ranged in orderly manner upon a pole shelf above the bunk. A larger table placed against the wall beneath a window in the exact middle of the room was evidently common property, its two ends showing the same contrast as did the rest of the cabin—one end unscrubbed and cluttered with a heterogeneous collection of odds and ends; the other clean, and neatly arranged.

The chechako stepped into the room with two pails of water which he placed on the stove in which he had built a roaring fire.

"That used to be our dining table," he explained, "till we—kind of split up. Then we each made a separate one."

"Uh-huh," replied Black John. "He sort of bogged down gradual on you, till you couldn't stand it no more, eh?"

"That's it!" exclaimed the other, eagerly grasping at the understanding in the big man's words. "That's just exactly what happened. I can't figure it out. Bill was a damn good fellow. But somehow he got to slipping."

"Yup. A lot of 'em does. They ain't got no guts. They can't take it. They'd ort to stayed to home."

"But Bill has got guts! He's the best friend I ever had."

A grin twisted the corners of the big man's lips. "Yer kind of rough in yer expression of friendship, ain't you? But there'll be time to talk later. Have you got any clean rags? We've got to see what we kin do fer this guy."

"I've got some clean underclothing. I boil it every week."

"Rip it up into strips as wide as you kin git 'em, while me an' Cush dumps the stuff off'n this table an' cleans the top. We'll drag it out in the middle of the floor, here, an' scrub it with soap an' b'illin' water, an' then we'll slosh some whiskey over it. I fetched along a quart fer beverage purposes, but we kin forego a drink in the interest of humanity. We've got to guard agin blood pizen. There ain't much danger, way out in a place like this, an' if he'd of kep' hisself as clean as you, there wouldn't of be'n practically none, an' we could of gone ahead an' drunk the quart."

A few minutes later as they were about to lift the patient from the bunk, the chechako paused. "Shouldn't we spread a blanket er somethin' on the table to lay him on?" he asked.

Black John shook his head. "No, we scrubbed that table top good an' wet it with whiskey. It stands to reason a hard surface couldn't hold as many germs as a soft one—like a blanket. Git holt of him now an' we'll h'ist him up."

The man was lifted from the bunk and deposited on the table, and Black John cut away the trousers and underclothing just below the mid-thigh, where the chechako had applied a tourniquet. Slitting the legs of the garments to the bottom, he carefully removed them, to disclose an ugly wound where a soft-nosed bullet had completely shattered the knee.

"That leg's got to come off," he decided, at a glance. "But first, we've got to loosen up this tourniquet fer a minute or two."

"I'm afraid he'll bleed to death," objected the chechako. "He lost quite a lot of blood before I got it stopped."

"What blood he loses in a couple of minutes won't kill him," replied Black John. "But if we don't let some blood into that leg above where we're goin' to take it off, he'll die of gangrene, shore as hell. We'll tighten it agin in a few minutes."

"You seem to know exactly what to do," said the chechako, with an air of vast relief. "Have you ever studied surgery?"

"Only in a general way," replied Black John. "Like cuttin' up a moose. Surgery is jest like anything else. It's one of them damn things that pops up along a crick that a man's got to do. If he knows how to do 'em; so much the better. If he don't; he goes ahead an' does 'em anyhow. You won't find but damn few specialists out amongst the cricks—but there's a hell of a lot of men that goes ahead an' does a specialist's work, an' gits away with it. This here is a country where common sense has got to pinch-hit fer education, as a ball player would say. An' it's surprisin' how often it scores."

"I sure hope it scores this time," exclaimed the chechako fervidly. "Good God—if Bill should die, I'd—I'd—" his voice broke, and he paced up and down the floor nervously clenching and unclenching his hands.

"Git holt of yerself—an' keep holt!" ordered Black John, roughly. "There's only the three of us here, an' we're all needed. Like I said—if he dies, you ain't goin' to have long to worry. It'll be murder—an' we hang murderers quick on Halfaday. In your case, this here job's got a personal angle, so you better do your damndest to make it a success."

Thanks to the tourniquet, the operation was nearly bloodless. The chechako stood by, white-faced and shaking, and handed Black John such implements as he called for.

As the business proceeded, the patient writhed and started to struggle. Old Cush sought to hold him, but the man rose to a sitting posture, his eyes staring wildly, his arms flailing. Only for an instant did Black John hesitate, then shifting the implement he was using to his left hand, he swung with his right—a swift, powerful blow that landed squarely upon the point of the man's chin. His head snapped back, and he collapsed upon the table, and the next moment Black John, himself, staggered from a blow that landed just under his own ear. He whirled just in time to dodge another blow, as the chechako leaped toward him. Once again his mighty right shot out, and the chechako crashed backward against the wall and slumped to a limp heap upon the floor.

"Why—the damn cuss!" cried Old Cush. "An' you with yer hands full, doin' all you could fer his pardner!"

"Oh, I ain't very busy," grinned Black John. "It's all in the day's work. Don't blame the pore devil. His nerves is all shot. He'll be good fer a while, now. An' the patient here, too. That anesthetic took holt quick, didn't it? I hope it didn't onhook his neck. Come on—let's git this over with."

III

AS THE OPERATION neared completion, the chechako on the floor stirred, and rose groggily to his feet. "What—happened?" he asked, pressing a hand gingerly against his jaw.

"You took a little nap on the floor," replied Black John, without looking up from his work of tying stitches.

"I—I must have passed out," said the man, apologetically. "I remember I felt awful shaky. I—I had a bad dream. I dreamed you socked poor Bill one in the jaw, and I was defending him."

"That wasn't no dream," replied Black John. "Whatever dreamin' you done come later. Come on, now, an' help git him onto his bunk."

"Just a minute, till I change blankets—mine are cleaner." The filthy blankets were stripped from the bunk, and a few minutes later the three stood looking down at the injured man who reposed between clean blankets. "He looks awful white," said the chechako. "Do you think he'll live?"

Black John shrugged. "A hell of a lot of one-legged men has," he replied. "Anyhow, he's got a chanct. We done the best we could fer him."

"I—I don't know how to thank you men," faltered the chechako. "If I'd had to go clear to the fort for help, I'm afraid he'd have died."

"Most likely," agreed Black John. "An' that would of left you in a hell of a spot. Even with things as they be, you've got some explainin' to do. You see, on Halfaday, where most of us is outlawed for one thing an' another, we don't favor no gunplay. It's liable to result fatal, an' fetch the police. We live moral as hell up here—not because we want to necessarily, but as a matter of policy. All major infringements on morality, like murder, robbery, claim-jumpin', an' the like, is dealt with by a miners' meetin'. So is skullduggery, it bein' any other offense that is deemed hangable—like, fer instance, maimin' whilst shootin' with intent to kill. We'll set on your case this evenin', but if there's any extenuatin' or mitigatin' circumstances connected with it, it might be jest as well if you'd sort of outline 'em to me an' Cush. It's jest possible that we might be able to kind of, in some way, head off the boys from runnin' hog-wild in the matter of hangin'."

"Oh, I shot him, all right. I won't try to lie out of it. I'd have killed him if I could. Maybe I went crazy. I don't know. I never wanted to kill anybody before—least of all Bill. It was such a little thing that started it, just—"

"Hold on, son," interrupted Black John, in a voice that was gruff, but not unkindly. "Better start further back than the little spark that touched off the powder. I don't know what it was—an' it don't make no difference, nohow. You mebbe don't know it—but us older heads does—this here shootin' was the result of a build-up. One little thing on top of another—nothin', mebbe, amountin' to a hell of a lot by itself, but added together they bulked important as hell."

"THAT'S IT!" exclaimed the younger man, with evident relief. "That's exactly what happened. I know it's going to sound foolish; I've been thinking about it—since—since the shooting. It's so foolish I didn't think anyone would understand. Bill never was very orderly, and early in the winter he began to get sloppier an' sloppier. He quit shaving—said there wasn't any use in it. Then he quit combing his hair, and taking baths, and finally he hardly ever even washed his hands and face. He wouldn't sweep the floor, nor help wash up the dishes. He quit washing his clothing and blankets, and when I'd remind him about it, he'd get mad, and grouch around and tell me I ought to have been born a girl, and a lot of stuff like that.

"I tried not to pay any attention to it, and while we were out working in the shaft he was all right—the same old Bill—but in the evenings, and days when we couldn't work, he seemed morose and sour. It would make him grouchy when I washed up my own clothes, or took a bath, or scrubbed the floor.

"Soon after Chris'mas, I couldn't stand it any longer, and I told him that if he wanted to live like a hog he could—but he couldn't make me live that way. So we each took an end of the cabin, and divided up the dishes and supplies, and each did his own cooking, on his own territory.

"By that time, we'd got to bickering over trifles—things that didn't amount to a damn—like a couple of spoiled kids. Sometimes we wouldn't speak for days at a time. Then this morning while I stepped to the creek for a pail of water, he did that!" The man paused and pointed to a picture pinned to the wall, just above the little table at his end of the cabin.

"Done what?" asked Black John, as he and Cush stepped up for a closer inspection.

"Why—he drew a mustache on that girl!"

"Oh," said Black John, as he peered at the picture of a beautiful young woman upon whose upper lip an absurdly flowing mustache had been penciled. "Your girl?"

"No, not my girl. I cut it out of a magazine. But she's just what a man would want his girl to be like—if he had one. She's kind of an ideal girl, I guess. She's so clean and wholesome looking—and good! I used to lie there on my bunk and just look at her, and wonder whether any real girl could be just like that.

"Well, when I got back with the water and saw what he'd done, something seemed to bust inside of my head, and I saw red. I stood there just staring at the picture, and then he laughed—a nasty, sneering laugh. I dropped the pail, and went for him. He's a lot bigger than I am—and stronger—and he just kept on laughing that sneering laugh, and slapping me, and pushing me away. I couldn't hit him—and finally I turned and grabbed up my rifle and cocked it, and swung it on him.

"He said, 'Good God, Jack—don't murder me!' I remember the word 'murder' made me pause. 'I won't murder you,' I cried, 'but I'll kill you! Get your gun and we'll have it out, for good and all. Pick it up—and we'll shoot it out!'

"'Not in here,' he said, and I could see that his eyes had narrowed to slits, as he reached for his rifle. 'Outside!'

"'Outside it is,' I agreed. 'But get going. You take one side of the crick and I'll take the other.'

"He went out the door, and I waited till he stopped beside that big rock across there at the edge of the timber, then I stepped out and got behind the corner of the cabin. I don't know who shot first—but we both were shooting. We kept it up for a long time. I slipped into the timber, and so did he—and whenever we'd catch sight of each other, we'd fire. We kept it up—mebbe an hour, maybe two or three hours—I don't know. Then I saw his handkerchief waving at the edge of a bush, and I dropped my rifle and ran over there. He'd tied it to the barrel of his rifle. He looked up and smiled—and suddenly I saw that it was that same old smile of Bill's, no sneer in it, no animosity. 'I guess you got me, Jack,' he said. 'It was a while back. I guess I'm bleeding to death. But it's all right, kid. It was all my fault. I can see it—now. I was a damn rotter.' Then he fainted, and I put on that tourniquet to stop the bleeding, and picked him up and carried him here, and then ran for help.

"But it wasn't all his fault—by a damn sight! Bill was a fine fellow. It was my fault—I started the fight. I'll take what's coming to me, and I'll take it standing up."

BLACK JOHN nodded slowly and turned to Old Cush. "What did I tell you—about women? *Even their picture kin raise hell with a crick.*" He regarded the chechako. "You've got to make a trip down to the fort," he said. "Me and Cush will stay here with the patient. There'll be some men come back up with you. We'll git this miners' meetin' over with. We'll hold it up here. You'll find a one armed man behind the bar." The huge man picked up a pencil and scribbled a note. "It's to One Armed John," he explained to Cush, "tellin' him to send Pot Gutted John, an' Long John, an' Red John, an' Big Nosed John, an' Little John right up here, an' fer 'em to fetch up a dozen quarts. We need a drink an' there'll be some left fer the patient."

The chechako took the note as his glance flashed about the room. "Couldn't I just wait and clean up here a bit?" he said.

"I—I'd kind of hate to have anyone see poor Bill's end of the cabin looking like this. They'd think he—"

Black John grinned. "We'll leave things jest as they be, son," he said. "This here cabin will talk louder than any lawyer you could hire! Git goin' now, an' tell them boys I said to hurry back."

When the man was gone, Old Cush turned to Black John. "Who is them quarts on?" he asked.

"Me an' you. We're splittin' the expense. You know damn well, Cush, that now an' then I ain't averse to takin' a moderate profit on some venture. But this case is different. These boys has got theirselves in a psychological jam—"

"Is that some form of skullduggery?" asked Cush.

"That's fer the miners' meetin' to decide."

"Seems kind of too bad, in a way, to hang that young feller—even if he is a chechako," ventured Cush. "I kind of like him."

"Yeah. It looks like he might amount to somethin'—when he learns to leave women alone. An' what with that handpicked jury, it's just barely possible he might git a break at that."

A LOW moan from the bunk drew the two to the injured man's side. He stared up at their faces with a look of perplexity.

"Who—are you?" he asked, in a feeble voice. "And where's Jack?"

"He's gone down to the fort. He'll be back after a while. We're stayin' with you while he's gone. How you feelin'?"

"My—jaw hurts. And my leg hurts like the devil!"

"Yeah," replied Black John soothingly. "Yer jaw—that's due to the anthesthetic. It works like that on some folks. An' don't worry about yer leg—there ain't enough of it left to hurt much. We took it off jest above the knee."

"Took it off! Are you a doctor?"

"My occupations is varied," said Black John. "Sometimes I'm one thing—an' sometimes another. I was a doctor this afternoon. This evenin' chances is, I'll have to be a lawyer—an' that's the way it goes. I sort of turn my hand to anything that shows up. I'll fetch you a drink of water now, an' then you try an' ketch you some sleep. Yer pardner'll fetch back some licker, an' then you'll git a proper drink."

After Black John held a cup of water to the man's lips he closed his eyes and relapsed into silence, and the two seated themselves at the clean end of the cabin.

"We've got to sort of figger out some kind of a wooden leg for him," said Black John, as he filled his pipe. "Spruce is best—it's tough, an' light, an' handy to git. There's plenty of sticks in that old burnin' down the crick; we kin find a piece that's fire-killed an' dried out tough and stout."

"Take it in a country like this," said Cush, "an' a peg leg is goin' to be hell, anyways you looks at it. Every time he steps in the snow, he's goin' to sink clean to his stump. An' the same in muskeg. An' if he hit slick ice with it, he's goin' to spin around like a button on a smoke house door, an' set down."

"We might rig the end of it so he could fit on different things—like snowshoes fer snow, an' a kind of a spike fer slick ice."

"Yeah," scoffed Cush, "an' a wheel fer summer, an' a ski fer winter. But every time he steps into a canoe, that peg leg's goin' right through the bottom of it."

"He could take it off fer canoein', but we could make him a knee, too, if we could git holt of a hinge somewheres."

"We could whittle out a foot an' fasten on the end of it, too," suggested Cush, "an' nail a shoe on it. Then if he kep' his hinge oiled so it wouldn't squeak it would be as good as any other leg."

"Better," grinned Black John. "His toes couldn't never git cold, an' black flies an' mosquitoes couldn't bother it, an' if a dog bit him, er he got shot in it, it wouldn't hurt him none."

"Shore," agreed Cush, "an' he could roll up his pants an' paint a sock on it to match his other one—an' by the way—a pair of socks is goin' twict as fer with him, as what they used to—he kin only wear one to a time."

Black John chuckled. "Looks like about the only worry he's goin' to have from now on is to keep the squirrels an' woodpeckers from buildin' nests in his leg. I jest happened to think—we kin use moosehide fer a hinge—it's tough, an' it don't squeak. Guess I'll slip out an' see if I kin find a chunk of wood. We might's well be workin' on it, as doin' nothin', whilst we're waitin'."

IV

IT WAS LONG after dark when the chechako returned, accompanied by the men Black John had named as a jury. After several rounds of drinks, in which the injured man joined, Black John called the meeting to order.

"Miners' meetin' called fer the purpose of tryin' a chechako named Jack fer the shootin' of another one named Bill, said Bill's leg havin' been shot in the knee. I'll app'int myself chairman of this here meetin', an' it's yer dooty to listen to all the evidence an' give a verdick accordin' to it.

"In the first place, I'm askin' you to take notice of this here room. It's plain to see that instead of a two-man camp, like it started out to be, it's two one-man camps in under one roof—an' you men know what that means.

"Take notice of the condition of the two halves of the room. I'll explain that the dirty half belongs to the man that got shot, an' the clean half to the defendant in this action. While dirtiness, per se ain't no shootin' offense, yet it is one of them straws that shows who broke the camel's back.

"On top of livin' filthy, an' not helpin' keep the cabin clean, this here, to wit, Bill layin' there in the bunk feloniously draw'd a mustache on that lady in the picture there on the wall—her bein' the property of the defendant, to wit, Jack.

"Now, gents, you all know that the purest an' most sentimental sentiments that there is is inspired by women. Women, gents, is the crownin' glory of the human race—barrin' men. When a man loves a woman he's—he's well—he's got the world by the pants with a downhill pull—or so he thinks. We've all got to remember, gents, that there ain't a man in this room which his mother wasn't a woman! And we've also got to remember that the crownin' glory of women is that they ain't got no whiskers! Now, therefore, when some damn miscreant comes along, an' with malice aforethought, takes a pencil an' deliberately draws a, to wit, long and curvin' mustache on the face of a fair an' beautiful woman he's committin' a sacrilege that there can't no depths of human depravation be compared with. An' we got to consider that this here heinous offense was committed on top of six or seven months of filthy livin' an' grouchiness.

"With such facts before us, we come down to the pax vobiscum of this case. When the defendant come in this mornin' an' seen what his pardner done, he went haywire—but instead of murderin' him on the spot, as any right-mindin' citizen would of done off Halfaday—what does he do? Gents, he offers to shoot it out with him. Yes, sir—he lets him git his rifle, an' he takes his'n—an' then they got on opposite sides of the crick an' began peckin' away at one another. The results of this here gentlemanly duel, gents, proves exclusively, that right is bound to prevail. The mustache-drawer got shot in the knee, an' then this here defendant, to wit, the chechako named Jack run to the wounded man's side an' carried him in here an' laid him in his bunk after stoppin' the blood, an' then he run fer help. He met up with me an' Cush, an' he continued to help us take off the man's leg—an' he done yeoman's service at it, too—an' you all know what that means, gents. It means that his acts saved a human life.

"Now, then, with all them facts in mind, we're bound to consider that, taken by an' large, an' as a general rule, shootin's, as such, has been frowned on on Halfaday—but there's always mitigatin' an' extenuatin' circumstances—which I've hinted at. An' they must be considered in renderin' a verdick, which in this case, if it should turn out disadvantageous to the defendant, any damn cuss on the jury that voted agin him will have to settle with me! All we want is a fair an' impartial verdick on this case.

"Them favorin' conviction, signify by sayin', 'Aye.'"

Silence.

"Contrary, 'No.'"

A lusty chorus of 'No's greeted the words, and Black John turned to the defendant.

"Yer acquitted of wrong-doin'," he announced. "But an' however, such acquittal carries a conditional sentence. Fer yer own good, the two of you are commanded to appear at least onct a month at Cushing's Fort, an' mix with the boys. You won't find us a bad bunch—an' you'll find that you'll git along together hereafter, jest as if nothin' had happened."

The chechako nodded. "I can see that now," he said. "I—want to thank you men."

"Me, too," the words came weakly from the bunk, where the injured man raised himself to his elbow. "I can see it, too. I was listening to what you said—it was my fault. It's all true."

Black John stepped to his side, as white teeth flashed beneath his black beard. "Listen, fella," he said, "don't you pay no heed to what I said about you a while back. Didn't I tell you I'd prob'ly have to do a lawyer's job this evenin'? Well, that was him talkin'—not me, personal. There wasn't practically no truth at all, an' damn little sense in what he said, but he won his case—so fergit it."

HARDLY HAD he finished speaking than the door opened, and Corporal Downey of the Northwest Mounted Police stepped into the room. Black John greeted him effusively:

"Hello, Downey—well, I'll be damned. Step in an' have a drink! We was jest about to open a new quart."

"What about this shootin' up here?" asked the officer, his glance traveling rapidly about the room.

"Shootin'? What shootin' was you referrin' to?"

"Listen," said Downey, "I stopped in at the fort and overheard One Armed John and another man talkin'. They was discussin' a miners' meetin' that was goin' on up here. What about it?"

"Oh—yeah. The miners' meetin'. Well, it's all over with."

"Did you hang someone?"

"Hell no, Downey! Up here on Halfaday we only hang a man when he's guilty."

"But there was a shootin'." The young officer stepped to the bunk, and threw back the blanket, disclosing the bandaged stump. "How did this man lose his leg?"

"Who—him?" asked Black John. "Well now, Downey—since you mentioned it, I'll tell you. He got pretty drunk, last night, an' went to sleep in the river, an' a steamboat run over him."

Corporal Downey joined in the roar of laughter that greeted the words.

"That's all right, John, but you can't laugh off a shootin'. Shootin' off a man's leg is a crime in the Yukon—even though he wasn't killed. This case will stand investigation."

"Yeah?" drawled Black John, a twinkle in his eyes, "an' who's goin' to do the investigatin'?"

"I am!" the words snapped crisply from Downey's lips, as he eyed the big man sternly.

Black John shrugged. "Go to it, if you want to," he said. "But it's the first time I ever know'd the Mounted was interested in Alasky shootin's."

"Alaska!" exclaimed Downey.

"Why shore. Didn't you know the line cuts this feeder about a mile back down the crick?"

"No," replied Downey. "I knew of course that you're close to the line up here, but I didn't realize I'd crossed it."

"No harm done," laughed Black John. "Come on—drink up. This case has already be'n investigated—an' justice has been done. After you'd looked things over you wouldn't of made no arrest, even if it was in yer own territory. Jest a case of too much chechako—an' some snapped nerves. It'll work out all right. Hold on now till I tole off the boys to help this chechako take care of this man. There better be two here with him fer a while. I'll fix it so one man from the fort will be here on twenty-four hour shifts. They kin rotate till he gits well."

Pot Gutted John took the first shift, and the others started for the fort, Black John explaining the case to Downey as they walked down the creek in the moonlight.

Late that night, after Downey had gone to bed and the others had returned to their cabins, Old Cush poured himself a drink and shoved the bottle toward Black John.

"Take one more fer a nightcap, John," he invited. "An' say, I didn't know that there cabin was over in Alasky territory. Damn if I believe it is."

Black John grinned. "Me neither, but I don't know—an' neither does Downey. Cripes, I had to think of somethin', didn't I? There ain't no use in quibblin' over technicalities—so what the hell!"

REWARD—$1,000

CORPORAL DOWNEY, IN charge of the Northwest Mounted Police detachment in Dawson looked up from his desk to greet the black-bearded man whose huge frame darkened the doorway of the little office.

"Hello, John! Pull up a chair an' fill your pipe. What's on your mind?"

"Not a thing, Downey! Not a damn thing," Black John Smith grinned. "What I claim, if a man keeps his conscience clear he ain't got a damn thing to worry about."

"Wish I could agree with you," growled the officer. "My conscience is reasonably clear—an' I've got plenty to worry about."

"Meanin', I s'pose, that robbery up on Quartz Crick? It shore don't give me no pain in the neck if some big outfit loses a few ounces of dust, now an' then."

"It was four thousan' ounces of dust, an' the Pacific Dredge & Minin' Company's squawkin' plenty."

"Shore they'd squawk. But accordin' to the talk in the Tivoli, last night, it was an inside job. If it was, it's their own fault. They ought to be more partic'lar who they hire."

Corporal Downey frowned. "I'm not so sure it was an inside job. It might have been. But there's another angle."

"The night watchman skipped out, didn't he? An' he claimed he couldn't give no description of the man he said tied him up an' gagged him?"

"That's right. He's considered a tough baby, too. He's taken shots at several prowlers since spring, includin' one Company official who attempted to visit the office one night without botherin' to make himself known. The robbery took place on the night of the second—an' this is the sixth, an' we haven't got anywheres with it. All we know is that the next mornin' some employees found the watchman layin' unconscious in front of the strong room, bound an' gagged. Some cloth had be'n stuffed in his mouth, an' a bandage wrapped so tight over his mouth an' nose that he was nearly suffocated. The doctor said it was a wonder he was alive. A few more minutes an' they'd never have brought him to. When he was able to talk he told about bein' grabbed from behind an' thrown down an' choked till he lost consciousness. He claims he never saw his assailant—don't know if it was one man, or a dozen. The night was black dark, all right—we checked on that. So his story might be true."

"If it's true, why would he disappear that same day?"

Downey shrugged. "Your guess is as good as mine. His disappearance makes it look like a frame-up. But on the other hand his experience might have scairt him out. Or he may not have told all he knows—he may have an idea who attacked him, an' hit out to get him, single handed."

"If he was as tough a hombre as what folks claim, he wasn't scairt out," opined Black John. "An' why would he go after the robber single handed, instead of playin' in with the police? The thousan' dollar reward the Company offered fer the thief, dead er alive, wasn't posted till yesterday—an' he'd already be'n gone three days. He shore as hell wasn't after that reward."

"That's right. But if it was a frame-up, why would he let his pardner gag him so tight it nearly killed him?"

BLACK JOHN grinned. "He prob'ly couldn't help himself. If it was a frame-up his pardner ondoubtless tied his hands an' feet first. Then he shoved the rag in his mouth an' proceeded to do the bandagin' to suit himself, the man bein' helpless. It's my best guess he done it with the thought in mind that four thousan' ounces is better than two thousan'. An' that he acted on the theory that you don't have to divide no loot with a corpse."

"You mean—he doublecrossed his pardner, the watchman!"

"Well," grinned the big man, "if he'd of done me like that I'd be tempted to suspect that it savored of the doublecross."

"I hadn't thought of it that way," Downey admitted. "From that angle, it looks more than ever like an inside job."

"Shore it does," Black John agreed. "An' if I was you I'd go ahead an' arrest all the officers of the Company fer aidin' an' abettin' a felony, er accessories before the fact, er some sech crime, on the theory that a corporation is responsible fer the acts of its employees."

Downey laughed. "I'd like to, for all the trouble they're causin' us—squawkin' their heads off! I've posted men up an' down the river—Whitehorse, an' Forty Mile. When are you goin' back to Halfaday?"

"Right now. I done fairly well in the stud game last night, an' I don't see no reason to let the boys git even—at least not this quick."

"I'd go up with you, but I've got to be in court tomorrow on another case. But I'll be up as soon as I can. In the meantime you might keep yer eyes open fer any suspicious characters that might show up along the crick."

"Cripes, Downey—ninety-nine an' forty-four hundreths percent of the folks that shows up on Halfaday is suspicious characters! What fer lookin' is this disappearin' watchman?"

"He's kind of smallish—right around five foot-six. Hard lookin' greenish eyes. A scar runs from the right hand corner of his nose out onto his cheek. Smooth face. Brown hair. About thirty-five. If it was an inside job, his pardner might be a large man with a stubble of beard on his face, an' wearin' a black felt hat with a piece of the brim tore off. We ain't got much of a description of him. No one paid much attention to him, except that he was known to have struck the foreman fer a job the day before the robbery, an' hung around the works a while after he got turned down."

"All right, Downey. I'll keep an eye open. We wouldn't want no damn pardner-stranglin' skunk on Halfaday."

"Remember—there's a reward out, if you locate 'em."

"Huh—reward! One thousan' dollars—when there's a matter of sixty-four thousan' dollars in dust involved! Sech reward is trifln', not to say right down penurious. Them big corporations shore invites my contempt!"

"The reward is payable for the robber, or robbers, dead or alive—regardless of whether or not the dust is recovered," Downey explained. "But don't go takin' the law into yer own hands up there, John. I'll be along in a few days. If the robbers are there, I'll arrest 'em myself—an' when I do, I'll expect to recover that dust! You can keep the reward. The police are not interested in that."

"Yer expectations is laudable, Downey," grinned the big man. "An' no one could blame you fer not bein' interested in that thousan' dollar reward. It ain't no interestin' amount. Well, so long! I'll be seein' you!"

II

ON AN AFTERNOON, ten days after his departure from Dawson, Black John beached his canoe before a cabin that stood in a tiny clearing, a little way back from the water, on a low bank across the creek from a broad willow flat, and nodded to the two men who had haled him. One, he noted, was a smallish man, with piercing green eyes that stared unwinking, like the eyes of a snake. A scar extended from the corner of his nose out onto his cheek. His companion was a large man whose features were concealed behind a stubble of whiskers. This one wore a black felt hat with a piece missing from the brim. It was the larger one who spoke as Black John stepped from the canoe.

"Ain't this Halfaday Crick?" he asked. "An' if it is, where in hell's Cushing's Fort? Accordin' to what we heer'd a man could git anythin' he wants, up here—an' we're damn near out of grub."

"Yeah, this is Halfaday," Black John replied, stretching prodigiously. "Paddlin' all day shore cramps a man."

"Yeah. But where's this here Cushing's Fort?"

"It's about five, six mile further up the crick," Black John replied, with a glance at the empty canoe beside which he had beached his own. "You boys campin' here?"

"Yeah. Jest hit here this mornin'."

"You wouldn't be Black John Smith, would you?" asked the smaller man, his unwinking eyes on the huge man's face.

"I would."

"Glad to meet up with you. We heard tell about you holdin' up the U.S. Army, one time, somewheres over in Alaska."

"Oh, shore. But the incident has ondoubtless be'n greatly exaggerated. It was jest a prank—the gratification of a passin' whim, as you might say."

"I can't figger how a man could hold up a army," grunted the larger of the two, a gleam of skepticism in his eye.

"It ain't so hard, if you surround it," Black John replied. "Didn't you ever read no hist'ry?"

"You mean like all about George Worshin'ton, an' a lot of old fellas, like that? Hell, no! What I claim, a man's wastin' his time readin' about a lot of folks that's dead. I quit school in the fifth grade. Couldn't see no p'int in keepin' on."

"There prob'ly wasn't none," Black John agreed, and noted that the smaller man's lips had twisted into a wry grin.

"The talk is, along the river, that you kinda run things, up here."

"Well, me an' Cush sort of sees to it that there ain't nothin' pulled off along the crick that would fetch the police in on us. Whatever a man done before he come to Halfaday ain't no one's business but his own. After he gits here he's got to refrain from committin' any sech crimes as murder, larceny, claim jumpin', er general skullduggery."

"What does a man do, up here?"

"We work daytimes. In the evenin' most of the boys drifts into Cush's fer a session of stud, er mebbe to do a little drinkin', in a quiet way."

"Suits me," observed the snake-eyed one. "I'm a man which loves his quiet."

"What's this here kind of work you was tellin' about?" asked the larger man.

"Why, the boys works their claims. Most any location on the crick pays wages—an' some of 'em does a lot better'n that."

"How about this here claim?"

"It's all right. I always figgered it ought to be one of the best claims on the crick."

"Huh—there's three, four shallow shafts sunk on it. Why would it be abandoned, if it's so damn good?"

"It never be'n what you'd say, 'abandoned,'" Black John replied, producing his tobacco pouch and filling his pipe. "This is Olson's old claim. He was shot, an sence then there's be'n several parties moved in here. But what with gittin' killed, one way er another, er hung, er arrested, they didn't none of 'em stick with it. It's got so the boys figgers it's onlucky."

"To hell with that!" the smaller man exclaimed. "Believin' in luck is nigger stuff. This here's a good cabin, an' if they ain't no one got any rights on it, we'll move in.

"All we want is a chanct to make us an honest livin'."

"Yeah," agreed the larger man, a bit vaguely. "Which way is the line from here? An' how fer is it?"

"It lays about a mile straight back up a gulch from Cush's. From here I'd say it was three, four mile back—if you cut out over the rim."

"Oh, it ain't that we give a damn about the line," the smaller one hastened to say. "We was jest kinda gittin' our bearin's."

"They're a good thing to git," Black John agreed. "Well, guess I'll be shovin' along er I won't make Cush's by supper."

"We might be up later. We need some grub. An' we might set in that stud game."

"Okay. An' it ain't no more'n right I should tip you boys off that if you've got any heft of dust you'd better fetch it up an' bank it in Cush's safe."

"Why not cache it?" demanded the stubble faced one.

"Well, that's a good way, too," Black John admitted. "But most of the boys, realizin' as they do the frailties of human nature, prefers to bank with Cush an' take his receipt fer their dust. There's be'n cache robberies—even here on Halfaday. In most instances the robber was hung. But the dust they got was hardly ever recovered, owin' to them havin' time to recache it before the fatal event come off."

"The hell with bankin' it with this here Cush! How do we know he wouldn't doublecross us?"

BEFORE BLACK JOHN could reply, the smaller man laughed, as he flashed a meaning glance at the speaker. "Guess we won't need to worry about what we'll do with our dust till we git some."

"Oh, shore!" the other hastened to agree. "I was jest figgerin'—

in case. If this here claim's as good as what Black John figgers, we ought to have plenty of dust 'fore very long."

"I see you've got a stampedin' pack there," observed the smaller man, as Black John was about to step into his canoe. "Be'n off on a prospectin' trip?"

"No. Be'n down to Dawson."

"Dawson, eh? What's the news along the river?"

"Oh, nothin' to speak of. The Detroit-Yukon outfit is openin' up a new proposition on some crick back from the river. Boat-load of chechakos got drowned in Five Finger Rapids. The *Sarah* run aground down on the Flats, an' they had to onload her before they could float her agin."

"Any excitement on the cricks—Bonanza, er Ophir, er Hunker, er Quartz Crick?"

"Nothin' much, I guess. Oh, yeah—Quartz Crick! The Pacific Dredge & Minin' Company's strong room was robbed of eight thousan' ounces of dust, couple weeks ago."

"Eight thousan' ounces!" The words fairly exploded from the lips of the smaller man. "Hell—they never had no eight thousan' ounces in that strong room at once! I use' to work fer 'em—an' I know. They cleaned up every two weeks, an' the clean-up run right around four thousan' ounces, stidy."

Black John grinned. "I s'pose you was the one that counted them ounces fer 'em, eh?"

"What do you mean by that?"

"Meanin' that the talk around Dawson is that the Pacific Dredge & Minin' outfit has be'n takin' out jest about twict what they've be'n claimin' they was takin'. The officers give out the figgers, an' no one—not even them that worked there—know'd any different. It was on account of 'em figgerin' on some kind of reorganization, er somethin'. They wanted to make out like they wasn't doin' as good as they really was.

"Some kind of shenanigan they was cookin' up to gyp the stockholders. Them that was in on it was prob'ly figgerin' on buyin' up the shares cheap. But this here robbery sort of put a crimp in their game. Seems that the treasurer got rattled an' spilt the beans by blabbin' out the real amount that was stole. The talk is in Dawson that all the other officers is sore as hell at him. But what I claim, it would serve the damn skulldugs right if the stockholders would kick the whole kit an' kaboodle of 'em out."

"It's a damn lie!" the stubble faced one blurted. "There was only—" He paused abruptly, and Black John caught the venomous glance of suspicion that the smaller man darted the speaker.

"Yeah?" he encouraged. "What was you goin' on to say?"

STUBBLE FACE had caught the gleam, too, and he floundered among his words. "Why, I—er—I wasn't goin' to say nothin'—except it don't stand to reason that no big outfit like that would doublecross their stockholders. What I claim, if they said they was takin' out four thousan' ounces, they was takin' out four thousan'—an' not a damn ounce more!"

Black John shrugged. "You've got a hell of a lot more faith in them big outfits than I have."

"What's the police doin' about it?" asked Snake Eyes abruptly.

"Well, the talk is sort of this way an' that. No one doubts, the police included, that there was eight thousan' ounces lifted out of the strong room that night—an' the police know what the fortnightly clean-up was, because they collect the royalties. An' no outfit would be damn fool enough to pay royalties on eight thousan', when they was only takin' out four.

"There's considerable difference of opinion as to how the robbery was pulled off. It seems that after the night watchman had told the police, next day, that he never got sight of the one that over-powered him, he disappeared. So most folks figger that him an' the robber was in cahoots—that he let the robber tie him an' gag him. An' that they j'ined up, later, an' divided the loot. The police leans toward this theory—an' I'm inclined to agree with it, too.

"The main argument agin it is that if the robber was a pardner of the watchman, he wouldn't never of gagged him like he done. They p'int out, an' with more er less reason back of it, that the robber wouldn't of had to gag the watchman, except jest enough to make it look like a practical gag—because the watchman wasn't goin' to put up no holler, anyhow. Instead of which, that watchman was gagged to within an inch of his life! It took a doctor an' two nurses to fetch him to. An' the doctor claimed that if he'd laid there five minutes longer he'd of be'n dead as a door nail! Not only the robber rammed a rag in his mouth clean down to his throat, but to make shore he couldn't breathe he wrapped a bandage 'round an' 'round his head so he couldn't hardly git no air at all. The doctor couldn't figger out how he got enough to live till they found him. He claims it looked like a deliberate attempt on the part of the robber to suffocate the man. An' that's why some folks are claimin' it must of be'n an outside job—that the robber wouldn't of tried to murder his pardner. But shucks, I—"

"They're right, too!" Stubble Face cried vehemently. "'Course he wouldn't try to murder him! He had to make that gag look good. Cripes, he wouldn't dast to leave him layin' there gagged loose—like so he could spit it out an' yell his head off! He couldn't do that, could he? Not by a damn sight, he couldn't! That would of give the play dead away. That there had to look like a damn good job of gaggin'. What I claim, if he got it too tight, so it shet off the man's wind, it was a mistake."

"I'll say it was," tittered Snake Eyes, in a flinty voice.

Black John grinned at Stubble Face. "Yer faith in corporations, an' robbers, an' folks of like ilk, is fer an' away beyond what mine is. Look at it from the robber's angle. Here's eight thousan' ounces in dust—"

"Four thousan' ounces!" interrupted the other.

"Well, fer the sake of argument, we'll say four thousan', sence you insist on maintainin' the integrity of them damn crooks. But the figger is eight thousan', jest the same. Even the rest of the officers of the company are admittin' it, sence the treasurer squawked. But whatever the amount was, the robber know'd damn well that he'd git twict as much if he didn't have to divide it with a pardner. So, after tyin' the watchman up hand an' foot so he couldn't offer no resistance, he crammed that gag down his throat—an' him helpless. Then he wound that bandage around to make shore he couldn't breathe in no air through his nose. He wouldn't of needed to shet off his nose, if he hadn't wanted to kill him. A man kin breathe through his nose—but he can't holler through it, by a damn sight! Then he gits the dust an' hits out fer whatever place they'd agreed to meet.

"Of course, he don't never expect the watchman to show up. But he stays there, jest in case the onexpected would happen, an' some one should find him an' cut him loose before he passed out. An' the way things turned out, that's jest what did happen." Black John paused and laughed. "Boys, I'm tellin' you, I'd liked to of be'n there an' seen that damn doublecrosser's face when the watchman did show up, next day! An' him realizin' he had to divide them eight thousan' ounces, instead of keepin' 'em. Of course, if he'd of be'n damn good an' smart, he could of cached four thousan' of them ounces—knowin' that the watchman only figgered there'd be four thousan', all told. That way, he'd of got six thousan' to the watchman's two thousan', even after dividin' up with him. But that's prob'ly givin' him more brains than he had. Anyhow, I'd shore liked to of heard him tryin' to explain' about gaggin' him so tight! He prob'ly give him the same line of dope you jest put out," he said, glancing toward Stubble Face, "about havin' to make it look like a bony fido gaggin'. An' the damn sap of a watchman prob'ly believed him! Oh, well—what the hell! If he didn't know no better he's prob'ly satisfied. It's like the old sayin' 'what a man don't know don't hurt him none'. They'll prob'ly git picked up, anyway. The police are watchin' the river.

"Well, so long, boys. Be seein' you later. Here I be'n fritterin' away my time, an' I ought to be halfway to Cush's!" Taking his

place in the canoe, he shoved off, slanting a glance toward the bank where the two were standing, Stubble Face staring stupidly after the canoe with mouth agape, with the green eyes of the other fixed upon him in a glare of venomous hate.

AT THE second bend of the creek, Black John beached his canoe and drew it into the bush. "Hell," he muttered to himself with a broad grin, "I left my tobacco pouch' layin' there in the grass. Guess I'll loaf back an' git it."

As he slipped noiselessly through the bush a loud voice reached him from the clearing.

"I tell you it's a damn lie! There was only four thousan' ounces. Heck, you worked there—you ought to know!"

Pausing at the edge of the clearing, Black John peered between the branches of a small spruce tree to see the two men facing each other just where he had left them at the edge of the creek. The voice of Snake Eyes reached his ears—not loud bawled, like the hysterical voice of the other, but steady and hard as chilled steel.

"Yeah, I thought I knew. But I didn't. You heard what Black John said—about the big guys aimin' to doublecross their stockholders. Jest because I worked there wasn't no sign I knew what the real cleanup was. It was claimed to be four thousan' ounces—an' that's what I thought it was, along with everyone else that wasn't in on the know."

"But I tell you four thousan' ounces is all there was! Everyone that's robbed always lies like hell about how much they lost! Hell, you know as well as I do, I didn't git no more out of it than you did. You was right there an' helped divide it!"

The smaller man's lips curled in a sneering grin. "Yeah, I helped divide what there was in sight when I got there. Black John called the turn—to a gnat's hind leg. You'd already cached four thousan' ounces before I got there."

"It's a lie, I tell you—a damn lie! Hell, if I'd wanted to doublecross you I could of took the stuff an' kep' right on goin', couldn't I? I wouldn't needed to go to that place acrost the river where we agreed to meet!"

"No, you couldn't. An' you know damn well you couldn't! Where could you have gone to? If you hadn't of be'n there when I got there, I'd of got back my mem'ry damn quick—an' the police would of had yer description—an' they'd of had you, by night! How in hell could you of got away with it—an' the police watchin' the river, both up an' down it? An' if you'd of come on to Halfaday like we'd planned, I'd of be'n right on yer tail. An' when I got here I'd of knocked you off without battin' an eye. An' I'll knock you off yet, if you don't come acrost with them other two thousan' ounces!"

"But I tell you there ain't no more ounces. That damn treasurer lied!"

"Not on yer life, he didn't. What with the scheme they was hatchin' up, it would of be'n agin his interest to make the amount bigger'n what it was. He got rattled, jest like Black John said, an' blatted out the truth. An' what's more—you did try to knock me off with that damn gag. Black John's smart—he called the turn right down the line. You waited till you had me tied up so I couldn't do nothin' an' then you rammed that rag clean down my goozle! I wiggled an' struggled to let you know it was damn near chokin' me to death—but you kep' right on! An' on top of that you wound that bandage so tight it pressed my nose flat! An' when I j'ined up with you next day you did look s'prised as hell—an' guilty, too! An' you give the same excuse he said a damn doublecrossin' skunk would give—that you had to make it look like a good practical job of gaggin'!"

"An' by God, that's jest what I did have to do—make it look good! If I'd gagged you loose they'd know'd damn well it was a frame-up."

"You made it look good, all right—too damn good! I'm takin' them four thousan' ounces we fetched up here fer my share. You kin go back to the Yukon an' dig up the other four thousan'—from wherever you cached 'em."

With a roar like the bellow of a bull Stubble Face leaped toward the other, a belt knife in his hand. The slanting rays of the sun flashed on another blade as Snake Eyes sought vainly to sidestep the onrush. The next instant the two bodies merged in a writhing, twisting tangle of flailing arms and flashing blades.

So sudden had been the attack that by the time Black John plunged into the clearing, both men were on the ground. One glance showed him that Stubble Face was done for, as blood spurted in a stream from a gash in the side of his neck that had half severed his head from his body. Snake Eyes rose to his hands and knees, sought vainly to withdraw the knife that was buried to the hilt in his chest, and sank to the ground again.

Picking him up bodily, Black John carried him into the cabin and laid him upon the blankets that covered the freshly cut boughs on one of the bunks. Drawing the knife from the wound, he ripped the man's clothing off and proceeded to bandage the wound, together with several other clashes, with strips torn from a shirt he found in one of the packsacks. Covering him with a blanket from the other bunk, he hastened outside to find Stubble Face already dead.

"You shore got what was comin' to you," he muttered to the

corpse at his feet. "Tryin' to murder a helpless man—an' him yer own pardner!"

Returning to the cabin, he searched the two packsacks, removing a heavy package from each.

"About a hundred an' a quarter apiece," he muttered, hefting them judicially. "That figgers four thousan' ounces, all right. There ain't no use leavin' the stuff layin' around loose. What with some of the shady characters that infests Halfaday, it might git stole."

Carrying the packages into the bush, he buried them beneath the low hanging branches of a small spruce tree, and returned to the cabin.

III

ON THE DAY following Black John's departure from Dawson Swiftwater Bill and Moosehide Charlie stepped into Corporal Downey's office at detachment headquarters.

"Hear you got a robbery on yer hands," Swiftwater said.

"Yeah. Pacific Dredge & Minin' Company's clean-up on Quartz Crick got lifted. A matter of four thousan' ounces."

"What we heard—the night watchman was found bound an' gagged next mornin', an' after claimin' he didn't know nothin' about who done it, he skipped out."

"That's right."

"Well, mebbe we kin help you a little. Me an' Moosehide was comin' downriver, an' yesterday we camped fer a b'ilin' of tea jest above the mouth of the White, an' whilst we was there we seen a canoe with two men in it comin' upriver, huggin' the shore. They headed up the White, an' I put the glass on 'em an' seen that the man in front was the Pacific Dredge outfit's night watchman."

"You sure?"

"Shore as hell. You know my claim lays next above Pacific

Dredge, on Quartz Crick. I've seen him a hundred times."

"Who was the other one?"

"Never seen him before. He was bigger'n the watchman. Couldn't see his face plain on account it was covered with whiskers."

"Was he wearin' a black felt hat with a chunk gone out of the brim?"

"He might of be'n. I didn't pay no partic'lar heed to him."

"You say this was yesterday noon? You fellas got down here damn quick. It's eighty mile to the mouth of the White."

"Yeah, we flagged down the Hannah along in the afternoon an' come on down on her. Ridin' a steamboat has got canoein' beat all to hell, even downstream."

Corporal Downey drummed on the desk top with his fingers. "Black John headed upriver yesterday on his way to Halfaday," he said.

"I told him to keep an eye out fer that watchman."

Moosehide Charlie grinned broadly. "He will, all right— 'specially if he knows he's packin' four thousan' ounces of dust."

"Hell—Black John wouldn't stick no one up!" Swiftwater Bill exclaimed. "He's got too much sense fer that. Outlaw er no outlaw, Black John's a damn good man fer the country. He wouldn't never admit it, but us old sourdoughs knows he's helped you out on more'n one case, Downey."

THE OFFICER nodded. "Yeah, Black John's a kind of a law onto himself. If them four thousan' ounces them birds are prob'ly packin' had been lifted off'n some individual prospector, I'd be willin' to bet any amount a man would name that I could go up to Halfaday an' fetch back the robbers—an' the ounces. But with the dust lifted, as it was, off'n a big outfit—well, I'll prob'ly get the robbers all right, but I wouldn't bet a thin dime on locatin' them ounces. Dust from big outfits has got a way of mysteriously disappearin', on Halfaday!"

Swiftwater Bill laughed. "Well, hell, Downey, after all—look what them damn dredge outfits is doin' to the country! It's gittin' so a pore man ain't got a chanct, no more, the way they're goin' in an' rippin' up cricks."

"Yeah—but a robbery's a robbery, jest the same—no matter whose dust is stolen."

"Oh, shore. An' like you say, you'll prob'ly git the robbers all right. It shore don't give me no headache if the Pacific Dredge don't git back their dust. An'," he added with a broad grin, "I'll bet it won't give Black John none, neither!"

"I'M HITTIN' fer Halfaday right now!" Downey exclaimed. "It's upstream work all the way to Halfaday, an' there was two of them an' only one of Black John—an' they had four days' start of him. He might not overtake 'em before they hit Halfaday. He'll have only one day's start of me—an' I can travel as fast as he can. Like you say, he's got too much sense to pull anything so raw as a hold-up—an' I'll crowd him so close he won't have time to figger out any scheme fer fanaglin' that dust out of 'em—even if he aims to."

"What was the amount you was willin' to bet on fetchin' back them ounces?" grinned Moosehide Charlie.

"Get to hell out of here!" Downey related. "I've got to throw my outfit together."

Toward the middle of an afternoon, ten days later, Corporal Downey beached his canoe opposite the willow flat and leaped ashore to stare down at the body that lay close to the water's edge with a gaping wound in its throat. A belt knife lay close beside the body, its blade stained with dried blood. The officer glanced toward Olson's old cabin from the stovepipe of which smoke curled lazily.

"Hey!" he called loudly. "Who's in there?"

A moment later Black John Smith stepped from the doorway and joined him.

Downey pointed to the corpse at his feet. "What the hell

happened to this man?" he cried.

"He died. Looks to me like he'd had some trouble with his neck," the big man replied.

"Who killed him?"

"Fella in the cabin, there. I mistrust he's that night watchman you was tellin' me about."

"Why did he do it?"

"They must of had some kind of a dispute."

"Is the other man hurt?"

"Yeah, he's cut up pretty bad. I carried him into the cabin an' pulled a knife out of him. It was drove in plumb the len'th of the blade. Couldn't of missed his heart more'n an' inch."

"Is he still alive?"

"Yeah—jest about. He comes to every little while an' mutters an' mumbles about gittin' doublecrossed. Mostly he's out of his head."

"Did you see the fight?"

"Yeah—what there was of it. It was over so damn quick I really didn't git no good look at it. I heard loud talkin'—like an argument of some kind, an' I landed an' slipped through the bresh an' seen the two of 'em standin' here, callin' each other liars, an' what-not. It seemed like the other one was accusin' this one of doublecrossin' him in the matter of some four thousan' ounces in dust. I figger it's ondoubtless them four thousan' ounces you was tellin' me about bein' lifted off'n the Pacific Dredge outfit.

"Anyways all at once this fella draws a knife an' jumps the other one. Then he draw'd a knife, an' they flew at it—stabbin' an' slashin' somethin' awful. It was all over in a jiffy—with both of 'em on the ground. I run in, an' seein' that this one was done fer, I picks the other one up an' carries him into the cabin an' lays him on the bunk, an' pulls the knife out of his gizzard, an' done what I could fer him in the way of bandages.

"That was day before yesterday, an' I've be'n here ever sence, waitin' fer someone to show up. I couldn't hardly go away an' leave the pore devil all alone—the shape he's in. He's runnin' a fever, an' keeps mutterin' an' moanin' fer water. I feed him water, an' now an then git a little hot tea down him. I figger he's a goner, though. I don't think even a doctor could save him—the way he's slashed up."

"How about the dust—them four thousan' ounces? What become of that?"

Black John shook his head. "That's what's puzzlin' me. Accordin' to what I kin make out from the fella's mutterin', he claims the other one cached it on him somewheres down on the Yukon. An' mebbe he did. It shore as hell ain't in their packsacks."

FROWNING, DOWNEY led the way into the cabin and glanced down into the face of the man who lay in the bunk, covered to the neck with a blanket.

"He's the watchman all right," he said. Then, as the man stirred uneasily and muttered, he stooped over him.

"Where's the dust?" he asked sharply, his lips close to the man's ear.

The eyelids fluttered open and the watchman stared up into the officer's face. A gleam of recognition flickered in the fevered eyes, and the lips moved.

"Police—go git him," he muttered weakly. "Go git—the damn—doublecrosser—tried to murder me—so he could have all the dust. He cached—four thousan' ounces on me—down on the river." The lips ceased to move, and the eyelids closed.

"Yes, yes!" Downey said. "I'll get him! Tell me—where did he cache the dust? Where'bouts on the river?"

Again the eyelids fluttered open. "Across the river—up half a mile—a gravel point—with a dead tree—an' three big rocks— he waited there for me—but he doublecrossed me—he cached four thousan' ounces—the damn—dirty—" The words ceased, the man's hand clutched suddenly at his chest beneath the blanket, and he half rose on his elbow, his eyes staring wildly.

As Downey reached to ease him back onto the makeshift pillow he retched violently, and a torrent of blood gushed from his mouth, and he dropped back—dead.

For several moments the two stood in silence, staring down at the figure beneath the blood drenched blanket. Black John glanced at Downey.

"Well," he said, "I guess that clears up yer case. If you want to be gittin' back I'll git some of the boys to come down an' help bury these two damn miscreants fer you. That is, onlest you'd rather I'd go along back with you an' help you hunt fer them four thousan' ounces. That's what you claimed they lifted off'n that dredge outfit, wasn't it—four thousan' ounces?"

"That's right. An' I don't mind tellin' you that if that dust had be'n lifted off'n some prospector, I'd be damn glad to have you help locate it. But," he added, with a twinkle in his eye, "as things stand, I guess I'll jest take a chanct on locatin' them ounces, myself."

"All right, Downey—you're the doctor! You can't say I didn't offer to help. Anyway, here's one case where you can't suspect that I had anything to do with concealin' a big outfit's loss. Hell—them two damn thieves was a hundred an' fifty mile back off the Yukon before I ever seen 'em!"

"That's right, John. I guess that lets you out, this time. With the start they had you couldn't possibly have overtaken them on the big river—an' that's where that bird claims the dust was cached."

"Don't it beat hell how them damn crooks deceives one another? It jest goes to show that human nature ain't what it ought to be—by a damn sight!"

"Yeah—an' it goes to show that they can't make crime pay, in the long run," Downey added, as he turned from the room and headed for his canoe.

"Y-e-a-h, I s'pose it does—lookin' at it from that angle. Well, so long, Downey. Be shore an' let me know what luck you have locatin' them ounces. I'll be interested to know!"

"So long, John. I'll let you know. An' by the way—after all, it was you that captured these robbers. I'll make out the report on it, an' you can put in a claim fer that reward."

Black John made a deprecatory gesture. "No, no, Downey, fergit about the reward. I didn't rightly capture 'em, nohow. An' besides, I wouldn't claim no reward fer doin' what little I could fer a dyin' man. Hell—it wouldn't be ethical!"

BONUS MATERIAL

TEN THOUSAND NEW LAKES

THEY'RE BUILDING HIGHWAYS TO PARADISE IN ONTARIO—HIGHWAYS THAT'LL TAKE YOU TO VIRGIN LAKES AND STREAMS TEEMING WITH HUNGRY NORTHERNS, WALLEYES AND TROUT

IT WAS LATE in May, and cold up there north of Lake Superior. The day before it had snowed, and the portage was slippery. Easing the canoe into the water, we flipped a coin for seats. Frank won the bow and, selecting a large yellow wobbler, rigged his casting rod. Preferring a fly rod, I tied a smaller plug on a heavy nylon leader, took the stern seat, and shoved off.

After casting into the chop where the fast water of a little river broke into the lake, Frank had reeled in half his line when *wham!* The rod arched, and for the next few minutes the 6-pound northern he had hooked gave him plenty to do. I let out line and trolled slowly for perhaps a hundred yards. Then I got a strike, and believe me, brother, a 5-pound walleye can give you a lot of action on a 5-ounce fly rod.

Frank hooked a walleye from under an overhanging cedar and tied into two more northerns—one a 10-pounder—and I netted another walleye and a northern before we had paddled a quarter of a mile.

I swung the canoe ashore, and we stepped out. "Boy, this is it!" Frank exclaimed. "This is what we've been looking for—been dreaming about for a year. This is the new country that Nap told us about—lakes full of hungry fish, and nobody to catch 'em."

I grinned. "Talkin' ain't fishin'," I reminded him with a glance at the lowering sky. "Let's get back to work before it rains."

Tying on a small red wobbler, I took my place in the bow,

and after changing to a spoon Frank picked up the paddle and shoved off. It was all the same—no matter what we offered, the northerns and walleyes grabbed. A cold drizzle set in, and a few minutes later, after netting a walleye and a northern at the same time, we called it a day and paddled back to where Bill and Johnny were just landing. They had shoved off and drifted along with the light breeze, casting with anything they took out of the box, and found plenty of action.

We had been on the water an hour and had taken eight walleyes and six northerns, while the other canoe counted five walleyes and seven northerns. After releasing the northerns and all but four of the walleyes, we hit back to camp. And that evening we gorged on luscious fillets fried in butter.

At seven o'clock the same morning we had checked our baggage, consisting of two aluminum canoes, tent, packsacks, sleeping bags, cameras and fishing tackle, and boarded the Algoma Central train at Sault Ste. Marie, Ontario, on the St. Marys River, at the outlet of Lake Superior and readily accessible by train or car, some 350 miles northward from either Detroit or Chicago. Our destination was Magpie, a whistle-stop on the spur line running from Hawk Junction to Michipicoten, a village with an excellent harbor located on Michipicoten Bay, the extreme northeastern reach of Lake Superior. This spur line maintains daily passenger service, though its main function is the transportation of thousands of cords of pulpwood, cut and loaded along the main line to the northward and hauled on long freight trains drawn by two heavy diesel engines to Michipicoten for transshipment by water to the mills.

A year ago, as the Dubreuil brothers were closing out their logging operation on Mountain Ash Lake, some seventy miles to the eastward, Nap Dubreuil had predicted that we would find good fishing when he invited us to visit their newly acquired timber holdings north of Magpie, in the heart of the hitherto inaccessible spruce and jack-pine country.

At Magpie, Marcel Dubreuil placed a panel truck at our

disposal with brother Gus as driver, and after loading the outfit we jolted over a dozen miles of newly bulldozed road and pitched camp on the shore of the little lake into which the logs were dumped for the sawmill. We were all set by four o'clock. Although the sky was heavily overcast, we were raring to go; so with the canoes and tackle in the truck we hit for Tray Lake, over a so-called road on which we made good time—three miles in forty minutes!

Arriving at the lake, Gus produced an outboard motor from a cache, and we lowered a square-end canoe from a rack where it was kept out of reach of the bears. Towing the two light canoes, we crossed Tray Lake, landed at the outlet and made the quarter-mile portage to Sutherland Lake. It was there on Sutherland that we tied into those walleyes and northerns which gave us that hour of real sport. Leaving the light canoes on Sutherland, we returned to camp, arriving just on the edge of dark.

Next morning we paddled the length of Sutherland, and down the slow-flowing river that leads to Davies Lake, some two miles distant. The channel of this river ran through a flooded marsh, half a mile wide, lying between high hills timbered with spruce, jack-pine and birch, with occasional splashes of light green where the poplars were just beginning to leaf out. This marsh is a lush feeding ground for the black ducks that we flushed at every bend. I counted 130 big blacks, probably 90 percent of them drakes, as the hens would be on the nests at that time of year. A big cow moose, standing belly-deep in the marsh, eyed us apathetically, allowing us to approach to within fifty yards before she turned and splashed into the bush.

The fishing on Davies Lake, which empties into the Magpie River some eight miles above Cedar Falls, was the same as on Sutherland. The walleyes and the northerns went for anything we tossed at them—even pieces of red gill cut from a fish. We caught them all over the small lake—along the shores, out in the middle, and the full length of the connecting river. After netting them, we returned them to the water, keeping only enough for a big feed for ourselves and our friends in camp.

After supper Frank spread out the Wawa sheet, a map recently issued by the Department of Lands and Forests, and we gathered around it. We had inspected it rather casually on the train and it looked good, showing countless lakes and streams. But now, with the fishing we'd had on the first two lakes we tried, we stared at it in awe.

"Look," Bill said. "Forty-one townships—fifteen hundred square miles—no roads to speak of—only a couple of small towns on the railway—close to a hundred lakes to a township—and not five percent of 'em even named!"

"Talk about a wilderness!" Johnny exclaimed. "Just think. This map covers only thirty-four miles north and south and forty-six miles east and west, and when you realize that the new road from Chapleau and the one from White River will open up three thousand more square miles, with no towns and not even a railway in 'em, we're looking at only a third of the wilderness that can soon be reached by car!"

"That's right," Bill agreed. "Ten thousand new lakes!"

"And most of 'em full of hungry fish," Frank added.

"Uh-huh," I grinned. "Walleyes and northerns furnish plenty of good sport—good to eat, too, especially the walleyes. But they're not specs—and we haven't been taking them on flies."

"I'll bet that plenty of these lakes have got specs in 'em," Frank shot back. "You wait and see! And in the meantime you don't need to go high-hatting the walleyes and northerns."

Gus Dubreuil, who had strolled over for a game of cribbage, grinned from the doorway of the tent. "That's right," he said. "Speckled trout in plenty of lakes. Some lakes pike and dore, some lakes only gray trout, and some lakes nothing but speckled trout—big ones, too." Stooping, he placed a finger on the map. "Here's Goetz Lake—gray trout in that one. You cross Goetz and portage over into Parks, from there you'll strike a string of lakes—all easy portages. Plenty of speckled trout in those lakes. You try 'em and see."

So next morning we drove to Magpie, intending to make the mile-and-a-half portage up the railway track to Goetz Lake and on into that string of lakes for specs. It was Sunday, and Leo Nelson, the accommodating section foreman, offered to give us a lift on the handcar to Goetz Lake, where he and two of his crew were going for gray trout. It sounded good. Anything sounds good that promises to eliminate a mile-and-a-half portage with a canoe on your shoulders. But considering our two canoes and seven men, we eyed the vehicle dubiously.

Leo grinned. Producing a couple of 12-foot two-by-fours, he laid them lengthwise, one on each side of the handcar. With the canoes resting crosswise of the track at either end of the car, we climbed aboard, froze onto the handles and pumped the outfit upgrade to the lake, slowing to a crawl where the ends of the 17-foot canoes barely missed the walls of a narrow rock-cut.

With those big specs in mind, we didn't waste any time on Goetz. Paddling the length of the mile-long lake, we made the quarter-mile portage to Parks Lake, on the south shore of which the deserted buildings of the abandoned Josephine iron mine stand out stark and gaunt against the dark-green background of wooded hills. The Josephine functioned for a short time, shipping high-grade hematite ore to the furnaces until right after the war, when mud seeped in and filled the main tunnel, a thousand feet below the surface of the lake.

We flipped flies, spinners and tiny wobblers around for an hour without any luck, ate lunch on a little island, then shoved on to Endless Lake. That 600-yard portage from Parks to Endless is one for the book—a stiff upgrade through a deep ravine, and you make it on a wooden trestle! Some trestle— sixteen inches wide, and in places a good twenty feet above the rock-studded floor of the ravine.

This de luxe portage trail was not designed primarily for the convenience of fishermen. It is the insulation box surrounding the four-inch iron pipeline that supplied water by gravity from

Endless Lake to the mine. However, it's the easy trail up to Endless—if your nerves are steady. But, believe me, with a 17-foot canoe on your shoulders, you had better keep your eyes glued to that narrow bit of planking, or else! One misstep twenty feet above those jagged rocks, and your wife can collect your insurance.

We slipped the canoes into the water and did some fly-casting on Endless without getting a strike, then portaged a couple of hundred yards to Center Lake, a small round body of water with a tiny island in the center. The sun broke through the clouds for a few minutes, and we landed Johnny on the opposite shore, where he climbed to the top of a high rock cliff and took pictures.

After a half hour of futile fly-casting, during which we offered everything from gray deer-hair flies tied on No. 6 hooks that are sure killers on some Northern waters, on down through the book to Black Gnats on No. 13 hooks, I tied on a tiny wobbler, let out my line, and paddled slowly while Frank cast flies. A few minutes later I got a strike and landed a 14-inch beauty. The others took the hint, and the fun began. We stayed there a couple of hours and had great sport, bringing to net twenty specs—good full-bodied fish ranging from 12 to 17 inches in length.

Leaving the canoes on Endless Lake, we retraced our way down that narrow wooden trestle. The downhill trip seemed even more precarious, but we made it and walked around the shore of Parks Lake to the abandoned mine, where Bill Richards, the genial mining engineer, was holding forth with Poy Lor, his Chinese cook, while prospecting the rock-ribbed wilderness for another iron strike. I told Bill that I knew how Blondin must have felt when he crossed Niagara River above the falls on a tightwire. "Yeah," he replied, "it is a bit owly. I came down it one day last winter on skis." Which proves beyond doubt that Bill is either the best skiman or the damnedest liar I have ever met.

Bill drove us around Parks Lake to the railway in a station

wagon with a Virginia license, and we hiked down the track to Goetz Lake, where the two Finnish section hands were fishing while waiting for Leo, who was still out on the lake trolling for grays. At the end of a rocky point that jutted into the lake near the track they had wedged the butt of a slender 15-foot birch pole among the rocks so that it stuck out over the water. Both sat watching the wooden bobber, set for a 7-foot depth on a heavy linen line tied to the extreme end of the pole. So far the outfit seemed orthodox enough. I had fished that way hundreds of times in Minnesota when I was a kid.

Within a few minutes the bobber began to dip and move slowly out into the lake. As it disappeared beneath the surface we onlookers were treated to a method of landing fish that seemed a bit unique. Instead of raising the pole and horsing in the fish, one of the Finns took his place behind the other, who loosened the butt of the pole, straddled it and passed it back between his legs to the other, who also straddled it. Thus they pushed the pole into the bush behind them until the first man could grasp the line and ease the 4-pound gray trout in hand over hand and flip it onto the rocks.

As I walked back with one of the Finns to the railway track where they had left their minnow pail we crossed a slight depression and the man pointed to the track of a bull moose in the mud. "Big moose come here," he observed. Then, stooping closer, he added, "Dis mornin'—or mebbe tonight."

We heard the whine of Leo's motor, and a few minutes later he landed and tossed half a dozen 4- to 6-pound grays out of the boat. The handcar was placed on the rails, and we all piled on. It had been an uphill grind to reach the lake from Magpie, with all hands bearing down on the handles. But, believe you me, that down-grade return trip was some ride! The handcar shot along the rails, with no one daring to let go the flying handles for fear of getting knocked clear off the right of way. Grinning broadly, Leo kept a foot on the brake—but he didn't bear down, and we made the trip in six minutes flat!

At the Dubreuil lumber camp the crew is awakened at six o'clock each morning by a siren whose wailing whine is augmented by the howling of several dogs. Before the din had ceased next morning we rolled out of our sleeping bags, gulped a hurried breakfast, piled into the panel truck and hit for Magpie, reaching there just in time to catch a ride back to Parks Lake, where the section crew was making tie replacements.

Bill Richards had suggested that we try Cliff Lake for specs; so we returned to Endless Lake. It is a couple of hundred yards wide and half a mile long. Paddling to the west end, we portaged a third of a mile over a 500-foot rock ridge and enjoyed another day of rare sport with those big specs. I have no idea how many we brought to net, as we kept only a dozen, easing the rest back into the water.

Toward the middle of the afternoon we landed and dined royally on fried trout and the trimmings around a jack-pine fire on a flat rock on the shore of the little lake. Frank washed down the last bite of a 3-pound trout with a draft of hot tea and licked his fingers. "I don't get it," he said with a frown. "Here these lakes are full of big specs, and we haven't taken a single one on a fly—haven't even seen a rise."

"That's right," Bill agreed. "We've all had plenty of experience, and we've offered 'em everything in the book from gnats to streamers—and not a single strike."

"It's been cold and cloudly ever since we got here," Johnny observed. "Maybe they'll start hitting when it warms up."

"Richards told me it rained all last week," I ventured. "The chances are it washed in plenty of bottom feed. Then, again, you remember Gus mentioned that the district priest only visits this country once a month. It's my guess that these back-country trout haven't heard that the Lenten fast is over."

"That," Frank replied, "shows just how screwy a guy can get."

"Anyway," Bill said, "we'll tackle it again in August, when the weather will be warm, and I'll bet we'll get some action on flies."

The 300-mile reach of spruce and jack-pine wilderness north of Sault Ste. Marie, traversed by the Algoma Central Railway, has for years been a favorite stamping ground for sportsmen who each summer take advantage of the accommodations provided by the numerous camps and resorts along the line. But as yet there has been no practical way of reaching the innumerable unnamed lakes and streams that lie in the vast hinterland to the eastward and westward of the railway. Virgin water, these lakes and streams, teeming with fish—speckled and gray trout, walleyes and northerns. Literally thousands of lakes into which no one has ever dropped a line and which, with the exception of the men of the Lands and Forests air patrol, a few prospectors and wandering trappers, no one has ever laid eyes on.

Fishing on proven lakes and streams is good sport. But no matter how fast they bite or how big they come, there is no thrill like shoving out in a canoe on water that no one has ever fished. Maybe you will tie into walleyes, perhaps only northerns or gray trout—and possibly those big red-meated specs of dazzling, brilliant hue. There are several outfits in Sault Ste. Marie that will fly parties in to some of the larger lakes where good fishing may be had. But there remain thousands of smaller lakes on which no plane can land.

That's the picture at present. But in the very near future, if present plans materialize, it will be possible to penetrate much of this vast wilderness by car. Three years ago a highway reaching from Thessalon to Chapleau, 154 miles to the north, was opened. This will connect with the recently surveyed route of approximately seventy-five miles running northwestward to Hawk, where it will meet the highway being pushed eastward from White River, some sixty-five miles distant. These two projects, together with the highway following the shore of Lake Superior northward from Sault Ste. Marie, already available for some ninety miles to the Montreal River, will give access by car to a vast number of hitherto inaccessible lakes and streams as well as virgin areas of moose, duck and grouse hunting.

Eventually camps and more or less elaborate resorts will function along these highways, as they now function along the railway. But for the present the seasoned sportsman, to whom one virgin lake is worth a dozen proven ones, must provide his own accommodations—tent, camping equipment and canoe. And here's a tip. If from some high rock ridge you should spot an inviting-looking lake lying far back from the highway and the terrain is rough, don't bother to pack your canoe into it. Just take a couple of rolls of stovepipe wire, a pocketful of long spikes, a light ax, your lunch and fishing tackle, and when you reach the lake build a raft out of the dead cedar that can almost invariably be found along the shoreline.

The train leaving Sault Ste. Marie at seven o'clock in the morning arrives at Hawk (Mile 165) at one o'clock. Breakfast and luncheon are served in the dining car, and the round-trip fare ($13.75) allows the checking of equipment, including canoe. Rooms may be had at the Hawk hotel for three dollars a day— five dollars for two persons. Good meals are served at a nearby restaurant at a reasonable price. Ben Nelson, a competent guide, charges ten dollars a day for a party of four or five, and Toivo Nerkkola will transport an outfit in his truck to any of the numerous lakes of the region that can be reached by way of several short dead-end roads as well as along the highway connecting Hawk with Wawa and Michipicoten.

From Magpie, nine miles down the Michipicoten spur, gray trout may be taken in Goetz, Boulery and Loonskin lakes, and speckled trout in Parks, Endless, Center, Cliff and Andre lakes— all easily accessible by short portages.

Arrangements can doubtless be made with the Dubreuil brothers for transportation to some of the lakes reached by their bulldozed roads. Food, cigarettes, tobacco, soft drinks and a limited assortment of fishing tackle may be purchased at the lumber-camp store, twelve miles north of Magpie.

Walleyes and northerns are plentiful the entire length of the

Magpie River—good canoe water—and innumerable unnamed and unfished lakes lie within easy portaging distance from its banks.

THE
HALFADAY CREEK
LIBRARY

JAMES B. HENDRYX

James B. Hendryx's classic series returns to print! The author of more than 50 novels and anthologies, he's best known for his characters set around the outlaw community of Halfaday Creek in the Yukon. Set during the Gold Rush of the late 1890s, Hendryx penned over a hundred stories featuring these characters over the span of 25 years for a variety of pulp magazines.

Now, Altus Press has committed to return these to print. Using the original pulp magazines as the source material, along with the illustrations from their original pulp magazine appearances, these uniform edition books will be augmented with rare material taken from the James B. Hendryx archives held by the Leelanau Historical Society in Leland, MI.

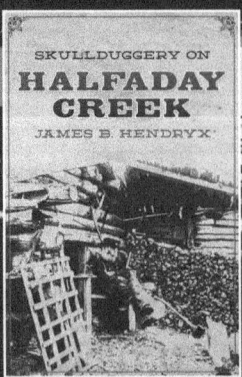

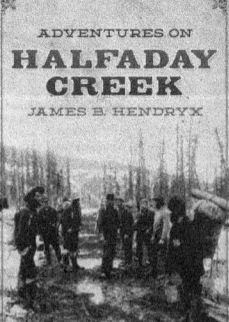

Leelanau Historical Society

Celebrating 150 Years of Leelanau History

Leelanau County was officially established in 1863 when the State of Michigan was a young 26 years old. People were attracted to the natural resources from the beginning—first as a way to earn a living and build a home, and later to enjoy recreation away from the cities. Early settlers arrived on the islands beginning in 1839, while Native Americans populated the Leelanau peninsula until pioneers began exploring the area in 1847. For the next 45 years, the villages known today—and some that are abandoned—were settled. North and South Manitou Islands and the Fox Islands officially joined the county in 1895.

The Leelanau Historical Society was launched in 1957 by a group of residents dedicated to collecting and preserving Leelanau's history. Leland, first established in 1853 and later the county seat, seemed the natural location for the Society. When the old county jail became available in 1959, the museum found its first home. Through generous donations and grants, a new museum was built in 1985 and later expanded.

Today, the collections and archives contain more than 11,000 items. Visitors to the museum learn about Leelanau life and maritime history from exhibits, educational programs and publications. The Society continues to collect, document and preserve items relating to Leelanau history.

203 East Cedar Street, Leland, MI 49654

Tel. (231) 256-7475

info@LeelanauHistory.org

http://www.leelanauhistory.org/

www.ingramcontent.com/pod-product-compliance
Lightning Source LLC
Chambersburg PA
CBHW071830020726
47502CB00004B/1307